LILAC MILLS

The Tanglewood Bookshop

1⊡ CANELO

Penguin
Random
House

First published in the United Kingd om in 2024 by

Canelo, an imprint of
DK Publishing, a d ivision of Penguin Rand om House LLC
1745 Broad way, 20th Floor, New York, NY 10019

The authorized representative in the EEA is Dorling Kind ersley Verlag
GmbH. Arnulfstr. 124, 80636 Munich, Germany

ISBN 9798217269846

Cover d esign by Jo Myler

Cover images © Alamy, Shutterstock

Look for more great books at
www.canelo.co | www.d k.com

–

154078558

The Tanglewood   Bookshop

Lilac Mills lives on a Welsh mountain with her very patient husband and incred ibly sweet d og, where she grows veggies (if the slugs d on't get them), bakes (bad ly) and loves making things out of glitter and glue (a mess, usually). She's been an avid read er ever since she got her hand s on a copy of *Noddy Goes to Toytown* when she was five, and she once tried to read everything in her local library starting with A and   working her way through the alphabet. She loves long, hot summer d ays and   cold winter ones snuggled   in front of the fire, but whatever the weather she's usually writing or thinking about writing, with heartwarming romance and   happy-ever-afters always on her mind .

Also by Lilac Mills

A Very Lucky Christmas
Sunshine at Cherry Tree Farm
Summer on the Turquoise Coast
Love in the City by the Sea
The Cosy Travelling Christmas Shop

Tanglewood Village series

The Tanglewood Tea Shop
The Tanglewood Flower Shop
The Tanglewood Wedding Shop
The Tanglewood Bookshop

Island Romance

Sunrise on the Coast
Holiday in the Hills
Sunset on the Square

Applewell Village

Waste Not, Want Not in Applewell
Make Do and Mend in Applewell
A Stitch in Time in Applewell

Foxmore Village

The Corner Shop on Foxmore Green
The Christmas Fayre on Holly Field
The Allotment on Willow Tree Lane

To Donald, who isn't a sheep, but a promise is a promise x

Chapter 1

Kazz Fernsby stifled a groan as the train lurched, and she put her hand to her mouth, praying she would n't be sick. Despite the dreary drizzly day, the train was warm – too warm – which did n't help with the nausea or the headache. She felt clammy, her palms were damp and her back was soggy, the long-sleeved T-shirt she was wearing underneath her fleece sticking to her skin.

Swallowing hard and trying not to throw up, she unwound her scarf, dropping it onto the seat next to her, and unzipped her coat. She would have taken it off, but she simply did n't have the energy to struggle back into it when the train arrived at her stop. What a state to be in on a Tuesday morning, she lamented. Days off were far too precious to waste feeling ill, especially when it was her own fault she was feeling like this.

A couple of years ago, she would have self-medicated the hangover with a fried breakfast and buckets of strong tea. But the thought of bacon, eggs and fried bread made her heave, and she swallowed again, her stomach roiling uncomfortably. Gingerly, she rested her head on the back of the seat and closed her eyes, only to quickly open them again when the nausea increased.

Why she had felt the need to knock back so many sambucas last night was a mystery. But she had worked all weekend and today was her day off, so she'd made the most of last night. The problem was, she had forgotten she'd promised to help her mum sort through the house this morning, and she only remembered when Mum had rung (three times, because Kazz had slept through the first two calls) to check she was on her way.

Feeling decidedly unwell, Kazz had rolled clumsily out of bed and stumbled into the kitchen, only to be glared at by Freya, the most uptight of her three flatmates. Apparently – and Kazz didn't know how true this was, because last night was rather fuzzy around the edges – Kazz had rocked in at one twenty-three a.m. And the reason Freya knew it had been one twenty-three was because Kazz had woken her and Mona up. Dorian, bless him, would sleep through a volcanic eruption, so at least there was one person who wasn't cross with her.

After apologising profusely and promising to cook dinner for everyone this evening, Kazz hoped she had done enough to appease her angry flatmates.

The train rattled over the tracks, jostling her, and she burped, pulling a disgusted face at the taste of second-hand flowery aniseed. The first thing she would do when she got to Mum's house would be to make a cup of tea. She would also try to force down a piece of toast while she was at it, in the vain hope she would feel better with something in her stomach.

The idiotic thing was, Kazz didn't usually drink much. Her idea of letting her hair down was a couple of single malts. But Rossiter – one of the front-of-house staff at the restaurant where she worked – also had today off, so when he'd suggested going to a bingo session last night, Kazz had thought it a great idea. She had never played bingo before, believing it to be the domain of old ladies with purple hair, but she had been sed uced by talk of two-for-one cocktails and big prize money.

She had n't won anything (who knew bingo could be so viciously competitive?), but she had enjoyed several d rinks. This morning, she bitterly regretted enjoying quite so many, and vowed never to touch sambuca again. Or nachos with cheese, because she d istinctly remembered eating a sharing plate all by herself.

Kazz stared listlessly out of the wind ow, watching the familiar East Lond on land marks roll by. She had lost count of the number of times she had mad e this journey over the years. The house had originally belonged to her grand -parents – although *belonged* was a bit mislead ing because they'd rented it. However, they had lived there for as long as she could remember, and when Nana d ied and Grand ad flatly refused to move into somewhere smaller and more manageable, Kazz's mum had eventually been forced to give up the lease on the little flat she'd lived in above the convenience store that sold mainly Russian food , and move in with him when he became too ill and frail to look after himself. Her mum had kept the place on after he'd passed away from cancer. That had been over a year ago, and Mum had n't got around to sorting out the house until now.

Kazz id ly wond ered what had prompted her mother to d o it tod ay, and wished she had d ecid ed on next wee or the week after, but she supposed it was long overd ue and she only had herself to blame if she wasn't firing on all cylind ers this morning. Never mind not d rinking sambuca again – Kazz vowed never to touch another d rop of *alcohol* for the rest of her life.

When her phone trilled , she thought it might be her mum, making sure she was actually on her way this time.

3

Or it could be the restaurant, because Fred d ie French (or Fred erique, as he preferred to be called) was renowned for summoning his staff into work on their d ays off. Something she objected to frequently and vociferously, much to Fred d ie's annoyance, even though she invariably went in to help him out.

Thankfully, it wasn't her boss, and she managed to d red ge up a smile when she saw that she had a message from Stevie, even though it was a photo of a cake.

Today's special, the message said *Toasted marshmallow and ginger cake.*

Kazz grimaced ; Stevie was one of the best pastry chefs she knew, but Kazz wasn't in the right frame of mind to appreciate it. Stevie had been Kazz's best friend since they were in infants' school. The pair of them were opposites in looks – Kazz short and d ark-haired ; Stevie tall with ginger hair, although she insisted it was chestnut – and in personalities, Stevie being flightier and a bit of an airhead .

Another message from Stevie followed .*Watcha doing today? Working?*

Kazz's thumbs flew over the screen. *Helping Mum clear out Grandad's house.* She ad d ed a sad face emoji.

Gotta be better than work tho?

Would rather be in bed. Heavy night. She ad d ed the green-faced emoji to that one.

Ha ha. I thought you were supposed to be
the sensible one!

Yeah, Kazz used to think that too, until Stevie's Aunt Peggy had left Stevie enough money to open a little tea shop in a village on the English–Welsh bord er – which was a far cry from Lond on, where they had both lived and worked . Stevie's inheritance had n't stretched to buying a space in the city, so she had been forced to look further afield .

Kazz had been there at the start, from being at Stevie's sid e d uring Peggy's funeral (Kazz had had a soft spot for Stevie's aunt and had wanted to pay her respects just as much supporting her friend) to attend ing the auction where Stevie had bought the property. Kazz had even helped to set up the tea shop, trawling around boot sales for china and other bits and bobs with which to fill it. Kazz d istinctly recalled how envious she had been at the time – not about moving to Wales, but about being able to afford a business of her own. She would love to be able to d o that, but as things stood at the moment, she could n't afford to open a burger van on an ind ustrial estate, let alone a cute tea shop in a chocolate-box village. And neither was she likely to be left any money in a will. Her grand ad , bless him, had n't had a bean to his name when he'd d ied , and her mum wasn't exactly rolling in money. Stevie was one lucky, lucky cow!

To top it all off, Stevie had settled d own with a gorgeous man, whom she would be marrying next year, and now it was Kazz who was getting blotto on a Mond ay evening, when that had been the sort of thing that Stevie used to get up to.

Another message pinged onto her screen.*Why out on a Monday? Party?*

Bingo?!!!!

Kazz was about to respond when her phone rang. Stevie had got bored with messaging.

'Here's me imagining you going to load s of parties and clubs, and you're going to *bingo*?' was her friend 's opening salvo.

Kazz sighed . 'What can I say? I'm living my best life.'

'Who d id you go with? *A guy*?' There was a whole world of innuend o in the word .

'Rossiter.'

'Ooh, are you and he…?'

'We're just friend s. Why are you phoning me on a Tuesd ay morning? Are you bored ?'

'I'm waiting for some d ough to rise. And I wond ered what you'd got up to at the weekend .'

'Work, mostly.' She sighed again.

'OK, my lovely, what's wrong?' Stevie d emand ed . 'It's not like you to sound so d own – even if you d o have a hangover. Is it Fred d ie?'

'It's always Fred d ie.' Her boss treated his staff like second -class citizens, and when it came to foul language, even Gord on Ramsay would be shocked at what came out of Fred d ie's mouth. Kazz tend ed to stand up to him (which cheesed Fred d ie off no end), but the others were too scared .

Stevie said , 'You need to start looking for another job.'

'I know, but I've got a big case of *out of the frying pan and into the fire* heebie-jeebies. Anyway, I d on't want to d o anything d rastic right now because Mona is moving out. If we can't find anyone to take over her room, my rent will be going up by a third .'

'Ouch.'

'I wish I could afford to rent a place of my own, but you know how rid iculous prices are in Lond on.'

'You sound royally fed up. What you need is a holid ay.'

'I can't afford that, either. Not on the measly salary Fred d ie pays me. Even by Lond on stand ard s, it's poor. Every time I ask him for a pay rise, he bursts out laughing.'

'That's why you need to get yourself another job − a better-paying one.'

'I promise I'll start looking when we find another flatmate.' Kazz crossed her fingers. The likelihood of her looking for another job was slim; she operated on the premise of better-the-d evil-you-know and she had worked hard to scramble up the lad d er in Fred d ie's kitchen. As sous chef, she was one rung below head chef, but as Fred d ie himself occupied that role and was also co-owner of the restaurant, she was unlikely to go any higher.

Stevie exclaimed , 'I've got an id ea! Why d on't you come to stay with me for a few d ays? We haven't seen each other in ages and the break will d o you good .'

A little break sound ed lovely and Kazz's spirits lifted ; then they promptly sank again as she wond ered whether Fred d ie would be willing to spare her. Although she had holid ays still to take, the restaurant was alread y gearing up for the forthcoming festive season, when it would be all hand s on d eck. The restaurant was even open on Christmas Day, so there would be no respite then, either. But even if Kazz had been able to visit Stevie over the holid ays, she would n't, because she had her mum to think of. On second thoughts, her mother had a boyfriend −

a nice bloke called Vince – so would probably spend the day with him, which would free Kazz up for some good old partying. If she had the energy. Or the enthusiasm. Or the funds. All three appeared to be sadly lacking lately. It seemed that bingo was as much as she could manage these days. More, actually…

So maybe a few days in the lovely little Welsh village would be just what she needed. Set in the bottom of a wide green valley, with mountains all around and a river running through it, Tanglewood had a picturesque high street with all kinds of artisan shops, a narrow stone bridge that forded the river, and lots of wonderful walks. It was a friendly place, where everyone knew everyone else, and that was another thing that Kazz was envious of – the caring atmosphere. Stevie had made some good friends, even if one or two of them were rather… *quirky*.

Tanglewood was the perfect place to recharge her batteries and have some fun with her bestie at the same time. Kazz missed her. They used to be inseparable, but since Stevie had moved to the village, visits had been few and far between.

Noticing that Wanstead Park was the next stop, Kazz hurriedly said, 'I'll see what I can do. Got to go,' and made some loud kissy noises, before ending the call and shoving her phone back in her pocket as she lumbered to her feet.

The cold air on the platform made her shiver, and she huddled deeper into her coat, having gone from overly warm to chilled in a matter of seconds.

To add to her woes, the sky was as cloud-laden and sullen as when she'd set off an hour earlier, and a steady drizzle was falling again. It hadn't stopped raining for weeks and the city was overcast and miserable-looking. Not even the Christmas decorations that were already festooning many of the shops and businesses could dispel the early November gloom.

Kazz made her way out of the station and onto the street, but before she had managed to pull her hood over her head, she felt a drip plop down the back of her neck.

Cursing, she took an extra-long stride to dodge a puddle, as she hurried along the pavement. Her mum lived off Woodgrange Road, a four-minute walk away, and when Kazz reached the turning into her mother's street and was about to cross to the other side, a white van cut the corner, going far too fast.

Both off-side tyres splashed into the gutter, sending a wave of dirty rainwater over her legs and feet, and forcing her to leap back.

To add insult to injury, the driver tooted his horn, as though it was *her* fault. Then he gunned the engine, releasing a cloud of black noxious fumes into her face, which made her cough so hard that she felt sick again and nearly threw up.

Cold, wet and feeling thoroughly done with the day already, Kazz stared miserably at the van, smoke billowing after it down the street, and wished all sorts of nastiness on its rude and inconsiderate driver.

Could this day get any worse?

Chapter 2

Kazz hesitated when she reached her mum's front d oor and saw that there was a soggy note sellotaped to it, the word s barely legible.*Gone to the charity shop. Back in 5.*

It seemed that Mum had mad e a start on clearing out Grand ad 's things without her if she was alread y taking stuff to the charity shop, Kazz thought as she unlocked the d oor and stepped insid e. This was confirmed when she noticed a stack of bin bags in the front room. There must be twenty of them, and she id ly poked a finger through the tied -off end s of the nearest. A jumper she recognised as being one of her mother's (it had a very d istinctive and rather garish pattern) could be seen sitting on the top, and she guessed Mum must be having a sort through of her own stuff at the same time. Which was just as well, consid ering her mother had brought everything with her from her old flat when she'd moved in with Grand ad , so she probably had load s to get rid of.

Kazz carried on into the kitchen, kicking off her shoes and wriggling out of her jeans as she went. Ugh, even her socks were wet and she peeled them off with a grimace, then glanced around the old -fashioned but spotless kitchen, wincing when she saw the wet footprints she had tracked across the floor. Scooping up her d amp clothes, she bund led them into the washing machine, threw a laund ry tablet in after them and turned the d ial to a fast wash.

Barefoot, she hurried upstairs in search of some d ry clothes, and prayed that Vince had n't stayed the night. Vince was a lovely chap and he thought the world of her mum, but Kazz d id n't want to bump into him on the land ing when all she was wearing from the waist d own was a pair of knickers and a rash of goosebumps.

'Hello?' she called , but the house was silent, and she guessed he must be at work.

He d id n't live with her mum, but Kazz assumed it was only a matter of time before they moved in together. As she began to hunt through a chest of d rawers, searching for some fluffy socks and a pair of pyjama bottoms, she paused as a thought occurred to her. Maybe that was the reason for the clear-out. Her mum could hard ly expect to take all of Grand ad 's things with her when she went to live with Vince, and Vince would hard ly want to move in here when he had a perfectly nice – and consid erably more mod ern – home of his own. The other factor was that Grand ad 's house was rented , so it would make sense for her mum to give up the tenancy and go live with Vince.

After stuffing her legs into a pair of brushed cotton pyjama bottoms, Kazz perched on the ed ge of the bed to put on the socks, and as she d id so, she happened to glance through the open bed room d oor and into the room opposite. A wave of sad ness swept over her.

The largest of the three bed rooms, it had been Nan and Grand ad 's. Kazz had n't stepped insid e it since Grand ad passed away, and she found herself walking toward s the d oor. Feeling sad , she shook her head (flinching when her hangover remind ed her of its presence) and glanced around the room.

It had n't changed .

A brass bed with a d usky-pink quilted coverlet sat against one wall, and a large d ark wood ward robe was up against the one opposite. It was a monstrous thing, and when she was little, Grand ad used to tell her it was magic. He used to say that, occasionally, it would let you catch a glimpse of Narnia, and Kazz had often been found trying to sneak up on it unawares, in the hope of find ing a magical country beyond the rail of musty suits and crimplene d resses. She used to be terrified of it, and every time she'd opened the d oor, she had always taken the key out of the lock and held it tightly, in case it d ecid ed to lock her in.

Trailing her fingers across its carved d oors, she moved toward s the mantlepiece and the books propped on top of it. The fire had n't been lit in a long time and she was surprised the land lord had n't taken it out; but it was a stunning period piece and ad d ed to the charm of the house. People loved those kind s of features and were scrambling to put them back in, so perhaps the land lord knew what he or she was d oing. Kazz had a feeling that not many houses in this street of late-Victorian build ings were as untouched as this.

She scanned the books, recognising many of the titles as being ones that she used to read when she was little. One in particular caught her eye. It was a big tome, roughly the height and wid th of a tabloid newspaper, and the spine was the d epth of her ind ex finger. Dark green with gilt lettering and embossed corners, only the title giving a hint to its contents, this had been her absolute favourite out of all the books her grand father had owned , and she had spent many, many hours lost in its pages. If she had thought the wardrobe was magical, it was nothing compared to this wonderful book.

Gently, she picked it up and placed it on the bed, and when she opened the cover, she was instantly transported back to her childhood. Breathing in the special perfume all old books seemed to have, her eyes feasted on the gloriously detailed illustrations of fairies that were dotted throughout its pages. It had been those, more than the stories they depicted, that had captivated her.

Filled with nostalgia, Kazz's heart swelled with love for the old man who had introduced her to books and had nurtured her love of reading, and she was grateful he hadn't sold this beautiful specimen.

Clutching it to her chest, she held it close. This book was definitely *not* destined for the charity shop. Mum could do what she liked with the others – the house was full of them – but this one was coming home with her.

Taking it with her, Kazz made her way along the landing, intending to go downstairs and make a cup of tea. But when she passed the closed door which led to the third and smallest bedroom, she hesitated. Not wanting to pry, but reasoning that she would see inside it at some point today, curiosity got the better of her and she turned the knob.

The door swung inwards, and Kazz gasped.

She had never seen so many books in one place outside of a library or a bookshop, and she couldn't believe her grandad had hung on to them. There must be hundreds!

Kazz had assumed that the stock had been sold off when his shop closed twelve years ago, but clearly it hadn't. Grandad, for whatever reason, had kept much, if not all, of it. Maybe these had been the most valuable, or the ones he hadn't been able to bear to part with. The living room had a couple of large bookcases, and there was a shelf or two in every room in the house (includ ing the d ownstairs cloakroom), but this was consid erably more than a shelf. Boxes of them were stacked one on top of the other, floor to ceiling, and you could n't put as much as a pin between the towering piles.

Kazz guessed it would have been a wrench to get rid of them. She would have felt the same way. Her grand ad had spent d ecad es build ing up his collection, selling books on and acquiring others to take their place. They had been a huge part of his life, and the bookshop had been a big part of her child hood . She felt rather sad that they would have to go.

Her mum would be feeling sad too, and Kazz wond ered whether Vince would set asid e some wall space in that mod ern house of his for a few d usty old volumes.

The sound of the front d oor banging open reached her, followed by her mother's voice. 'Karen, are you there?'

She wished her mum would stop calling her Karen, even though it was her given name. 'Karen' had such negative connotations these d ays, which was unfair, but what could she d o about it – apart from amend ing it slightly. Unfortunately, her mum d id n't agree, insisting that *she* liked the name and was going to carry on using it.

'Up here.' Kazz backed out of the room, her eyes scanning the piles in case another child hood favourite was hid ing in there, as she heard her mum trot up the stairs. 'I d id n't realise Grand ad had kept all these.'

'Hiya, love.' Diana gave her a look before following Kazz's gaze. 'That's not the half of it. You ought to see what's up there.' She jerked her chin toward s the ceiling.

'You mean, there are more in the attic?'

'Uh-huh.'

'How many more?'

'See for yourself.' Her mum opened the airing cupboard and took out a pole. Jabbing it at the ceiling, the hatch swung open and she used the other end of the pole to hook the loft ladder.

It rattled noisily downwards, setting Kazz's teeth on edge and making her still-fragile head pound.

'Go on, up you go,' her mother said, then frowned. 'Why are you wearing my pyjamas?'

'Rain, puddles and a white-van man,' she said. 'And it's only the bottoms; this is my own hoodie.'

'You're looking awfully pale and peaky,' Diana continued. 'I hope you're not coming down with some-thing.' She took a step back. Then another.

'Hangover,' Kazz explained tersely.

Diana blinked. 'On a Tuesday?'

'Blame Rossiter. It's his day off today, too. He wanted to go to the bingo last night, so that's what we did.'

'*I* never used to get blotto when I went to the bingo.'

'They were doing two-for-one cocktails. Rossiter said it would be rude not to have a couple.'

'If you ask me, you had more than a couple.'

Kazz ignored her. She had no defence, and neither was she proud of getting drunk. Once again vowing never to drink as much in future, she grasped the rails with both hands and proceeded to climb the ladder. When she was far enough up to see inside the attic, she located the light switch and —

Bloody hell! Surely not *all* of those boxes had books in them? It was going to take weeks to get rid of that lot. She'd hoped to only be here for a few hours. There were boxes stacked   joist to rafter, hund red s of the d amned things.

OK, maybe not hund red s, but there were are least sixty to eighty. It was a wond er the ceiling had n't collapsed und er their weight.

Kazz retreated   d own the lad d er. 'Are you sure you're read y to get rid   of Grand ad 's things?' she asked , hoping her mother would   change her mind . There was no rush – a week or two wasn't going to make the slightest bit of d ifference, and   next time Kazz would   make sure not to let a single d rop of alcohol pass her lips the night before.

She glanced   hopefully at her mother.

Diana had   a pained   expression on her face, but she quickly rearranged   her features. 'I'm read y. It's got to be d one. Shall we have a cuppa before we begin?'

Her mum left her to wrestle the loft lad d er back into position, and   by the time Kazz walked   into the kitchen, the kettle was boiling.

Feeling even more nauseous at the prospect of all the hard   work she was about to d o, she d ropped   a slice of bread into the toaster and   fetched   the butter from the frid ge. The interior was barer than usual, but a packet of bacon and   a small box of eggs seemed   to be laughing at her, and   she hastily closed   the d oor. Forcing a slice of toast d own her neck was the most she would   be able to manage this morning.

'Where d o you want to start?' she asked , as she waited for the toast to pop.

Her mum hand ed   her a mug. 'I've got something to tell you first. You might want to sit d own.'

Unease uncoiled   in Kazz's stomach and   her mouth was sud d enly d ry as she sank slowly onto a chair, the one Grand ad   used   to favour.

Her mother began, 'I've, um… The reason I… Oh, dear.'

'Mum! What is it?' Unease became dread, and Kazz put the mug on the scarred kitchen table and shoved her hands under her thighs to stop their sudden trembling. *Please don't let there be anything wrong with her*, she prayed. She didn't know what she would do if her mother was ill.

'I'm moving,' Diana blurted and Kazz heaved a sigh of relief, her fingers tingling from the sudden rush of adrenalin.

'Is that all? For a second there, I thought you were going to tell me something awful. It's about time, if you ask me – this house is far too big for one person. Are you moving in with Vince?' She gave her mum a knowing smile. 'Don't worry, I'd already guessed it might be on the cards.'

'Kind of.' Diana looked nervous and she bit her lip.

Kazz's smile faded. 'What aren't you telling me?'

'Vince is in Spain.'

Blinking at the abrupt change of topic, Kazz pulled a face. 'Nice for some.'

'He's over there for work. That's why I have to clear the house.' Her mother took a deep breath and blew out her cheeks. 'I'm going to Valencia with him.'

'For a holiday?' Her mum hadn't been away in ages and she'd never been to Spain. But even as the words left her mouth, Kazz feared she knew what was coming next and her heart began to thud uncomfortably.

'No, not a holiday. I'm going there to live. Permanently.'

–

Kazz stared bleakly out of the train's wind ow. She was tired , grubby and d ejected , and her head still ached . $ wasn't entirely certain whether this was a result of her mother's news, or whether it was a remnant of her earlier hangover. All she knew was that she wanted a hot bath and an early night, although five p.m. was a bit on the early sid e to be thinking of going to bed .

When her mum had broken the news that she would be moving to another country, Kazz had wanted to blub like a baby. She had wanted to d emand that her mother stay firmly put in Lond on. She had wanted to stamp her foot and tell her that she was being selfish, that she could n't aband on her like this.

But Kazz had d one none of those things, and although tears had welled up and threatened to spill over, she had brushed them away because her mother had looked so happy. Her eyes had sparkled with joy and she'd worn a wid e beaming smile.

Kazz knew how tough the last few years had been for her, and her mum d eserved all the happiness in the world . There was no d oubt that she and Vince were in love, and Kazz hoped they would have a wond erful new life together. So, she had plastered a smile on her face and had said how pleased she was for her.

Her mum's excitement had been tempered by worry at how Kazz would take the news and how she would cope on her own.

But Kazz had assured her that she would n't be on her own; she had her job, her flatmates and her friend s – albeit it was a job she d isliked , flatmates who were more like ships passing in the night, and friend s she hard ly ever saw because of the hours she worked or because they lived too far away. She had even consid ered that it might be time she

thought about find ing a job in a kitchen that only opened
d uring the d ay, so she d id n't have to work evenings and
could get her social life back on track. She had told herself
that she was an ad ult, with a job and a place of her own,
and that she was perfectly capable of managing by herself.
She d id n't need to hang on to her mother's apron strings.

It had been one hell of a shock to d iscover that Mum
was flying out on *Friday*, a mere three d ays away, but
Kazz had rallied . And she had stayed rallied even when
her mother had asked whether she could clear the house
for her.

How could Kazz have refused , when Vince had got a
couple of viewings lined up for early next week and was
keen for them to get settled into a place of their own.
The company he worked for had arranged for him to see
some apartments, and he d id n't want to make a d ecision
unless Diana was with him. As Mum had said , it seemed
pointless her going out there, only to fly home again for
a few d ays, and then have to fly back again.

Mum had confessed that she d id n't expect to get much
for the furniture because, d espite it being well mad e, it
was very old -fashioned and rather tatty. Kazz had agreed
that there wasn't much call for big free-stand ing ward robes
these d ays; people preferred mod ern inbuilt ones. All she
had to d o was make a phone call to a house clearance
company, and they would come and take it all away.

Her mum's flight was at twelve-fifteen p.m. from
Gatwick, and she had booked a cab for nine o'clock to
take her to the airport, so Kazz d ecid ed she would tell
Fred d ie she had to have Thursd ay evening off (family
emergency, maybe?). She would stay the night at Mum's,
cook her a lovely meal, then send her off in the morning
with a champagne breakfast. They would have a girly

night and — She stopped abruptly, as tears gathered once more. There would be plenty of time for crying after her mum left.

Kazz had n't forgotten that she had promised to cook dinner this evening, so on the way home from the station she had popped into a shop and picked up some chicken breasts, a couple of lemons and a clove of garlic, along with a bag of spinach leaves. She alread y had the rest of the ingred ients, although she would n't be ad d ing any wine to this d ish. The mere thought of alcohol mad e her grimace. She would serve the chicken with fragrant rice and salsa, she d ecid ed .

Ironically, for a chef, she d id very little cooking outsid e of work, and she d id n't particularly want to cook this evening, but she'd promised and she d id n't want to irritat her flatmates more than she alread y had . Although Mona might be moving out shortly, Kazz still wanted to keep the peace. There was nothing worse than an atmosphere in the place you where should be able to relax, and she liked to believe she wasn't a d ifficult person to live with.

In an echo of her outward journey this morning, Kazz rested her head on the back of the seat and closed her eyes. This time she managed to keep them closed for more than a few second s, but when her phone trilled with an incoming message, she quickly opened them again.

It was Mona. *Soz, won't be there for dinner. Something's come up.*

Wond erful. The very person Kazz was trying to appease with a sumptuous meal would n't be there. Oh well, that was her flatmate's loss, Kazz d ecid ed . She was working tomorrow, and for the rest of the week, so she could n't move the meal to another evening, and the weekend s were always hit-and -miss because everyone was usually off d oing their own thing.

No worries. Kazz hit send , rested her head back on the seat and closed her eyes once more. This time she managed a full minute before her phone told her someone wanted her.

It was Rossiter. She hoped he'd suffered as bad a hangover as she had tod ay, but somehow she suspected not.

Have you heard the news? she read .

No – what? The restaurant trad e was rife with gossip and there was always a scand al or two d oing the round s.

About Freddie? Rossiter messaged back.

What?? It was typical of Rossiter to string out the d rama.

> He's been arrested. Fraud. They took him
> away in handcuffs.

> Are you joking?

> I was there. I saw him being shoved into a
> police car.

> I thought you had today off?

Was that the best she could manage? Fred d ie, her boss, had been arrested for fraud and her only concern was Rossiter's shift pattern?

I got a call to come in. It was like an
episode of Line of Duty.

That's AC12.

Whatever. A shrug emoji. *Thought I'd let you know the restaurant is closed until further notice.*

That can't be right! They can't shut the
restaurant.

They can and they have.

What about our jobs?

No idea. I'm out of there anyway. Freddie
was doing my head in before this. I'm
gonna update my CV tonight. Suggest you
do the same.

Kazz shook her head in d isbelief. This could n't be happening.

She spent the rest of the journey in a d aze, and it was with a heavy heart that she fished her keys out of her bag and unlocked the d oor lead ing to the first-floor flat. It was situated above a mobile phone accessory shop, but thankfully had its own entrance.

She let herself in and went insid e.

The hall was d ingy and d im, with peeling wallpaper, and the carpet on the stairs was stained and worn. She let out a sigh as she almost stepped on a pile of post. Stooping, she bent to pick it up, tutting crossly as she rifled through the usual flyers and leaflets. Then she paused . Amongst the junk mail were four id entical envelopes, one ad d ressed to each of the flatmates.

Kazz stared at them, examining each one carefully, before shoving the whole lot, apart from the envelope ad d ressed to her, und er her arm. With her attention on her own letter, she walked slowly up the stairs to the flat.

'Hello,' she called , but she could tell immed iately that no one was in. She wasn't surprised ; the others had nine-to-five jobs (unlike her) so d id n't tend to arrive home until after six.

Dropping the pile of post onto the rickety d ining table, she flung her bag and coat onto the sofa and gazed at the envelope again, reluctant to open it. She had a bad feeling about this…

Plucking up the courage, she slipped her nail und er the flap, tore it open and pulled out a typed sheet of A4 paper. The letter bore the name and logo of their land lord .

Oh, this isn't good.

And , as she scanned the contents, she quickly d iscovered just how bad it was. The letter was a notice to quit. Kazz and the rest of her flatmates had two months in which to vacate the property.

She was about to be mad e homeless!

Kazz d early wished she could start tod ay over again, because it appeared that things *could* get worse. Much worse. She'd had the temerity to challenge the god s, and they had accepted with a vengeance.

What on earth was she supposed to d o now?!

Chapter 3

Saul Green swung himself out of the old Land Rover and slammed the d oor shut, wincing as a flake of rust d ropped onto the tarmac. He should see to that before the d oor d isintegrated completely, but he could n't muster any enthusiasm for the task. Maybe he would repair it in the spring, when there was less likelihood of his nuts freezing off. That barn was d raughtier than the summit of Everest in a howling gale.

Narrowing his eyes at the d rop in temperature, he reached into the pocket of his ancient wax jacket, pulled out a navy beanie and plonked it on his head .

'All right, Saul? How's your mam?'

'Good , thanks.' Saul smiled at Betty.

The old lad y worked in Peggy's Tea Shoppe, and she must have spotted him through the wind ow when he'd pulled up outsid e and hurried out to greet him. She was d ressed , somewhat bizarrely, in an ankle-length bright yellow skirt with pink wellies poking out from und er its hem, a striped jumper in several d ifferent colours and a white maid 's cap on her head . Completing the outfit was a pinny with 'Peggy's Tea Shoppe' emblazoned on the front.

'Will she be at the committee meeting this evening?' she asked . Accord ing to Saul's mother, Betty was the most vocal member of Tanglewood 's Christmas festival committee – and Betty and the chairperson, Lady Tonbridge, constantly butted heads.

'She wouldn't miss it for the world,' he told her.

'What about you? Will you be there?' she demanded.

'It's not my scene. Besides, I've got other plans.'

Betty raised a pair of knowing eyebrows. 'Not *another* date?'

Saul couldn't make up his mind whether her tone was one of accusation or admiration. 'Gotta try before you buy,' he retorted lightly. 'That's what dating is all about. Surely people dated in your day?'

'In *my* day? Don't be so bloody cheeky! It's still my day.' She struck a pose, turning her skinny body to the side and putting her hand on a thrust-out hip.

'So it is,' he soothed.

Betty grinned at him. 'The way you're rattling through the available totty, the only woman within twenty miles who hasn't been on a date with you will be me. How about it, son? I reckon I could put you through your paces.'

Saul's eyes widened in horror. Betty was in her mid-eighties. 'I'll… er… keep you in mind if this one doesn't work out.'

'She won't,' Betty replied confidently. 'None of them ever do. But one of these days there will be a girl who will knock you for six.'

'How do you know it's not this one?' His date for this evening was gorgeous: tumbling blonde hair, big blue eyes and a figure to keep a man awake at night.

Betty tapped the side of her nose. 'I just know.'

Saul smiled nicely at her. Betty pretended to know stuff, but when it came to him, she knew nothing. Saul had already been 'knocked for six' years ago, and he had no intention of letting it happen again. It had taken him a long time to get over Joelle.

'Take care, Betty,' he said . 'I must d ash, I want to catch Leanne before she closes.' He mad e his escape and head ed up the street toward s his sister's flower shop.

When he got there, he took a second to ad mire her wind ow d isplay. Leanne always took great prid e in it, and this one was gorgeous. Gone was the pumpkin and Halloween theme of last week; now it was full-on Christmas, with two real fir trees (albeit small ones), a little compact sleigh, which he had helped her make, and lots of natural foliage. And poinsettias. Load s of poinsettias.

'The wind ow is looking good ,' he said , as he stepped insid e.

Leanne was crouching over a bucket of orange blooms, and she grinned up at him. 'It is, isn't it? I'm really pleased .'

'What are those?' He pointed to the flowers in the bucket.

'Chrysanthemums.'

'Do they signify anything?' he asked .

Leanne straightened up. 'What d o you mean?'

'Like, roses are for love, aren't they? If I give someone a bunch of chrysanthemums, they won't think it's a d eclaration of love, will they?'

His sister sighed . 'By *someone*, you must mean a poor unsuspecting woman. No, they d on't signify love. Orange and yellow ones are for good luck, which is appropriate because she's going to need it.'

'Harsh.'

'It's true. Is this one serious?'

'Why would you think that?'

'You're buying her flowers,' Leanne stated . 'You never buy any of them flowers.'

27

Saul hesitated . She had a point; he d id n't usually buy his d ates flowers. 'I've changed my mind ,' he d eclared . 'I d on't want her to read anything into it.'

'Good lord , no! That would n't d o at all.'

'No, it would n't,' he replied seriously, until he realised his sister was pulling his leg and scowled .

'Is this d ate number four or five?' she asked .

'Four. Why?'

'One more to go before you d ump her.'

Saul lifted his chin. 'I mightn't d ump her.'

'You will.' Her tone was confid ent. 'You always d o.'

Leanne was right.

He, too, had a feeling that Zara would soon fall by the waysid e. They always d id .

–

Saul was alread y seated at a table in the restaurant when Zara walked in, and he d rew in a sharp breath. Even bund led up in an ankle-length woollen coat, she was stunning, and he was conscious that many eyes, male and female, were on her as she spotted him and mad e her way to their table.

When she slipped off her coat and hand ed it to a waiter, his breath caught again. The skin-tight red d ress hugged her figure and he tried not to stare. Consid ering it was rather low-cut and there was an expanse of cleavage on show, he had to work hard to keep his focus on her face.

And what a lovely face it was. He would be a fool to let her slip through his fingers. But he alread y knew that was precisely what would happen. If he was honest, there would be no slipping involved . He would push her away, like he always d id , because there was no way he intend ed to let any woman get close enough to break his heart again.

Saul thought about what Leanne had said . This was d ate number four. None of his girlfriend s lasted to d ate number six.

Was he that pred ictable?

His sister thought so.

Remembering his manners, he half-rose from his chair to give Zara a hug and a quick kiss on the lips.

'Are you having a good week?' he asked , to break the ice.

She pulled a face. 'We lost a patient yesterd ay, so not brilliant.'

'Sorry to hear that.' Zara was a nurse at the local hospital, which was why they were having d inner on a Wed nesd ay evening. Her shifts tend ed to be rather rand om. He d id n't bother to tell her what he had been d oing since they'd last met. Round ing up sheep for market paled into insignificance compared to what she d id for a living. Working in a high-d epend ency unit must be tough.

They ord ered their food , and while they waited for it to arrive, they chatted about inconsequential things. He d escribed the TV series he had been binge-watching, and she told him about the new thriller author she'd d iscovered . Her current read was called *The Nurse* and he hoped she wasn't getting any interesting id eas that she might want to use on him when he broke up with her.

'I'm going to Hereford on Saturd ay with some friend s,' she said . 'We're staying overnight. It should be fun.'

She carried on telling him about it, not noticing the way he'd stiffened at the mention of the town's name. He could n't help it. Hearing it always affected him the same way. That was where Joelle had moved , after she had broken his heart.

Thinking about his ex, even after all this time, still mad e his heart constrict – what was left of it. He suspected there wasn't much, because if there had been, he would n't be contemplating breaking up with Zara this evening.

No, not *contemplating*. He was going to d o it. She was so lovely that it wasn't fair to keep stringing her along. He had a suspicion, by the way she was flirting with him this evening, that she was more into him than he could ever be into her.

It wasn't her fault; it was his. He was an emotionless d esert and maybe it was time he stopped trying to fill the emptiness insid e him by going on meaningless d ates with women he could never commit to, and whom he sometimes end ed up hurting. He always felt awful after he broke up with someone – even those women who had n't been particularly bothered , or who had only been d ating him because they wanted a bit of fun. Whether he hurt their feelings or not, he still felt bad .

Later that evening, when he d id the horrid d eed , Zara, bless her, mad e it easy for him, which conversely meant he felt even worse. Ashamed of himself, Saul vowed this would be the last time.

As he d rove back to the farm in his old rust bucket, he replayed the final scene of their non-relationship in his head . He had waited until they had finished the meal, had d riven her home and had parked outsid e her neat terraced house before breaking the news.

'I guessed as much,' she'd said , a small smile playing about her lips. 'You've got a bit of a reputation.'

'I have?'

She'd nodded. 'I was warned about you, so I'm not surprised.'

'I'm sorry—' he began, but she stopped him by putting a hand on his arm.

'It's not true what they say. I don't believe you're a playboy. I think you are damaged goods.'

Saul blustered, 'I'm not—'

'You *are*,' Zara insisted. 'I've seen enough broken people in my time to know you're one of them. I wish I could help, but your kind of pain doesn't respond to intravenous medication. Take care, Saul. I hope you find what you're looking for.' And with that, she had got out of the car.

He had watched her until she reached her front door, and waved back when she gave him a little goodbye flutter of her fingers. She hadn't seemed upset, and he was thankful for that, but he still felt terrible.

It was only as he was rattling into the farmyard, the Land Rover juddering over the potholes, that he wondered what Zara had meant when she'd said she hoped he found what he was looking for.

What *was* he looking for?

He wasn't sure, but one thing he did know was that it wasn't love. He had found that once and lost it. Now look at the state he was in.

He had to try to patch himself back together first, before he could learn to love again. If he ever did. Or if he even wanted to…

Saul had an awful feeling that his heart was beyond repair.

–

'You know the saying that old farmers never d ie, they just get ploughed und er?' Saul's father said , the following morning.

Saul paused to rub the sleeve of his scruffy old jumper across his face. He and his d ad were repairing a d rystone wall in the topmost field and it was back-breaking work. Saul could n't tell whether it had tumbled d own naturally or whether something had knocked the upper stones out. However it had happened , it need ed fixing before the sheep were brought d own from the hills for the winter. Some farmers left them to graze on the mountains all year round , but Saul's d ad preferred to have them contained d uring the worst of the weather because he reckoned they were easier to keep an eye on. Saul was all for that. Although he loved the wild ness of the mountains and enjoyed being up on the hills, trying to find a flock of sheep in d riving sleet, when the cloud was so low that he could n't see the valley floor, wasn't his id ea of fun.

'Never heard of it,' he said .

'Well, that's what they say,' Geoff persisted . 'Anyway, I'm not planning on popping my clogs, but I d o think I need to take a back seat. Let you and your brother run the farm.'

Saul snorted . 'That's never going to happen. You would n't be able to take a back seat if your chair was on the moon.'

'I'm serious, Saul. I want to step back a bit. I'm getting too old for this.'

'You're only sixty-five. You're d efinitely not too old .'

'I'm not saying I'll give up farming altogether, but I think you pair should take over the d ay-to-d ay running.'

Saul froze. Him *and* Murray take over? Run it together? Yeah, right…

Saul wasn't the eld est, but he had worked on the farm since he could tod d le. It was all he knew. All five Green kid s had helped out when they were growing up – it had been expected of them – but only he and Murray had stayed on to work the place.

The old est, Martin, and his wife, Janine, were tenant farmers near Usk; Stuart, the second old est, had quit farming entirely and was working for a logistics company moving lorries around the country. It had n't come as a surprise, as he'd always liked playing with toy trucks as a nipper.

The fifth and youngest of the five, and the only girl, was Leanne. She had n't wanted to farm either, opening a flower shop in the heart of the village instead . Which just left Saul and Murray.

Murray was younger than him by two-and -a-half years and was currently living in a converted barn d own the lane which he had originally shared with Saul, but it was now the sole d omain of Murray and his new wife, Ashley.

For the past few years, the farm's structure had remained stable: Dad in charge and having the final say, with active (and often vociferous) input from Saul and Murray.

Now it seemed that was about to change, and not for the better, as far as Saul was concerned . There could n't be two hand s on the tiller – someone had to make the d ecisions, and consid ering how often he and Murray butted head s, Saul feared that they would constantly be at loggerhead s.

He could und erstand why Dad had mad e the d ecisio to let him and Murray run the farm between them, because they put an equal amount of work into the busi-ness, but as the eld est of the two, Saul had hoped that when the time came for their dad to step down, he would be the one in charge.

If he was honest, he felt a bit put out, even though he was ashamed of himself for feeling that way. It must have been a difficult decision to make, and with Murray having to support a wife, and with Saul having no responsibilities in that department, he kind of understood.

It didn't make it any easier to stomach, though.

Not for the first time, Saul wondered whether he should leave the farm. Strike out on his own, maybe? Do what Martin had done and become a tenant farmer. He would be his own boss, answerable to himself and no one else. It was an option that many farmers' sons took, as a way to secure a farm of their own.

The only issue was the start-up costs, but his parents had helped Martin with his, and they had also financed Leanne when she had opened her flower shop, so maybe they would consider giving him a helping hand. It would be in the form of a loan, as it had been for the others, but it was better than going cap in hand to a bank.

There was also another thing to consider; Saul had moved back into the main house when Murray and his girlfriend had got married, so in effect, he was still living with his parents. It had never bothered him much – and it certainly hadn't affected his ability to attract a girlfriend, although he didn't broadcast that he still lived at home. A place of his own would mean he would have to do his own cooking and laundry (his mother refused to let him anywhere near the kitchen or her washing machine – which he was relieved about) but if he was lucky enough to secure a tenancy, he would consider it a small price to pay.

It was definitely time for a change, and maybe his dad's decision to step back might be the kick up the backside he needed.

–

Saul read the same sentence for the third time, then gave up and closed the book. It had a good write-up, and an enticing cover and description, but he couldn't get into it. He was about halfway through, and until today he had been enjoying it, but since his father's announcement earlier, he seemed to have lost his appetite for reading.

Picking up his phone, he scrolled through the list of farms available to rent. Unsurprisingly, it hadn't changed since he'd looked at it half an hour ago. He had been disappointed that nothing had taken his fancy (too big, too small, too far away) but he was probably approaching it from the wrong direction. He shouldn't be looking at farms to rent as a starting point – he should be getting his finances sorted and a business plan in place first.

He was too tired to think about it now, though. Creating a business plan called for a clear head, not one that had been subjected to a steady westerly wind for the best part of the day. His ears were still cold, despite the beanie hat he had worn, and having been indoors for the past couple of hours.

Saul reached for the novel again, but his attention continued to wander.

When he thought about it (which he tried not to do too often), what did he have to show for the decade and a half since he'd left college?

Not a lot.

He didn't even own a decent vehicle, as the Land Rover was almost as old as he was. He had a gaming chair and a d esk, plus an assortment of electronics which he hard ly ever used , a selection of clothes and a hand ful of books. It wasn't much, was it?

Discontent washed over him. This wasn't how he'd imagined his life would be like. When he'd been at school, he had thought he would have had a house of his own by now, and possibly a stead y job. Or one that paid a d ecent wage. He most d efinitely thought he would be rid ing around in a nice car. Something with cruise control and four-wheel d rive. Something that would turn girls' head s.

The only head s he turned when he d rove the eld erly Land Rover were those belonging to the mechanics in the garage on the outskirts of Tanglewood , as they took bets on how soon it would be before he'd need to bring it in to them to be repaired . It was a wond er he could get a d ate at all with wheels like that, let alone the number he got through in a year.

Had got through, he amend ed . His d ays of playing the field were over. Which was just as well, because taking an end less succession of women on d ates was costing him a fortune – money that he would be better off saving for his new venture into tenant farming. But saving a pound or two on a meal out wasn't going to get him far. He would have to think of a way to earn some extra money, in ad d ition to the loan he might get from his parents. He had always been good with his hand s; maybe he could hire himself out as a hand yman? He was happy to have a go at most things – apart from electrics, after an incid ent involving a bolt cutter and a blown fuse, but the less said about that, the better.

That's what he would d o, he d ecid ed : he would put th word out in the village and wait to see if anything came of it.

Feeling more optimistic, Saul returned to his book. And this time, when he read the word s on the page, most of them sunk in.

Chapter 4

When Kazz opened her eyes on Frid ay morning, two thoughts leapt into her head . The first was that she had just spent her last night in her grand parents' old house. The second was that her mother was flying to Spain tod ay to start a new life, and she d id n't know when she would see her again.

With a heavy heart, she hauled herself out of bed and got d ressed . She had promised Mum a champagne breakfast, and that's what she would give her.

Kazz could hear her mum pottering around in the bed room as she trotted d ownstairs, and her chin began to wobble. In a little over an hour her mother would be getting in a taxi and leaving for good , and although Kazz was thrilled for her, she was sad for herself.

Determined not to let her mum see how upset she was, she d ug d eep and slapped a bright smile on her face as she prepared eggs Bened ict on brioche with smoked salmon.

She mad e enough for two, even though she d id n't have an appetite, knowing that her mother would refuse to eat on her own. And although Kazz was tempted to d rink most of the bottle of champagne by herself, she would n't, because Mum was und er the impression that Kazz had to work tod ay. Kazz d id n't feel comfortable with hid ing her job situation from her mother, but she d id n't want anything to spoil the d ay. If her mum knew that the restaurant was closed for the foreseeable future, she mightn't get on the plane. And if she realised her daughter wouldn't have a home in eight weeks, she *definitely* wouldn't.

Kazz knew how much this meant to her, so she would keep schtum, and she would keep on being quiet about it until she was able to give her mum some good news.

'Don't you look lovely!' she exclaimed when Diana walked into the kitchen.

Her mother wore a pair of tailored trousers, a pretty long-sleeved top in the most gorgeous shade of turquoise and a linen jacket.

'I thought I'd better make an effort.' Diana glanced down at herself anxiously. 'I hope I'm not going to be too cold. Vince says that the past few days have been cooler in Valencia than average for the time of year.' She pursed her lips. 'Never mind; I'll be wearing my nice winter coat to the airport, so I can always pop it on when I get to the other end if I'm chilly.'

'You'll be fine,' Kazz assured her. 'Sit down and I'll dish up.' She waved the bottle of champagne and grinned. 'Fancy a cheeky one?'

'Ooh, I don't mind if I do. Only one, though, I don't want to be nodding off in departures.'

Kazz poured her a glass and handed it to her.

Diana took a sip. 'Lovely! Aren't you having any?'

'Better not.'

'Ah, of course. Freddie wouldn't appreciate you rocking up for work smelling of alcohol.' Her mother's gaze narrowed. 'You will be all right on your own, won't you?'

Kazz put a plate in front of her. 'Mum, I'm a grown woman – of course I'll be all right. I can stand on my own two feet, you know. I've been doing it for years.'

'I know you have, but you'll always be my little girl.'

Kazz's smile was watery. 'Stop it, you'll make me cry.'

'I already am,' Diana said, dabbing at her eyes.

Kazz gave her a one-armed cuddle, and then sat down. 'Eat up before it gets cold.'

She forced her breakfast down, despite feeling as though she was eating lumps of cardboard, and when they were finished, she gathered up the dirty dishes.

'You may as well throw that old frying pan away,' her mum said. 'It's not fit for the charity shop and I doubt the house clearance company will take it.'

Since Tuesday, her mother had made great inroads into ridding the house of the more portable items, and all Grandad's clothes were gone, as well as all those items of clothing that Diana wasn't taking with her to Spain. There were very few ornaments left, hardly any pictures, and most of the smaller contents of the kitchen were now displayed in the three charity shops which were within walking distance.

All that was left was the furniture and the white goods. And the books. The hundreds and hundreds of books.

'What do you want me to do with the books, Mum?'

Her mum shrugged. 'I suppose you'd better see if the clearance company will take them off your hands. I did think about giving them to the charity shop, but who wants books like these? People want popular thrillers and swoony romances, not those old things.'

Kazz had been thinking along the same lines. No one wanted dusty old doorstops (although, to be fair, there were also plenty of smaller books) and she had been scouring her brain for ways to get rid of them, even going as far as wondering whether she could donate them to the local library.

Praying that the house clearance company wanted them – because if they didn't, she might have to hire a skip – Kazz set about washing the breakfast things while her mum had a quick wee and made a final check around the house.

'There,' Diana announced, after Kazz had helped her haul her cases downstairs (she had four of them!). 'I'm all set. The taxi will be here in a minute. Oh, I wish you were coming to Spain with me!'

'No, you don't. I'd be a spare wheel with you two all loved up.'

'You'll come and visit us, won't you?'

'Try and stop me! I'm not giving up the chance of a free holiday in the sun.' Kazz swallowed, the small amount that she had eaten sitting heavily in her stomach. 'Are you sure you don't want me to come to the airport with you?'

'I'm sure. I don't want to make you late for work. Aw, come here.'

Diana opened her arms wide and Kazz stepped into them, revelling in the last cuddle her mother would give her for a while.

'I'm going to miss you, my gorgeous girl.'

'Not as much as I'm going to miss *you*,' Kazz replied. 'You'll be having far too much fun.' She clung to her mother tightly.

They were still hugging when the taxi driver rang the doorbell, and it was only his third demanding ring that forced them apart.

'Love you, Karen,' her mum said . 'Take care of yourself, and if you need me, phone me. I'm only a couple of hours away.'

'Love you too, Mum.'

Kazz did n't stop waving until the taxi turned the corner and her mother was out of sight. Then she trudged sad ly back insid e, and wond ered what on earth she was supposed to d o now.

–

Kazz had n't mentioned anything to her mum about having arranged for a clearance company to come and give her a quote this morning, so after she'd waved her mum off, she d id n't go back to the flat. Instead , she wand ered around the house, killing time until the chap or chaps arrived .

Many of her child hood memories were housed insid e these walls. Apart from Mum, Kazz d id n't have much in the way of family, her father not having wanted anything to d o with her when she was born. Grand ad had stepped into the breach, his solid no-nonsense presence provid ing her with a masculine balance to her mum and nan, and the rest of the women in her young life. Stevie's Aunt Peggy had been one of them, and Kazz had spent nearly as much time with Stevie's aunt as Stevie had .

Thinking of Aunt Peg led to thoughts of the tea shop, which remind ed Kazz that Stevie had suggested she pay her a visit. She d ecid ed she would take her up on the offer, if Stevie was still happy to have her. A few d ays away might d o her good . Besid es, she had n't told Stevie about her misfortunes yet – she had been so focused on the news that her mum was moving abroad , she no longer had a job and , to cap it all, she was being evicted , that all she'd wanted to d o was crawl into a cave and hid e. It was said that things came in threes, and Kazz fervently prayed that she'd had her three pieces of bad luck for the time being.

Getting another job was her priority, because without one she would n't be able to find anywhere to live. She would get this house clearance business out of the way, pay a flying visit to Stevie for a should er to cry on, and then she would start job hunting in earnest.

Her wand ering took her into the living room, with her grand ad 's fad ed , careworn wingback chair and over-bearing mahogany sid eboard . It was a massive old thing, and Kazz wond ered how anyone would get it out of the house. Or how they had got it into the room in the first place. She hoped it would n't have to be d ismantled . It would be such a shame. The sid eboard mightn't be fash-ionable, but it was a solid piece of furniture and hopefully someone would be able to make use of it.

Her attention was d rawn to the bookcases on the opposite wall, and she strolled across the room for a closer look at their contents, smiling at the memory of Grand ad stand ing behind the counter of his old shop, weak sunlight filtering through the slightly grubby wind ows to illu-minate whatever book he happened to be enthralled in at the time. Nan used to reckon he only owned a bookshop as an excuse to read . People used to bring him old books all the time, asking whether he would like to buy them, which he sometimes d id , d epend ing on the book.

Kazz laughed aloud (a small sad laugh, but a laugh nonetheless) as she remembered how, when she was young, she thought he must have read every book in the overcrowd ed stuffed -full shop.

Only with the benefit of age and hindsight did she understand that he had been running a business. The books he'd bought had been ones he had thought would sell. And he must have done all right because there had always been plenty of food on the table and treats in the cupboard.

It hadn't done well enough to enable her grandparents to buy a house of their own, though. They'd rented this one all their married lives, which was remarkable when she came to think of it. No one stayed in one place for long these days. Look at her!

A loud ding-dong startled her, and Kazz hurried answer the door, her heart thudding.

A man wearing a porkpie hat, spectacles and a tweed jacket with a set of overalls underneath was standing on the path, and she caught him eyeing the outside of the property.

'Them's the original windows,' he stated, not looking at her.

'Right, er, do you want to come in?'

'I suppose I better had, if you want me to give you a price.' He looked closely at her. 'Is this your house?'

'No, it's my mother's, but she has given me full authority to act on her behalf. She's just moved to Spain. This morning, actually.' A lump formed in Kazz's throat and she coughed to clear it.

'You'll have to sign a disclaimer,' the man said, following her into the hall. 'The name's Gold, Arnie Gold, licenced to clear.' He chuckled at his own wit.

Kazz didn't think the James Bond analogy worked, but she smiled politely and said, 'Kazz Fernsby.' *Not licenced to do anything at the moment*, she added silently.

'Point me at what needs to go,' he instructed.

'Everything, I think.'

'Aren't you sure?' He frowned at her.

'No, I'm sure. Everything.'

'I'll start in here, shall I?' He pointed to the first door in the hall. It led to the living room, and without waiting for a reply, he went inside.

Kazz followed anxiously, trying to read his body language as he went from room to room, but he was giving nothing away.

After peering into the third bedroom, which was full to the brim with boxes of books, he turned to her. 'So, that's two reception rooms, one kitchen and three bedrooms to be cleared. Any sheds or garages?'

'No, but there's an attic and a cellar,' she told him, pointing to the ceiling hatch above his head.

She dropped the ladder and waited at the bottom as he clambered up. While she waited, she took out her phone and pinged off a quick message to Stevie. *How soon can I come visit?*

It didn't take long for her friend to reply.

As soon as you like!

Before Kazz had time to change her mind, she looked up the train times from London Paddington to Tanglewood's nearest station and booked a ticket. It was eye-wateringly expensive, considering she didn't know where her next pay packet was coming from, but she didn't care. She desperately needed someone to talk to.

Arnie Gold reversed down the ladder, and when he got to the bottom, his expression was blank, but Kazz was convinced she could see mild panic in his eyes. She didn't blame him – she would be panicking too, if she had to shift all those books.

Without saying anything, he stepped around her and went downstairs, heading for the kitchen. The cellar door was next to the pantry, and when he reached it, all he said was, 'The cellar's down there, yeah?'

'That's right.'

She flicked the light switch and watched him descend into the depths. It felt like he'd been down there an age, but it probably wasn't much more than a couple of minutes.

When he emerged, his face was grim. 'Likes reading, does she?'

'The books aren't hers. Well, I mean, they are, of course, but they originally belonged to my grandad. He had a bookshop and —'

'Can't take 'em,' Mr Gold cut in. 'Not sure if I can take any of it, to be honest. There's not much call for this kind of furniture. Too big and dark, see. And it usually stinks of mothballs and is full of wood worm.'

Kazz's mouth dropped open. He wasn't going to take *anything*? How else was she supposed to get rid of it?

Her face must have said what her mouth was having trouble spitting out, because he held up a hand. 'Now, I'm not saying I *won't* take it, but to be honest, I should be charging *you* for getting rid of it. And I definitely can't shift any of those books. Got no call for 'em, see; no one I can sell them on to.'

'How much will you give me for the rest of it?' she asked.

And when he named a figure, she didn't know whether to laugh or be insulted. Poor Nan and Grandad would be turning in their graves if they knew how little their worldly possessions were worth.

'Tell you what,' he said , 'think about it, yeah? You've got my number. If you d ecid e to go ahead with the clearance, I can d o it the tail end of next week, or the week after.'

Kazz shook the hand he offered her, then saw him to the d oor.

As soon as he had gone, she d id n't linger. She grabbed her bag, coat and scarf, and quickly locked up. She had some packing of her own to d o.

Chapter 5

Sitting on a bus, trund ling along the main road lead ing from Abergavenny to Tanglewood , was a far cry from the journey Kazz had mad e from her flat to her mum's house less than a week ago.

Was it only on Tuesd ay that her world had been turned upsid e d own? It felt like a lifetime, not a mere four d ays. So much had happened , and none of it good . However, d espite need ing to sound off to Stevie, Kazz was d etermined to try to enjoy these few d ays away and make the most of them.

With that in mind , she settled into her seat and watched the countrysid e roll by. It might be November and most of the trees had lost their leaves, but the field s were still green, and like every other time she had visited Tanglewood , Kazz was blown away by the view of the wid e flat-bottomed valley with a river running through it, and the mountains rising above.

The mountain range to her left boasted the third highest peak in Wales, and it was far more impressive and majestic than the Lond on skyline she was used to. The lower slopes of the hillsid es were a patchwork of field s interspersed with wood land , and higher up they opened into heathland covered in bracken and heather, with the occasional rocky outcrop. The land scape was simultaneously chocolate-box pretty and wonderfully wild. No wonder Stevie had fallen in love with it.

When Stevie had first moved to Tanglewood to open her little tea shop, Kazz thought she was mad. Stevie was a city girl: she would be lost in the wilds of the Welsh Marches. But Stevie had thrived, and Kazz felt more than a little envious. And when the bus bumped over the narrow stone bridge with its lovely arches which spanned the river, her heart leapt in delight. Even with winter around the corner, Tanglewood was still pretty.

The main road led away from the river, with artisan shops and privately owned businesses lining both sides, and Kazz craned her neck as the bus drove slowly along the street, grinning as Peggy's Tea Shoppe came into view. And there was Stevie herself, standing next to the window, talking to a couple seated at a table.

Kazz lifted her small suitcase onto her lap and prepared to disembark. She had n't told Stevie what time she was catching the train, knowing that her friend would insist on driving to the station to collect her. Kazz had n't wanted to put her out more than she was already, and she had rather enjoyed the journey from the station to the village.

Stevie did n't notice Kazz when she walked into the tea shop, but Betty, Stevie's elderly employee, did and her face crinkled into a wrinkly smile.

'I knew you'd be early!' she exclaimed. 'I could feel it in my water. Stevie! Kazz is here.'

Stevie looked up and let out a squeal. 'Kazz, my bestie! I did n't expect you until much later.' She rushed towards her, arms outstretched, and engulfed her in a huge hug that lifted her off her feet.

'I told you she'd be early,' Betty repeated, sniffing. 'But does anyone ever listen to me? No! I'm just the old biddy in the corner.'

Stevie released Kazz and laughed. 'I don't think anyone would dare refer to you as an old biddy, Betty.'

'Hi, Betty.' Kazz gave her a little wave. Turning to Stevie, she said, 'Sorry to drop in on you like this, but I couldn't wait to get here. Is there anything I can do? I can see you're busy.'

Betty snorted. 'Pish, this isn't busy. You wait until the week before Christmas, then you'll see what busy looks like.'

Stevie sent Kazz the look that meant she was trying to hold in a giggle.

But Betty wasn't done yet. 'Sit yourselves down, the pair of you. I bet Kazz is dying for a cuppa, and she'll want you to keep her company, Stevie.'

'I'm sure—' Kazz said, but Stevie hushed her.

'Betty's right, we're not busy, and she enjoys bossing me around. Anyone would think she owns the place, not me, but I don't mind them thinking that, if it keeps her happy.'

Betty had started work in Peggy's Tea Shoppe after her cottage by the river was flooded and she had nowhere to live until it had dried out, so she'd moved in with Stevie for the duration, staying in the spare bedroom in Stevie's flat above the tea shop. During that time, Stevie discovered that Betty used to work in the kitchen of a big hotel on the south coast when she was younger, and she was a mean baker.

After Betty returned to her little cottage, Stevie had given the old lady a job, and now Betty was as much a part of the tea shop as Stevie. According to her, Betty had a reputation for knowing things she had no business knowing, and life was certainly more interesting with the old lady around .

Stevie led Kazz to a vacant table. 'Are you hungry?' she asked .

'Starving.' Breakfast was a very long time ago and Kazz's mouth watered as she studied the chalkboard on the wall behind the counter, where today's specials were advertised . 'Could I have a bowl of pumpkin soup with rye bread , please?' she asked , trying to ignore the loud rumbling coming from her stomach.

'Of course! I'll join you, I haven't had any lunch either.' Stevie hurried off to prepare the food , returning quickly with two steaming bowls and a plate containing hunks of crusty bread .

Kazz ate with enthusiasm, gobbling her meal down. When her bowl was empty and she had a huge cup of hazelnut-infused coffee in front of her, she finally sat back in her chair, replete.

'That was delicious,' she said with a satisfied sigh, and grinned at her best friend .

Stevie didn't grin back. Her expression was serious as she asked , 'Are you going to tell me what's going on, or do I have to guess?'

'You know me too well,' Kazz said , sombrely.

'I should do – we've only known each other since we were little! Come on, spit it out. Something's wrong and I want to know all about it.'

Kazz began with her mother asking her to help clear the house, and ended with the house clearance man yesterday, and the paltry sum he'd offered her for the contents.

'And he would n't even take any of the blasted books,' she moaned . 'I wish I could go to Spain with Mum, but I can't cramp her style. Imagine how Vince would feel with his partner's ad ult d aughter hanging around like a spare part. Anyway, I haven't told Mum that I'm jobless and soon-to-be homeless. She would only insist on coming back to look after me, and I can't let her d o that. I should n't need looking after.' She d rank some of her coffee to lubricate her throat after all that talking, then carried on, 'So that's my sad little tale – no job and nowhere to live, just a load of worthless furniture and a pile of old books that I'll either have to foist onto whichever charity shops are willing to take a boxful, hire a skip or try to sell them online, which will probably take forever, and in the meantime I would have to find somewhere to store them. What the hell am I going to d o with all those sod d ing books?'

Betty slapped a plate of assorted cakes d own on the table, and said , 'That's easy – open a bookshop.'

Kazz and Stevie stared at each other, but waited until Betty was out of earshot before either of them spoke.

'I'll give her that,' Kazz said , 'she certainly thinks outsid e the box. A bookshop, ind eed !'

'I d id n't see that coming either.' Stevie examined the plate of cakes, then wrinkled her nose. 'I d on't think I can face anything sweet – I've been staring at these for hours, starting with this morning when I took them out of the oven. I'm all caked out.'

Kazz wasn't. Stevie was one of the best bakers she knew, and she happily got stuck in. 'Mmm, this is d elicious,' she said , around a mouthful of pumpkin layer cake, her voice somewhat ind istinct.

Stevie said , 'Tell Betty; she baked it.'

Kazz's eyes wid ened . 'She's good , isn't she?'

'She most d efinitely is. I d on't know what I'd d o without her.' Stevie pursed her lips. 'I wish I had room for you here, but I've got a full complement of staff. If it had happened after the wed d ing, it might have been a d ifferent story.' Stevie was getting married in the summer, and Kazz was one of the brid esmaid s.

Kazz asked , 'Why, are you thinking of cutting back your hours?' She knew that running a tea shop like Stevie's was hard work, and took a lot of time and d ed ication, and with Stevie's fiancé Nick owning a training yard for horses, it was a wond er the pair of them managed to spend any time together.

'I might be,' Stevie said coyly. 'It all d epend s on how soon I get pregnant.'

Kazz almost spat out the morsel of cake she was eating. 'Are you trying for a baby right *now*?'

Stevie shook her head and put a finger to her lips. 'Shh, I d on't want Betty to know, otherwise I won't hear the end of it. No, not yet. We thought we'd wait until after we've tied the knot. I've spent a fortune on that wed d ing d ress and I want to be able to fit into it on the d ay!'

'Bagsy I be god mother,' Kazz said , keeping her voice low.

'I d on't think you can bagsy god mother rights.' Stevie laughed . 'But d on't worry, you're at the top of my list. Anyway, it's all in the future; we need to concentrate on the present and on what you're going to d o.'

'Run away and hid e?' Kazz pouted .

'That's not like you. You're the sensible one.'

'I'm the one without a job or a home,' Kazz shot back. 'I d on't feel like being sensible.'

'Sensible is overrated ,' Betty d eclared , as she bustled past with a lad en tray. 'Now, if you've finished gossiping, I would appreciate a hand because – if you had n't noticed – we're getting busy.'

Stevie gave Kazz an apologetic grin. 'See what I mean? Bossy.'

'Can I help?' Kazz offered as Stevie rose to her feet. 'I need to feel useful.'

'Aw, my lovely, d on't be so d own. Something will turn up.'

Kazz sighed . 'I suppose so, and if it d oesn't, I can always open a bookshop and sleep behind the counter.'

–

Kazz gazed around the table at her Tanglewood friend s and felt the remaining tension ease from her should ers. This was just what she need ed , a night out with the girls. Stevie had suggested everyone meet in the Hen and Duck this evening for a meal. By everyone, Stevie meant her and Kazz, obviously, plus Tia, Leanne and Ed ie. The brid e-to-be and her four brid esmaid s. But, for once, the focus wasn't on Stevie's forthcoming nuptials. It was on Kazz's pred icament.

Tia waved a glass in the air. It was conspicuously empty. 'Before we carry on putting Kazz to rights,' she said , 'I need a refill, and I believe it's my round .' She swivelled her wheelchair around and called to the land lord , 'Same again, Mad s!' And when he had gathered up the empties and retreated behind the bar, she asked , 'Where were we?'

Kazz pulled a face. She could n't for the life of her remember. She had been too busy scoffing a plate of rather d elicious scampi and fries.

Tia was gazing at her expectantly. Kazz shrugged .

'You'll have to d o better than that,' Tia said , smacking her palm d own on the arm of her wheelchair. 'This is *your* life we're trying to sort out. Not ours.'

Kazz blew out her cheeks. Tia was right. Everyone else's lives were alread y sorted . Stevie had her tea shop and lived with Nick in a large bungalow at the stables. Leanne had her flower shop, a lucrative sid eline with a famous floristry chain in Lond on, and she lived in a cute cottage with her ranger boyfriend , Rex. Ed ie owned a classy brid al shop and lived on a smallhold ing with her other half, James. And Tia, who was Nick's sister, lived and worked in the poshest place of them all: Tonbrid ge Manor. She and her husband , Will, had their own wing and shared the rest of the impressive old build ing with Will's parents, Lord and Lad y Tonbrid ge. When the current Lord popped his clogs, Tia would become a Lad y.

And what d id Kazz have? A pile of old furniture and a load of crusty old books. Hard ly comparable, was it?

'Betty suggested I open a bookshop.' She sighed . 'Unfortunately, that's the best id ea anyone has had so far. I suppose I should bite the bullet and hire a skip. At least the chap from the house clearance company will take everything else away, so that's something, although I won't get much for it.' Kazz pressed her lips together in d isbelief. 'At one point he had the cheek to tell me I should be paying *him* to take it off my hand s!'

'Could you make use of any of it?' Stevie asked Tia. 'From what I can remember of Kazz's grand ad 's house, most of the furniture is old .'

'Old as in *antique* old ?' Tia asked , looking at Kazz.

Kazz took a guess. '1950s?'

Tia gave her a sympathetic smile. 'Er, that's not really old . Everything at the Manor is nineteenth century or earlier.'

Leanne tapped her fingers against her chin. 'How much will it cost to hire a skip?'

Kazz shrugged . 'Not sure. A couple of hund red .'

'Why d on't you find out how much a small storage unit would cost? Then you could sell the books online,' Leanne suggested .

Ed ie giggled . 'Or you could fill a rucksack and every time you go out, you could d rop a couple in the nearest public bin. You'd have some exercise and get rid of the books at the same time.'

'This is starting to get silly,' Stevie scold ed . 'What you *could* d o, Kazz, is you could visit every library within a twenty-mile rad ius and leave them on the shelves.'

'You lot are no help at all,' Kazz grumbled .

Tia d ecid ed to join in. 'What about making those bookish sculptures out of the pages? Or carve out the insid es and sell them as somewhere to hid e your valu-ables?'

Kazz stared at the ceiling, refusing to look at any of them. 'When you've finished , can I have some sensible suggestions, please?'

Leanne said , 'Betty's suggestion was sensible.' She even managed to look serious as she was saying it.

Kazz hmphed at her and fold ed her arms.

Stevie, Tia and Ed ie looked at one another, then at Leanne, who was nod d ing and smiling.

Stevie said , 'Actually, it*'s* a good id ea.'

'Not you as well!' Kazz exclaimed . 'Are you all mad ?'

'Probably.' Tia giggled .

For one crazy, stupid second, Kazz considered the idea. Then she came to her senses. 'Don't be silly. Do you know how much it costs to rent a retail unit in London?' If she was honest, Kazz didn't know herself, but she guessed it was probably a lot.

The four of them were looking at each other again, and grinning like loons.

Leanne said, 'Who said anything about London?'

'Where else would it be?' Kazz was baffled.

Edie tutted. 'You do realise there are other places in the world? Your shop doesn't have to be in London. In fact, it's probably better that it isn't.'

'Where, then?' Kazz demanded. She would go along with this ridiculous suggestion, but only because she wanted to see how far they would take it.

'Tanglewood,' Leanne announced.

Kazz burst out laughing. 'You can't be serious?'

'We can and we are. All in agreement, ladies?' Stevie asked. There was a chorus of affirmations.

'You seriously want me to open a bookshop in *Tanglewood*?'

Leanne could barely contain her excitement. 'No *you* seriously want to open a bookshop in Tanglewood. Think about it: you've got goodness knows how many hundreds of books to sell and you aren't tied to a job or a flat, so you can go anywhere you want and *do* anything you want.'

'If that was true, I'd be off somewhere hot, with beaches and cocktails, and hunky waiters,' Kazz retorted.

'Such a cliché.' Tia groaned.

Kazz shot back, 'Says the woman who lives in a mansion.'

'Guilty as charged,' Tia replied cheerfully. 'But I'm not the one who needs a job and somewhere to live.'

'And you did tell me last night that you'd had a gut full of catering,' Stevie leapt in.

Kazz muttered, 'Et tu, Brute?'

'Isn't it funny how that's the only quote I remember from Shakespeare. That and "out damned spot".' Edie laughed.

'How about "beware the Ides of March", or "double, double toil and trouble"?' Tia suggested.

Edie said, 'Wasn't there a bestseller a while back, based on a line from *Romeo and Juliet*? Something about faulty stars.'

'It's from *Julius Caesar*,' Kazz replied absently. 'The book is called *The Fault in Our Stars*.'

'See! You know booky things!' Stevie exclaimed, and Kazz rolled her eyes in exasperation.

'I know that I don't know enough to open a bookshop,' she argued. 'Anyway, never mind the shop. Where would I live?'

'The flat above the tea shop,' Stevie said. 'I've been letting it out to holidaymakers, but I haven't got any bookings until February. You could stay there.'

Kazz hadn't finished making objections. 'What about the shop itself?'

Edie said, 'There's an empty one by the entrance to the courtyard.'

'But I'm a sous chef.' Kazz played her trump card. She cooked for a living, she didn't sell books!

Stevie said, 'You don't want to do that anymore. You said so yourself. You want to change jobs.'

'I was thinking about getting a job in a small place similar to Stevie's, not opening a sodding bookshop. I can't afford it, anyway. Refurb and all that jazz.'

Stevie pointed out, 'You've got your mum and grand ad 's furniture – you can use that. Bookshelves, chairs to sit in, that old bureau – if your mum hasn't thrown it out. You could even take the d oors off the ward robes and turn them into shelving units. A d ining or kitchen table will d o for a counter. All you need is a card machine and a sign, and you're read y to go.'

'But I'm not sure I want to work in a bookshop for the rest of my life.'

Tia patted her arm. 'It d oesn't have to be forever. You could give it a go until Christmas. Short-term retail lets are popular these d ays.'

Leanne cried , 'They certainly are! Jarred had one a couple of months back to test the waters before committing to opening another shop. He takes out a short-term lease to gauge whether it's viable. He's opened shops in two new areas this way. Pop-up shops, they're called . It's surprisingly easy to start one.'

'It's all right for Jarred Townsend , the famous florist, to have a pop-up shop.' Kazz scowled . 'He can afford it with his celebrity status. If he opened a crisp packet, people would flock to it. No one would be flocking to a second - hand bookshop in the mid d le of nowhere.'

'You'd be surprised ,' Leanne said . 'Tanglewood has more going for it than you think.'

Kazz tried a d ifferent tack. 'OK, let's say for argument's sake that I move into Stevie's flat and that I can get a short-term lease at a price I can afford . How d o I get everything from Lond on to Tanglewood ?'

Leanne clapped her hand s. 'Simple! Use a trailer. The farm has a rud d y great big one. It'll need a good clean-out, but it'll d o the trick.'

'For one thing, I don't have a car, and for another, even if I did, I'm not driving a trailer.'

'You don't have to, my brother will.'

'Your brother?'

'Saul.'

'I don't think I've met him,' Kazz mused.

'He's nice,' Stevie said. 'I went out with him once.'

Leanne wrinkled her nose. 'I'd forgotten about that. You had a lucky escape.' She turned her attention back to Kazz. 'A word of warning: he might look pretty, but pretty is as pretty does. If you take him with a pinch of salt and you understand that he's a good-time guy, you won't get hurt.'

Kazz declared, 'I won't get hurt anyway. Don't you think I've got enough to be getting on with? I don't want a man in my life right now.'

Leanne sighed. 'Yeah, that's what they all say – until they meet him.'

Chapter 6

Kazz always slept well when she was in Tanglewood . She put it d own to not having a bunch of flatmates making going-to-work noises at six in the morning, when she'd only been in bed for about five hours. She was an eight-hour-a-night girl – any less than that and she was as grumpy as old Mrs George on a bad d ay. Mrs George was the little old lad y who frequented the tea shop on a regular basis and with whom Betty had the occasional spat. Kazz had only met her once, but the woman's sheer grumpiness had mad e an impression.

The bungalow was quiet, although she could hear the rumble of an engine outsid e and a horse making the whickering noise that Stevie had told her meant hello in horse-speak.

Kazz stretched luxuriously, feeling slightly guilty that Stevie had let her sleep in. Although tod ay was Sund ay, last night Stevie had said she was popping into the tea shop this morning, having muttered something about a Christmas festival meeting she was hosting, and told Kazz to relax and enjoy herself.

Those had been Stevie's last word s to her before she'd gone to bed . Along with the parting shot of, 'I'm so excited ! You're going to open a bookshop in Tangle-wood !'

Kazz, in the cold light of day, definitely was going to open a bookshop. Not in Tanglewood , nor anywhere else. It was the most ridiculous idea she'd ever heard . She didn't know anything about running a business, and although she'd spent a considerable chunk of her child - hood in Grandad 's old shop, she didn't know much about books, especially old ones. And she had a feeling a love of reading didn't count.

Looking at it logically, her love of reading would probably be more of a hindrance than a help, because any book knowledge she had was of relatively recent publications; and by recent, she meant within the last twenty years or so, apart from childhood favourites like Noddy Goes to Toyland and the Kipper books. And although she had read a few of the classics, such as *Jane Eyre* and *Wuthering Heights*, in her time, she wasn't sure those counted either. Because nearly all of the books she could remember seeing in her grandad 's house were obscure non-fiction titles and mostly well out of date. The fiction ones tended to be similar to the book of fairy stories she had decided to keep for herself. Few bookshops like the one her grandfather had owned existed anymore. The ones she frequented had current bestsellers, alongside arabica beans and slices of red velvet cake, and the fiction books were often literary-acclaimed titles and the non-fiction were shiny, glossy and enticing.

Kazz couldn't say the same for her books. They were old and musty, and although their smell reminded her of her grandfather, she didn't think many people would appreciate it.

Shelving the bookshop idea (she giggled aloud at her mental play on word s), Kazz had a quick shower, dressed and then wandered into the kitchen in search of breakfast.

She was touched to d iscover that Stevie had left a loaf of home-baked bread out for her, plus eggs, jam, honey and fruit, with a note telling her there was bacon and yoghurt in the frid ge and she was to help herself.

After a hearty breakfast, Kazz was d ebating what she should d o with herself until Stevie returned , when she heard the front d oor open and Tia's voice call, 'Hello! Anyone home? Nick? Stevie?'

Kazz hurried toward s her, wond ering whether she should offer to help, but at the same time aware of how fiercely ind epend ent Tia was and that she had also lived in this bungalow for several years before she married Will and moved into the manor.

'Just me, I'm afraid . Nick's out with the horses and Stevie is at the tea shop – something about a Christmas festival meeting?' Kazz said .

'Ah, yes, that.' Tia's tone was wry. 'How could I have forgotten? It's all Julia – Will's mother – can talk about. She d oes enjoy med d ling. I pity Stevie, with Julia and Betty in the same room, because Betty has very d efinite id eas about this festival, as d oes Julia. Anyway, it's you I've come to see.' Tia held up her hand . She was hold ing a set of keys aloft and she rattled them. 'Look what I've got,' she sang.

'Um… keys?'

'Can you guess what they're for?'

'To unlock something?'

Tia narrowed her eyes. 'There aren't any flies on you, are there? Don't you want to know what they are the keys to?'

'Only if you want to tell me.'

'You're not making this easy.' Tia turned the wheel-chair around in a nifty manoeuvre. 'Come on, what are you waiting for?'

'Where are we going?'

'You'll see. You'll need your coat. It's bloody freezing out there.'

Kazz fetched her coat, grabbed a scarf and a hat for good measure, and followed Tia.

Tia's husband was outside, waiting by the car. 'Don't mind Will, he's only here for his muscles,' Tia said, as he lifted her into the passenger seat.

Bemused, Kazz got in while Will loaded the wheelchair into the back.

'Do *you* know where we're going?' she asked him, when he got behind the wheel.

'The village,' he said.

'Why?'

'You'll have to ask Tia.'

Kazz clearly wasn't getting anywhere, so she sat back to enjoy the short drive into Tanglewood.

A few minutes later, Will eased into the car park off the main street. 'Call me when you're done,' he told Tia, after he had helped her out and back into the chair, and as she wheeled herself away, she gave him a cheery wave.

Kazz fell into step beside her and huddled into her coat. A keen wind blew across the river and there was a hint of rain in the air.

As they crossed the road, Kazz could see lights on in Peggy's Tea Shoppe and there were several people inside. She wondered if that was where they were headed, but Tia rolled straight past.

When Tia came to a halt outside an empty shop, she said, 'You can do the honours,' and held out the bunch of keys.

Kazz looked at them, then at Tia. 'I don't understand.'

Tia pressed her lips together and shook her head sadly. 'I do worry about you sometimes. Your *bookshop*? Remember? We spent ages talking about it last night.'

'But I wasn't serious. Not really,' Kazz objected.

'For pity's sake, go inside, will you?'

Kazz took the keys from her, and with a bit of fiddling to find the right one, she unlocked the door. A loud beeping blasted her ears.

'The alarm is on the wall,' Tia instructed, giving her the code.

Kazz hurriedly punched it in, and blessed silence descended.

'At least you know your books will be safe.' Tia laughed.

'Hmm.' Kazz wasn't sure how to respond, considering she didn't have any intention of opening a bookshop. It was a lovely idea, but it simply wasn't feasible.

'What do you think?' Tia's gaze roamed around the shop's interior.

The room was completely bare, stripped of anything that might have given Kazz a clue as to its original use. 'It's… um…'

'Perfect!' Tia clapped her hands. 'That's what it is: perfect.'

'You think?' Kazz's tone was full of scepticism. She eyed the bare walls and grubby windows doubtfully.

'A good clean, a lick of paint, and it will be good to go.'

'It most certainly will be,' Betty announced, stepping over the threshold, closely followed by Stevie, Leanne and Eddie.

Betty said, 'We had just finished our meeting when we saw you go past.' She beamed widely, her face a mass of wrinkles as she crowed, 'See, I told you opening a bookshop was a good idea.'

'It seriously isn't,' Kazz replied.

Stevie raised her eyebrows. 'You were all for it last night.'

'That was last night. I'd had a couple of glasses of wine.' Kazz strolled across the empty shop, her booted feet clumping on the floorboards. They reminded her of the wooden floors in her grandad's house, which Nan had covered with threadbare wool rugs. Kazz assumed they hadn't been threadbare when Nan had first laid them, but the worn bits were now ghostly evidence of countless footsteps.

A picture of the large rug in the main bedroom popped into Kazz's head, and she imagined how it would look in the centre of this room, with the two wingback chairs from the living room, and shelves filled with books along three of the walls.

A door at the far end caught her attention and she popped her head around it to discover that it contained a small storeroom and another door, behind which was a loo and a wash-hand basin.

When she walked back into the main part of the shop, her friends and Betty were in a huddle, whispering, but they quickly leapt apart when they saw her.

'Well?' Betty demanded. The others were staring at her hopefully.

'Why are you lot trying to bulldoze me into opening a bookshop?' Kazz asked, after a pause.

Stevie replied, 'Because you're not happy. Because you're at a crossroads. Because if you don't do it now, you'll regret it.'

Kazz wrinkled her nose. 'Let's say for argument's sake that I go along with this mad idea—' She glared at Betty, who had clapped and cried, 'Yes!'

Betty subsided and Kazz carried on, 'I can't afford it.'

The others exchanged glances. Betty held up her hands and backed away, shaking her head. 'That's for you lot to sort out,' she muttered, 'I'm just the ideas man.'

Stevie drew in a breath. 'You *can* afford it,' she said. 'Tia, tell her.'

'This place belongs to a friend of my father-in-law. He's been renting it out for years. It was recently a stationery business but when it folded —'

'People don't write letters anymore,' Betty piped up. 'It's all digital free-mailing and stuff, nowadays. I don't think you youngsters know what biros are. And don't get me started on fountain pens.'

Kazz had no intention of getting Betty started on anything.

Tia took up the baton once more. 'The owner hasn't had any luck letting it out since the stationery business closed, so I asked Edgar if he could ask him whether he would consider a short-term lease of a couple of months, and he jumped at it. Will picked up the keys for me this morning, and here we are.'

'I still can't afford it,' Kazz said.

'You can. The rent is peanuts. Honestly.'

Tia's version of peanuts probably wasn't Kazz's, considering the woman had a whole wing of a mansion all to herself and her husband, but when Tia told her the figure, Kazz was surprised. It did sound incredibly reasonable. Then a thought struck her. 'Is that per week, or per month?'

'For the whole two months,' Tia replied with a grin. 'Not bad , is it?'

Kazz's eyes bulged .*Not bad?* It was blood y brilliant. You could n't rent a park bench in Lond on for that! Her mouth was d ry and she swallowed nervously. Her heart was thumping and excitement fizzed along her veins. Maybe this id iotic id ea wasn't so id iotic after all…?

Trying not to show her excitement, because she d id n't want the others to sweep her away with their enthusiasm before she'd had the chance to think it through properly, she said , 'What if I d on't sell any books?'

'What if you *do*?' Ed ie countered . 'There isn't what I would call a proper bookshop for miles.'

'This would n't be a "proper" bookshop,' Kazz explained . 'It would n't be selling the latest Lucy Score or Felix Francis novel. The books I've got are old and musty.'

Leanne asked , 'Have you been to Hay-on-Wye?'

Kazz stared blankly at her, confused at the change of subject. 'No, should I have?'

'The Hay Festival?' Ed ie prompted .

'Oh, yes, I've heard of that,' Kazz said . 'It's a literary festival.'

'That's right, but Hay isn't just renowned for its festival. It's a town famous for its second -hand bookshops. There are over twenty of them, I believe. You should go take a look.'

'But my bookshop would be in Tanglewood , not Hay-on-Wye. Wherever that is.'

'It's roughly twenty miles away, but that's not the point,' Leanne said . 'What I'm trying to say is that there is a call around these parts for old books. People are used to coming to the Welsh Marches and seeing artisan shops,

68

quaint pubs and second -hand bookshops. Anyway, what have you got to lose?'

Leanne was right, Kazz d id n't have anything to lose. It wasn't as though she would be packing in a job to d o this or giving up her flat to move halfway across the country.

But what she would be d oing was d elaying the inevitable. Whether the bookshop mad e any money or not, the lease would only be a short-term one, and then she would have to start looking for a job, but with the ad d ed problem of not having anywhere to live. It hard ly seemed worth the effort. She might as well bite the bullet, hire a skip and get rid of the lot and be d one with it.

'I bet your grand ad would turn in his grave if you threw them away,' Betty said , into the silence.

'Excuse me?' Kazz blinked at the old lad y in astonishment. Had Betty read her mind ?

'You heard . Them books were his life's work. You can't simply give them away or chuck them out, not when you've got an alternative.'

Kazz was speechless. She had alread y begun to feel as though her friend s were ganging up on her, and now Betty was resorting to emotional blackmail.

Stevie moved closer and gave her a hug. 'It's up to you, Kazz, of course it is, but you haven't been happy for a while. You've got an opportunity to try something new, so why d on't you take it? If you d on't, you'll be spend ing the rest of your life wond ering what if. Look at me – I took a leap of faith and I've never been happier.'

Kazz bit her lip. It would be a very big leap, but maybe she *could* d o it? And Betty was right: Grand ad would be appalled at the thought of her d iscard ing his book collection like rubbish.

Hoping she wasn't about to make the biggest mistake of her life, Kazz took a d eep breath and announced , 'I'm going to d o it. I'm going to open a bookshop in Tanglewood . And if I fall flat on my face, I'm going to blame you lot.'

'You won't,' Betty said confid ently. 'This will be a whole new chapter in the story of your life.'

Ignoring the cheesy bookish pun, Kazz prayed the old lad y was right.

Chapter 7

Saul dried his hands on the towel draped over the radiator in the downstairs loo and caught a glimpse of himself in the mirror. Was that a grey hair? It *was*.

He tugged at it, wincing, but didn't pull it out. He supposed grey hairs were to be expected; he wasn't twenty anymore. Feeling disgruntled, he searched for another, and when he found it, he uttered a snort of disgust. Was this his body's way of telling him that time was marching on?

In a way, finding physical evidence that he was no longer a youngster gave credence to the feeling that he really did need to consider his future. Until recently, he had been content with his lot. But how much longer could he play the field? Moving back in with his parents hadn't been ideal either. And with Dad planning on stepping back…

Saul and Murray rarely saw eye-to-eye on anything. Saul thought it best to do something one way, and Murray thought it best to do it another. The only reason they had been able to work together for so long was because Dad had the final say. He made the decisions and the buck stopped with him. It made for a more peaceful life.

That peace was about to be shattered.

Ever since Dad had spoken to him, Saul hadn't been able to stop thinking about it, wondering whether it was a good id ea to strike out on his own, or whether he should stay and make the best of it, even if he and Murray were probably going to be at loggerhead s all the time. But with Murray married and no d oubt consid ering starting a family in the not-too-d istant future, he had responsibilities that Saul d id n't. If anyone had to walk away from the farm, it should be Saul.

He was brought out of his thoughts by the sound of the back d oor slamming shut and his mother's voice calling for his father.

'Geoff, d id you put the roasties in? And have you checked the beef?'

Sund ays usually meant lunch eaten around the big oak table in the kitchen, and his mouth watered . His mother was a d amned fine cook and her roast d inners were second to none. Even when he and Murray had been living in the converted barn d own the lane, they had continued to turn up every evening and on Sund ays to be fed .

Saul sauntered into the kitchen in time to hear his father say, 'Yes, and yes. I've even peeled the carrots.'

Mum said , 'You're a gem. Sorry we're late. The meeting end ed on time, but Leanne went with Stevie's friend to take a look at the old stationery shop. Leanne tells me that Kazz is going to open a bookshop. Isn't that right, Lea?'

Leanne was easing off her boots and rubbing her toes. For the life of him, Saul could n't work out why women put themselves through the torture of high heels.

'That's right. A second -hand one,' his sister said . 'Her grand ad used to have a bookshop and Kazz found hund red s of books when she was clearing out his house.'

He'd heard Kazz's name mentioned , but he'd yet to meet her. If he remembered rightly, she was one of Stevie's brid esmaid s, along with Leanne.

'I d on't like seeing empty shops in Tanglewood ,' his mother was saying. 'It's not good for the village.'

'How was your meeting, love?' his d ad asked . 'Did Betty hold court, as usual?'

Iris smiled . 'She d id . And so d id Lad y Tonbrid g Between them, they provid ed some fine entertainment. Still, we've got most of the planning for the festival in place. It should be grand .'

'I'm looking forward to it,' Geoff said . 'The festival marks the start of Christmas, as far as I'm concerned .'

'When will lunch be read y?' Saul asked , more inter-ested in his rumbling stomach than talk of bookshops or festivals.

Iris slipped an apron over her head and secured the ties behind her back. 'I'll get the veg on. I swear you've got hollow legs.'

'He's not the only one,' Geoff said . 'Clearing out the barn is hungry work.'

'Is it d one?' Iris asked , peering through the oven wind ow to check on the roast.

'More or less. Murray is still there, making sure we've got enough silage to see us through the winter.'

'Did you ask him if he and Ashley wanted to join us for lunch?' she asked .

Geoff replied , 'He said thanks, but Ashley is cooking lunch at theirs.'

'I suppose we've got to expect more of this, especially when they've got child ren,' Iris said . 'They're not going to want to come here every five minutes.'

There was a knock at the door and Rex walked in, bringing a blast of cold air with him. Leanne hurried over and stood on tiptoe to give him a kiss.

'How are the beavers?' she asked.

Rex was one of the rangers in the Bannau Brycheiniog National Park (it had been renamed, but he still referred to it as the Brecon Beacons National Park because old habits die hard) and he had a keen interest in wild life, especially in the beavers who had been released at a secret location on the Manor's land. It was an experiment instigated by Lord Tonbridge's son Will, in conjunction with Natural Resources Wales, as they tried to slow the run-off of rain-water from the hillsides in an attempt to reduce flooding. So far it was proving to be successful.

'The lodge is huge,' Rex said. 'And they've been busy cutting more trees down. I did n't see them today, but there are plenty of signs of what they've been getting up to. Gosh, lunch smells good.'

Saul quietly observed his mother. She was in her element with her family around her, and he knew she would be upset when she learnt of his plans, so he would n't tell her yet. For now, he would put the word out that he was available for odd jobs and say it was because he wanted to save up to buy some new wheels – which was true; the Land y was on its last legs.

When everyone was seated at the table and tucking into a sumptuous Sunday lunch, Saul said, 'I'm, um, thinking of doing a spot of moonlighting to earn a bit of extra cash.'

'What kind of moonlighting?' Leanne asked. 'Worming another farmer's sheep?'

'Ha ha. I was thinking of fixing things for people, or like, putting shelves up and stuff. Anything, really.'

'That's a stroke of luck!' She beamed   at him. 'I've got the perfect job for you.'

–

Saul pulled   onto Nick's d rive at eight thirty on Tuesd ay morning with a d egree of reservation. He d id n't fancy d riving all the way to Lond on and   back, especially with a strange woman in the passenger seat, but need s must.

It was od d   to think this was his first proper job outsid e of the farm since leaving college. Once upon a time, when they were teenagers, he and   Murray used   to hire themselves out d uring sheep-shearing season for a bit of extra cash. That had   been when Martin and   Stuart were still living at home and   were helping on the farm, and Dad   had   been able to spare him and   Murray for a couple of weeks. They used   to travel all over, sleeping in the back of the old   Land y at night (though it had   been newer then) or in a barn if the farmer could   n't offer them a bed . Three meals and   a couple of pints, washing themselves d own with ice-cold   water from an outsid e tap… Those were the d ays! Young, carefree, with the world   at their feet.

Then his old er brothers had   gone their own way, leaving him and   Murray to work on the farm. And   that had   been fun too, as he and   Murray had   converted   the old barn into a house. Despite squabbling over whose turn it was to push the hoover round , arguing over who was leaving tea bags on the sid e of the sink instead   of putting them straight in the bin or who forgot to buy the milk, Saul felt he'd   had   the best of both world s. Ind epend ence, plus the security of working on the family farm.

Then Murray had   fallen in love, and   Saul had   moved out so that Ashley could   move in, and   now Saul felt as though he had taken a step back. Living with his parents wasn't what he had envisaged d oing at thirty-three.

Once again, Saul felt a twinge of unease as he wond ered how his d ad and Murray would cope if he lef But he could n't remain on the family farm forever; too many cooks, and all that...

Turning the Land Rover and trailer combo around on Nick and Stevie's d riveway so it faced the right way, he brought it to a stop and got out.

Kazz was alread y waiting for him. She was petite, yet curvy, with d ark glossy hair cascad ing over her should ers, an upturned nose, and the most arresting eyes he had seen in a long time. Large and tawny brown, with long curling lashes, they remind ed him of a startled d eer, and she had the sort of translucent skin that might d evelop freckles if it saw enough sun.

At the sight of her, something that he had n't felt for a long time strummed in his chest, like the lingering echo after a guitar string had been plucked and the sound had almost fad ed away.

His attraction to her was instant and und eniable; and why would n't it be − she was gorgeous. But there was something else...

He cleared his throat, hoping to clear his head at the same time. His vow of abstinence when it came to the opposite sex appeared to be having a strange effect on him.

'I take it you must be **Kazz**,' he said , his voice gruff. He thrust out a hand for her to shake. 'I'm Saul, I d on't think we've met.' He would *definitely* have remembered if they had .

She took his hand and said , 'Hi, that's me, Kazz Fernsby.'

A bolt of d esire slammed into him and he quickly wrenched his hand from hers. Wond ering what the hell had just happened , he rubbed the back of his neck self-consciously.

Thankfully, she seemed oblivious. 'Thanks for this,' she said , head ing around the Land y to the passenger sid e and getting in.

This was going to be a very long d ay, he thought, when he caught a waft of her perfume as he slid into the d river's seat. She smelled so d arned good that it mad e his head spin.

'No thanks need ed .' She was paying him, so…

She buckled herself in. 'How long will it take to get to Lond on?'

'About four hours, give or take.' He'd never d riven to Lond on before and he wasn't looking forward to it, especially when towing a rud d y big trailer. A couple of bits of furniture, Leanne had said , and a tonne of books. The trailer might be overkill, but she had insisted on the big one, claiming that they would need it.

Kazz settled back in her seat, and as he started the engine, he sensed her staring at him. Feeling awkward , he said , 'Do you mind if I put some music on?'

'Not at all,' she replied .

He told Alexa to play a smooth tunes playlist, and the Land Rover's cab was immed iately filled with mellow music. Without warning, an image of pulling over and taking her in his arms flashed into his head , and he realised his music request was almost d efinitely the wrong choice. He should have asked Alexa for thrash metal, not music to make love to.

'So, a bookshop, eh?' he said after a while, feeling that he should make an effort at small talk. Not only was she his first client, but she was also his sister's friend. And he didn't want her to think he was a grumpy git.

'It appears so. I'm actually a chef, but…' She trailed off. 'It's a long story.'

His curiosity piqued, he wanted to point out they were on a long journey and that she would have plenty of time to tell it, but she didn't appear to want to talk about it, so he tried a different tack. 'What's it like living in London?'

His passenger immediately brightened. 'Fun, lively, never a dull moment.'

'Do you do any of the touristy things, like visit Buckingham Palace?'

'God, no! Nothing like that. Although the firework display on New Year's Eve is a sight to behold. I go if I'm not working.'

'A chef, you said. Any good?' He glanced at her, smiling to show he was teasing.

'Not bad. I've been known to cook a decent dish or two.'

The way she said it made Saul believe she was being modest, and he vaguely recalled a conversation where Kazz's name had been mentioned in relation to a posh restaurant. Stevie had worked in an upmarket restaurant before she came to Tanglewood, and he wondered whether it might have been the same one.

'Are you any good at farming?' she asked archly, and Saul barked out a laugh.

'Not bad. I've been known to shear a sheep or two.'

'Do you have a shepherd's crook?'

'Like Little Bo Peep?' he chuckled. Out of the corner of his eye, he could see a blush bloom on her cheek. The hint of pink was adorable. If he hadn't sworn off women, he might be tempted. Oh, who was he kidding! There was no *might* about it. He would have asked her out in a heartbeat.

He said, 'I do have a crook, as a matter of fact. It's handy for hooking sheep who don't want to be caught.'

'Don't you use dogs to round them up?'

'We do. We've got four dogs on the farm.'

'Do you have any other animals?'

'Chickens, a couple of cats, about fifteen head of cattle, but mostly sheep.'

'Did you always want to be a farmer, or did you drift into it because you were born on a farm?'

'A bit of both, I suppose. What about you? Did you always want to be a chef?'

'I wanted to have a bookshop like my—' She stopped abruptly and clapped a hand to her mouth, her eyes wide. 'Oh, my.'

Saul risked another look at her.

She met his gaze, and before he returned his attention to the road, he saw the shock in her eyes.

Clearly, Kazz Fernsby hadn't been expecting to say *that*.

Chapter 8

When Kazz had seen the battered old vehicle pull onto Nick and Stevie's expansive drive, she mightn't have been convinced it would get them to London but she wasn't about to look a gift horse in the mouth. Leanne, bless her, had managed to persuade her brother to drive Kazz back to the capital to pick up her belongings, plus the furniture from her grandad's house that she would need for the shop, as well as all the books. Kazz hoped Saul knew what he was letting himself in for. This wouldn't be a simple in-and-out job. It was going to take time and brute strength to shift some of the bigger pieces.

Mind you, she thought, he looked as though he was used to physical work. Along with a flat stomach and wide shoulders, he had dreamy eyes and was seriously hot. So hot that when he'd turned those gorgeous eyes on her and had held out his hand for her to shake, she had felt a fizz of excitement at his touch. This was one sexy guy, and her insides did a slow flip-flop of desire.

Wow – she hadn't had that kind of reaction to a man in a very long time, and it was a pleasant feeling. Life in Tanglewood had suddenly become rather interesting.

But then Kazz recalled Leanne's warning that her brother was a good-time guy. And she also remembered that she wasn't looking for a good time. Or a boyfriend. She was in Tanglewood purely to sell her grandad's books and give herself some breathing space to find another cheffing job: one with more sociable hours which meant that when she was read y for a boyfriend , she would actually be able to spend some time with him.

The only thing she should be interested in right now was whether Saul could load one of those big bookcases onto the trailer, d espite this particular ability being one she d id n't normally look for in a man.

From the way Leanne had spoken of him, Kazz had half-expected Saul to hit on her the moment she clambered into the d ilapid ated Land Rover, and she felt a little d isappointed when he d id n't, especially consid ering her instant attraction to him.

No wond er he played the field . He probably had women falling at his feet. In d ays gone by, she und oubted ly would have been one of them.

She had n't been looking forward to the d rive and had been worried that she would find the journey awkward . But then he had put on an easy-listening playlist and she had relaxed a little, only to tense up again as she wond ered whether this was part of his sed uction technique, and she wished Leanne had n't said anything.

But after they'd been on the road for about forty-five minutes and there had n't been so much as a hint of a flirt, Kazz started to relax, and d ecid ed that Saul mightn't be as bad as Leanne had mad e out.

Then they'd turned onto the M4 and he had seemed read y for a chat, and the word s that had issued from her mouth had shocked her to her core.

She could n't believe that she had wanted to own a bookshop, just like Grand ad , and she could n't believe that she'd forgotten. She used to beg Mum to take her to the shop instead of over to her nan's when she was busy at work. And more often than not, Nan used to give in, so Grand ad end ed up looking after her instead . He had mad a small counter for her, a replica of his much larger one, and she used to pretend to sell all kind s of things, not just books.

The memory came flood ing back, making her heart ache with sad ness. Her grand parents had been such a big part of her life. She had her nan to thank for her love of cooking, and it was she who had been partly responsible for Kazz enrolling on a catering course in college. She had never regretted her choice of career, d espite her growing d esire not to work such unsociable hours; but her subconscious blurting out that she had always wanted to own a bookshop was quite a shock.

And now she was being given the chance to d o precisely that. Everyone was right – if she d id n't take this opportunity she *would* regret it, and she knew in her heart it would never come again. Now was the id eal time to give it a go. She would n't get another chance.

A quiet excitement filled her, but it also competed with crippling anxiety and stomach-clenching worry. What if she mad e a total hash of it? What if she d id n't sell a single book?

The worry that she would end up worse off than she was now was a very real one, and she had to work hard to push it to one sid e.

Abruptly, what had only yesterd ay seemed like make-believe was tod ay fast becoming a reality, as what she was d oing sank in. Even signing a hastily d rawn-up contract in a solicitor's office yesterd ay for a two-month lease on the shop, and being given the keys to both that and the flat above Stevie's tea shop, which was to be her home until just after the New Year, had n't seemed real.

Yet, sitting in the passenger seat of a mud -splattered farm vehicle that held a d istinct whiff of animal, while barrelling along the brid ge spanning the River Severn which separated England from Wales, sud d enly brought it home to her: *she was going to open a bookshop.*

–

A vehicle as old as the Land Rover d id n't have a built-in satnav. The most mod ern feature was an ancient rad io and cassette d eck combo, which Kazz stud ied with interest, having never seen one before and d oubting whether she would see one again.

Thankfully, Saul had a smartphone, which he used to guid e them to the street her flat was on, because she d id n't have a clue how to get there from the M25. A d etailed knowled ge of the Und erground wasn't much help when travelling by road , and both her nerves and Saul's were frazzled by the time he found a place to park, not too far from the entrance to her flat.

'Blood y hell,' he muttered . His face was ashen and his eyes were haunted when he turned to look at her. 'I can't believe we mad e it in one piece.'

Neither could Kazz.

It had been a nightmare negotiating the vehicle and its trailer through the busy network of road s, and more than once Saul had been flummoxed by d iversions because of road works. The journey had also taken an hour longer than the guestimate he had given her. It was alread y one o'clock and she had n't even collected her belongings yet, let alone the stuff from her grand ad 's house. At this rate, there was no way they would be returning to Tanglewood tonight. They would be lucky if they got back by the end of the week!

'Oh, hell.' She sighed . 'I forgot to phone the house clearance man to tell him to meet me at the house tod ay.'

Saul gave a shaky laugh. 'I thought *I* was the house clearance man.'

'You are, kind of. But I'm not taking everything with me. It won't all fit in the trailer for a start.' She would send her mum's land lord a message and let him know that anything left at the house was his to keep or d ispose of. She hated being so d isorganised and unprepared , but this had all happened so fast that Kazz had n't had time to plan anything.

Saul was staring at her in d ismay. 'Please d on't tell me I'll have to make two trips,' he begged . 'I d on't think my nerves can stand it.'

'Neither can mine. It was a bit hairy, wasn't it?'

'I need a stiff d rink.'

'Will a cola d o?'

'It'll have to. We'd better grab something to eat too. I'm guessing it's going to be a long afternoon.'

'And the rest,' Kazz muttered und er her breath. She mad e a d ecision and reached for her bag. 'There's a d eli up the road . Do you want to get us some lunch while I make a start on the packing?' She held out a twenty-pound note.

Saul hesitated .

'Please take it,' she urged . 'We haven't got time to argue over who is paying for lunch.' Anyway, he was d oing her a massive favour, so it was only fair that she picked up the food tab. She pushed the money into his hand and turned to the d oor. 'I'll leave it on the latch. No need to knock.'

Without waiting for a reply, she shoved her key in the lock and hurried upstairs, scooping up the post as she went. There wasn't anything for her, and she d umped it on the table in the living room, before d ashing to her room, where she came to a halt, wond ering where to begin. Knowing that she would n't be back, she had to ensure she took everything with her.

Most of the items in her bed room were easy enough to gather together and stuff into her suitcase. They d id n't all fit, of course, so she resorted to using bin bags for the majority of it. She had just filled a second one, when she heard Saul's voice.

'In here,' she called , and when he appeared in the d oorway, her stomach d id that forward roll again that had nothing to d o with the sight of the paper bag of ed ible good ies that he was hold ing.

Telling herself to get a grip and that now wasn't the best time to have lascivious thoughts about anyone – especially Saul – she d ragged her gaze away and returned to her packing.

Out of the corner of her eye, she could see him looking around , taking it all in, and she wond ered what he was thinking. Looking at the flat through his eyes, she guessed that he probably wasn't impressed . It was small and cramped , only big enough for two people, yet it housed four. The land lord had wanted to get his money's worth, so what had once been a two-bed room property had now become a four-bed room one by taking a slice of what might once have been a generous living room, and splitting the larger of the bed rooms into two.

Kazz's room was a d ecid ed ly ungenerous two-point-four by three-point-six metres. She knew, because she had measured it. The upsid e of having such a small space was that she had n't been able to cram a great d eal into it. Neither the bed , the ward robe, the chest of d rawers nor the bed sid e table were hers (the flat had come furnished), so all she need ed to concern herself with were her clothes, toiletries, bed d ing and the framed photo of a New York skyline that she had bought when she'd first moved in. Actually, sod the photo. She'd fallen out of love with it some time ago.

'Do you need any help?' he asked .

She could d o with it, and she was about to say yes when the thought of him emptying her knicker d rawer (she had n't started on the chest of d rawers yet) mad e her think twice. And although she had yet to pack away her bed d ing, she d id n't want him hand ling her d uvet – seemed too personal somehow, especially since the cover and the sheet could d o with a wash. And he most d efin itely *wasn't* going to see what was in her toiletry basket in the bathroom. She would just slid e it out of the cabinet and tip the contents into a bag. Then she would tie it up and place it insid e a second . The thought of any man seeing the numerous potions, creams and lotions that it took to make her look presentable mad e her cringe.

And … Oh God ! Kazz spied a piece of card board o the top of her bed sid e cabinet that she had torn from an empty box of cond oms; it had been there for at least a year, and she had been using it as a bookmark.

She need ed to get him out of her bed room *right now.*

'Let's eat, shall we?' she suggested hastily, taking the bag from him and being careful not to touch him. The jolt that had gone through her earlier, when she'd shaken his hand , had thrilled her enough for one d ay.

She wished she could have blamed it on static electri- city, but the fact was that she fancied him rotten. And the five-hour journey had n't helped . Sitting next to him, his male magnetism washing over her (or had that been his aftershave?) had meant that she had been acutely aware of him the whole time. Whereas Saul appeared to be totally at ease and annoyingly unaffected by her presence.

Kazz supposed that was to be expected, if his reputation was to be believed. He'd probably had more girlfriends than she'd cooked steak au poivre. She doubted he would look at her twice.

They sat at the cramped dining table with its mismatched chairs to eat their lunch, Kazz guessing that the twenty pounds she had given him had n't been nearly enough, considering the amount of food. Saul seemed to have bought two of everything in the deli, although there wasn't much left of their meal by the time she declared she was full.

Saul had devoured his with the enthusiasm of a man who did manual work for a living and did n't need to concern himself with the number of calories he was consuming. Kazz ate because she need ed to keep her strength up, and although the food was delicious (she had bought loads from the deli in the past), she hard ly tasted it. She was far too on edge to enjoy it.

What the hell was she doing? Was she *mad*? The last time she had sat at this table, the furthest thing from her mind was moving to Tanglewood and opening a shop. Yet here she was, packing up all her world ly possessions, with a strange guy helping her do it.

'Are you OK?' The gentleness in Saul's voice and the concern in his eyes brought a lump to her throat.

She nodded uncertainly, pretty sure that she wasn't, but not wanting to show it.

He saw anyway. 'It's a big step,' he said. 'But if Stevie can do it, so can you.'

'She had a helping hand from her aunt Peggy.'

His smile was sympathetic. 'And you've had a helping hand from your grand ad .'

'Yes, but Tanglewood ? And a bookshop? I d on't know anything about owning a shop. At least Stevie is an expert when it comes to cakes and pastries.' Feeling tears prickling behind her eyes, Kazz flapped her hand s in front of her face. 'Don't mind me, I'm just having a wobble. So much has happened in such a short space of time that it's knocked me for six.'

She d id n't know how much he knew about her circumstances, but she guessed it was more than she had shared with him on the journey d own. Even if Leanne had n't said a great d eal, Tanglewood was a hive of gossip and news travelled fast.

'I reckon running a bookshop isn't much d ifferent to running a tea shop, but without the worry of giving someone food poisoning,' he said .

Kazz uttered a surprised laugh. 'There is that.'

'And books d on't have to be mad e fresh every morning.'

'True…'

'They d on't go stale, either.'

'Just musty and d usty.'

'Don't you just love the smell of old books!'

Kazz d id . It was one of her favourite aromas. And when Saul got to his feet, saying, 'You've got this. You'll be fine,' she caught a whiff of his aftershave and wond ered whether she should also ad d that scent to her list of favourite smells. She d ebated whether to ask him what it was, but d ecid ed against it, not wanting him to think she was flirting when she most d efinitely wasn't.

He gazed d own at her. 'What d o you need me to d o?'

'Can you start load ing this lot onto the trailer?' she asked , nod d ing her head at the pile outsid e her bed room d oor, feeling more in control. His quiet confid ence had given her the boost she need ed to hold her fears at bay. For the time being, at least. As well as being good -looking, and oozing confid ence and sex appeal, Saul appeared to be a nice guy – which was a lethal combination.

She watched him pick up the bulging and incred ibly heavy suitcase with ease, trying not to stare at the way the muscles in his arm bunched , or at his backsid e as he walked d own the hall.

Tearing her gaze away, she quickly d isposed of the remains of their meal in the bin, then hurried into the bed room, scooped up the cond om-box bookmark and stuffed it into her jeans pocket. Then she d arted into the bathroom and emptied her basket of toiletries and make-up into a bag.

Less than an hour later, she was d one and having a final check around .

She wasn't sure how she felt about leaving the place she'd lived in for the last four years. Regretful? Yes. Sad ? A little. Scared ? Definitely. But she was also excited .

As Betty had so aptly said , this was the start of a whole new chapter. All Kazz hoped was that it d id n't end on a cliffhanger.

Chapter 9

'Are you sure I won't get a ticket?' Saul asked . He was eyeing the street d oubtfully. 'Maybe I should find somewhere else to park?'

The parking in her mum's street was appalling, and Kazz shook her head . 'If you move it, you'll lose the space. If you get a ticket, I'll pay it.'

He frowned and she guessed that although he was unhappy with the parking situation, he d id n't want to move the Land y and trailer in case he then could n't get it close enough when it was time to load up.

'OK, I'll worry about it if, and when, a brown envelope land s on my d oormat.' He glanced up at the house and Kazz d id too, thinking that this was one of the last times she would see it, because she d oubted that she would visit this street again.

It was a mid -terrace property, built at around the beginning of the last century. It had bay wind ows up and d own, topped by pointy gables, and had a recessed porch. The stonework was grimy, but the wind ows were clean, even if they were the old -fashioned sash variety. Her mum had always been particular when it came to cleaning her wind ows.

Kazz opened up and Saul followed her insid e.

As she watched him gaze around , it struck her how old -fashioned the d ark hallway was, with its d ecad es-old wallpaper and cornicing around the ceiling and light fitting. The place was in serious need of mod ernisation, which would take a substantial chunk of money and time, and Kazz wished that her mum's land lord had d one something about it years ago. She wond ered whether he would sell up now that it was vacant, or whether he would finally get around to making it more presentable.

She felt the familiar prickle in her eyes as she realised that when she left tod ay, it would be the end of an era. The last part of her grand parents would be gone – except for Grand ad 's books, and they were about to be sold as soon as her shop was up and running.

Saul broke into her melancholy. 'Tell me what's staying and what's coming with us.'

She gave him a smile that she thought might be more of a grimace and beckoned him into the room at the front of the house, which looked out onto the street.

As he stepped insid e, he gasped , and she guessed the reason. It was the books. Hund red s of them filled two enormous bookcases that lined one wall, and inbuilt shelves filled with more of them sat on either sid e of the chimney breast. There was also a gold brocad e wingback chair with a saggy seat in front of the fireplace, which used to be her grand ad 's favourite, and an enormous sid eboard mad e out of wood so d ark that it was almost black. A couple of sid e tables with lamps on them, and another chair – this in a Chesterfield style – sat d irectly opposite the first. A large worn rug covered most of the floor.

'Er… all of it,' she said .

'All this?' Saul's voice rose an octave.

Kazz knew he would have a job to shift that sid eboard , even with her help, and he'd have fun and games with the bookcases too.

'Yeah. And …' She screwed up her face and pointed to another d oor lead ing off from the hall into the d ining room. It had a big old table and six chairs, and it also contained another wingback chair and a settee. And more books.

There were books in the bed rooms – although only one of the rooms had boxes of books stacked to the ceiling – and yet more in the cellar. And when Kazz informed him there was a fair number in the attic, he flinched .

'I'm not sure we'll get all this in the trailer. And I'm pretty sure we won't get everything load ed by mid night.' He froze, and his eyes wid ened as he ad d ed , 'You d want to bring the bed s and ward robes with you, d o you?'

'Do you think we should ?'

'No! Definitely not!'

Kazz frowned . 'You're probably right. I've got nowhere to put them, and Mum said to get rid .' She slapped a hand to her forehead . 'Damn and blast! I haven't told my mother what's going on. I'd better give her a call.'

'Don't you think we should make a start on this lot first? You can phone her on the way back.'

'Good id ea.' She rolled up her sleeves. 'Let's get on with it. The sooner we start, the sooner we'll be finished .' But she had a feeling that the 'sooner' she was hoping for would end up being much, much later.

–

The trailer was rammed to the rafters but Saul, bless him, had managed to fit in most of the stuff that Kazz wanted to bring with her to Tanglewood . The sofa had to remain behind , but the bookcases had gone in – although it had been touch-and -go for a while, until Saul had d iscovered they could be divided into two sections. He had even squashed the thread bare rug in by folding it rather than rolling it.

The Landy was also full, and there was barely enough room for Kazz and Saul to get in the front. But it was done, and now she was tired, dirty and hungry, and she suspected Saul felt the same. He had worked his socks off, and she couldn't thank him enough. What he had done today went above and beyond, and she was incredibly grateful.

Kazz was exhausted and she could barely lift one foot in front of the other as they trudged back inside after loading the last of it. Staggering into the dining room, she slumped onto the sofa.

Saul joined her. 'Bloody hell, I'm pooped,' he muttered.

'Me, too.'

They sat in silence, neither of them moving. Kazz didn't think she could. That sideboard had been a witch to shift. It had taken them forty minutes to manhandle it through the hall, into the street and onto the trailer. She was dreading unloading it at the other end. Maybe Saul could ask Nick to help? If she hadn't already checked it was empty, Kazz might have believed that her mum had hidden a body inside – it was heavy enough. Then there were all those boxes of books. She had stopped counting after 103. And that was without all the loose ones. Saul had taken care when loading them, not wanting them to rattle around on the journey home, in case one or two might turn out to be valuable.

'We'd better make a move,' he said, staying where he was.

'I suppose we should .' Kazz slumped even further into the sofa. 'Hungry?' she asked .

'I'm starving. You?'

'Famished .'

'Shall we see if there's something open before we go?'

Kazz smiled wearily. 'This is Lond on. There's always something open.'

Neither of them moved .

'If you could eat anything at all right now, what would it be?' Kazz asked .

'Tagliatelle Marinara.'

Kazz raised her eyebrows. Apart from her lips and the occasional blink, it was the only part of her that had moved for the past ten minutes. 'I would have put you d own as a steak-and -chips guy.'

'I'll eat most things,' he said , 'but Italian is my favourite. What about you?'

She d id n't reply and reached for her phone. If he wanted Italian, then Italian was what he was going to get. It was the least she could d o, consid ering how hard he had worked tod ay.

After pressing 'pay', she waited for the transaction to go through and then d ropped her head onto the back of the sofa. This wasn't the most comfortable settee in the world , and it clearly wasn't meant for sprawling on, but she was too tired to d o anything about the d iscomfort.

It d id n't appear to bother Saul either, because he lay in roughly the same position as her, except that his eyes were closed .

She gazed at him for a moment, d rinking him in and hoping he would n't catch her staring. He looked peaceful, and she sud d enly realised he was asleep. So much for him being a strapping farmer used to long hours and hard work, she thought with a smile.

Although, to be fair, it was he who had done the bulk of the carrying and loading. And he had taken most of the weight of the damned sideboard. She wished now that she hadn't bothered taking it, but she wouldn't tell him that. Not after all the effort, swearing and brute strength it had taken to get it on the trailer. Then there was the drive itself – busy, unfamiliar roads were bound to take it out of a person, and towing a trailer through London traffic couldn't have been easy. She would let him sleep for a while; he would need it, considering they had a long drive ahead of them, and he was the one who'd be doing the driving.

Despite her tiredness, she felt a tingle of desire as she gazed at him. His lashes were absurdly long, and his sandy hair was tousled. A hint of stubble on his jaw framed his lips, and she thought how kissable they looked: full but not too full. The skin on his face was tanned – from working outdoors, she assumed – and she wondered how far down his neck and chest the tan went.

He looked so relaxed lying there, sprawled on the sofa, his head tilted to one side, his legs stretched out in front of him. Even in repose, she could see how buff he was; there wasn't an ounce of fat on him, so that meant he must be all muscle under his T-shirt…

Kazz let her breath out slowly, her face flaming as heat rushed into it. *Calm down, lady…* She needed to get a grip, and a cold shower wouldn't go amiss, either.

Telling her mum about her situation would be the emotional equivalent, so she carefully eased herself off the sofa. While she waited for their food to arrive, she would give her mum a ring.

She guessed that her mother would be worried when she heard her news, but Kazz hoped she could allay her fears. Knowing that Stevie was helping might put her mum's mind at rest, hopefully enough to prevent her from catching the next plane back to the UK.

Kazz went into the kitchen to make the call, rolling her should ers as she went, feeling the stiffness in her neck. She would ache like the d evil tomorrow, and she groaned as she realised that she would be lucky to get any sleep at all tonight by the time they got back.

'Mum, how are you?' Kazz asked , a lump forming in her throat when she heard her mother's voice.

'Brilliant, I'm absolutely brilliant! We're having tapas in a little bar around the corner from an apartment we looked at earlier. It's got a lovely south-facing balcony, three bed rooms and three bathrooms. And there's a pool and a gym. I can't see myself in the gym, can you? Although I might give the pool a go. What's the time in Lond on?'

'Um, nine fifteen.'

'Aren't you working tod ay? Ooh, you'd love the food out here; it's so… *Mediterranean*. And I've d iscovered that I love chicharrón. And olives! Who'd have thought it!'

Her mum liking chicharrón d id n't surprise Kazz. Mum liked pork crackling and pork scratchings, and although chicharrón wasn't the same, it was similar enough. But Diana had always refused to try olives, saying that she d id n't like the look of them, and Kazz smiled to think that she liked them now. Moving to Spain had been just the ticket to spice up her mum's life and encourage her to try new things and broad en her horizons.

And Mum sound ed so happy that it warmed Kazz's heart to hear her. Diana had spent so much of her life struggling to bring her up as a single parent that she d eserved some happiness.

Kazz froze. *What had she been thinking?* How could she worry her mother right now? She should wait until the shop was up and running before she said anything. She would present it as a d one d eal, and even though Kazz knew her mum would still worry, she mightn't worry *as much.*

So instead , Kazz asked about her new life and the apartments that her mum and Vince had viewed , rather than share any d etails of her own circumstances. It was only the shrill ring of the d oorbell that end ed the conversation, as Kazz went to collect the food .

The d oorbell had also d isturbed Saul, who blund ered into the hall, bleary-eyed and half-asleep, to find out what was going on. His eyes lit up when he saw the bag and smelled the d elicious aroma that had begun to permeate the air.

Kazz had remembered to ord er some d rinks too, and she was looking forward to a cold can of cola. There were some plates and cutlery still left in the house from the breakfast she had cooked for her mum on Frid ay, so Kazz hand ed the food to Saul and hurried into the kitchen to fetch them.

'Eat your d inner before it gets cold ,' she told him as she tucked in hungrily.

Saul d id n't need telling twice and he lifted a lad en fork to his mouth. 'On a scale of one to ten, how would you rate this compared to your own cooking?' he asked , after he had tasted his first mouthful, a look of bliss on his face.

'About a five. But it fills a hole.'

'Stevie says you're one of the best sous chefs she knows.'
He ate some more before ad d ing, 'What is a sous chef, exactly?'

'A sous chef is second -in-command in a kitchen, und er the head chef. I am – I*was* – responsible for managing the kitchen staff, making sure the team is at its best, especially d uring service.'

'She also said you're a fantastic saucier. Am I right in thinking that a saucier makes sauces?'

'In a way. A saucier is also a position in a kitchen hierarchy, one below the sous chef.'

'I assume it takes years of training to get where you are?'

'It d oes.'

'Yet you want to give it up to become a bookseller?'

'I suppose I d o, for a couple of months at least. Although, I'm not sure I'm giving it up for good . Once a chef, always a chef.'

'Will you be sad to leave Lond on?'

'I d on't know.' Her reply was honest. She had never lived anywhere else. But maybe it*was* time for a change. New horizons, and all that.

When Stevie had first moved to Tanglewood , Kazz had shud d ered at the thought of not living in Lond on. She loved the vibrancy of the city; there was always something happening, somewhere to go, someplace to see, something to d o. It never slept, which suited the lifestyle she had chosen. Tanglewood would be a slower pace of life. It would give her much-need ed breathing space, and an opportunity to take stock. And with her mother out of the country, Kazz felt rud d erless and ad rift. Stevie and

Tanglewood offered an anchor and a safe haven. And you never know, she thought, if she liked the place, she might even stay.

Chapter 10

Kazz woke with a start as the Land Rover rattled over a pothole, and her head bumped against the window.

Glancing guiltily at Saul, she hoped she had n't been snoring. Or drooling. She felt bad for falling asleep and not keeping him company while he drove back from London, but she simply had n't been able to keep her eyes open. Karma was having the last laugh, though, because Kazz now had a stiff neck and she felt worse than if she had stayed awake.

'Where are we?' she croaked. It was difficult to tell in the dark.

'About ten minutes from Tanglewood.'

'You should n't have let me sleep for so long.'

'You needed it,' he replied.

'And you did n't?'

He sent her a quick smile, swiftly turning his attention back to the road. 'I'm kind of used to it,' he said. 'I can deal with the odd night without sleep.' Kazz's imagination began to run away with her as she remembered his reputation, but when he added, 'Lack of sleep is quite common during lambing,' she felt guilty for jumping to conclusions, and once again she wished that Leanne had n't said anything about his playboy ways.

Contrarily, though, she did feel vaguely aggrieved she had spent almost twenty-four hours in Saul's company and he had n't shown the least bit of interest in her. She might say that she felt slighted , if it wasn't so rid iculous.

She could see what attracted women to him, though. He was a seriously good -looking fella. Not too hand some that it was off-putting, but hand some enough to make her d rool a little. His most attractive feature, asid e from his face, was his self-assurance. He was quietly confid ent, with only a hint of cockiness. And he had also shown her a caring sid e to his nature. It was a combination guaranteed to have women fawning all over him.

'What's the plan?' he asked , breaking into her thoughts, and she saw they had reached the outskirts of Tanglewood .

To her d ismay, Kazz realised she had n't thought this far. Her focus had been solely on packing everything up and getting back, but she had no id ea what to d o now. She really should have had everything worked out before they'd set off yesterd ay. If Fred d ie could see how woefully d isorganised she was, he would ban her from his kitchen. Oh yeah, she was alread y banned – although it had nothing to d o with her – and she wond ered where her former boss was now. Was he behind bars, or was he out on bail, having found a hotshot lawyer who was at this very moment busily putting together a case to get his client off the hook? Or had she read too many crime and thriller novels?

Kazz realised she had n't respond ed to Saul's question, when he asked , 'You d o have keys to the shop, d on't you?'

'I d o.'

'Phew! For a second , I wond ered where I was going to put this lot.' He jerked his head toward s the trailer behind them.

She stared at him in d ismay. Oh, flip. He wanted to unload everything into the shop*now*? It was a reasonable assumption, but the place was nowhere near ready. It needed a good clean (although it wasn't really dirty, just a surface layer of dust) and a coat of paint wouldn't go amiss. A nice pale shade of dove grey, with white highlights and navy accents would look—

Kazz caught herself before her thoughts totally ran away with her. Decorating wasn't an option for several reasons, the foremost being that she couldn't afford to splash out on paint. And neither could she afford the time. The sooner the shop was open, the sooner she would start selling books (fingers crossed). She only had a two-month lease, so she had to make the most of it. She would have to settle for a good clean and be done with it.

Tanglewood's main street was empty except for the milkman, and Saul brought the vehicle to a halt directly outside the shop and switched the engine off.

'At least getting here before the birds are up has guaranteed us a parking space,' he said.

Kazz's lips twitched. This guy was obsessed with parking.

She got out, a blast of chill wind making her shiver. Hastening to unlock the shop, she flinched at the alarm's loud beeping. It took her two attempts to deactivate it, and when she did, she sagged in relief. The last thing she needed was a police officer turning up to see what all the noise was about.

She flipped on the bank of switches next to the alarm, and the shop was flooded with soft yellow light. Blinking owlishly, she headed for the room beyond, aware that Saul was behind her.

Kazz remembered seeing an immersion heater on the wall next to the sink in the loo, and she switched that on too.

'Not a bad set-up,' Saul said , glancing around .

'It'll d o,' Kazz agreed , walking back into the main part of the shop.

'Where d o you want what?' he asked , and her brain sud d enly began to function again, her tired ness falling away as she examined the interior and tried to work out where the big bookcases could go, and where was the best place to site the counter.

And sud d enly she could n't wait to get started ! She could see it now: the bookcases on that wall, the counter (aka the sid eboard) over there. She could put a chair there, and another there, with a little sid e table next to it with a lamp on it, and it was then she realised that even if she d id have time for a lick of paint, she would n't bother. Mod ern, fresh and new would n't be the right setting for her lovely old books. What was need ed was a nineteenth-century country-house library vibe, and her grand father's old -fashioned furniture was going to provid e exactly that.

Betty was right – she *could* open a bookshop. And for the rest of the d ay, Kazz set about turning the d ream into a reality.

–

'Blood y hell, it looks great!' Stevie exclaimed , later that afternoon.

It d id , Kazz thought, d espite very few books being on the shelves. Some were, though (although the categories were a bit haphazard), and the furniture was in the right place. The bookshop remind ed Kazz of an old e world e library.

Stevie hand ed her a wicker basket. 'I've brought food .'

Kazz's stomach rumbled at the word , and she realised she had eaten nothing all d ay apart from a bag of crisps and a chocolate bar. She had been living off ad renalin and copious cups of tea.

'You would n't happen to have a vacuum cleaner I could borrow?' she asked , taking the basket from her friend and peering into it.

'There's one in the flat,' Stevie said .

Ah, yes, the flat. Kazz had n't managed to take any of her personal possessions there yet. She would d o that later.

She sank into the gold wingback chair and unwrapped the parcels, her eyes wid ening as she saw lamb sausage rolls with a pot of harissa yoghurt, a slice of Gorgonzola, pear and walnut pie, a sliver of goat's cheese and spring onion galette, and several slices of cake.

'While you eat,' Stevie said , 'tell me what need s d oing, and I'll carry on.'

Kazz took a huge bite of the pie, and crumbs tumbled into her lap. With her mouth full, she said , 'You can't help with the books, but can you try to find the name of an insurance company? And I need an internet connection, and one of those card payment things. And a sign. I need a sign.'

'On it,' Stevie d eclared , peering at her phone. 'I'll send you the d etails of my insurance company – they're pretty good – and a number to call for a card machine. I'm not sure I can help you with the sign, though. The chap who painted mine retired , and even if he had n't, he wasn't the best. Do you remember me telling you that he got the name wrong? He painted *Poggy's* Tea Shoppe, not *Peggy's*.'

Kazz d id . It had mad e her chuckle.

'I'll ask on the group chat,' Stevie said . 'Someone will know someone who'll know someone. Tanglewood is like that.'

Kazz scoffed the rest of her impromptu picnic while Stevie jabbed and swiped at her phone, and when she was done, she gathered up the remains of her feast. 'Thank you, I needed that.' She gave Stevie the basket back.

'Don't forget to make yourself proper meals,' Stevie said. 'I remember when I first opened the tea shop, I was too tired to do much more than warm up some soup out of a tin. I would invite you to ours for supper tonight, but we're going out. Nick's got a new owner to impress; she has six horses and she's not happy with the yard they're in at present. They're not coming along as one would like,' Stevie added, putting on a posh voice.

'Aw, that's OK. I wouldn't have accepted anyway. I've still got loads to do here, and I haven't even started on the flat yet.'

'I'll see you tomorrow,' Stevie said, giving her a hug.

After the door closed behind her, Kazz plopped back into the chair. Weariness had crept up, ambushing her as she ate, and now she was so tired that she couldn't move. The thought of having to haul her suitcase and numerous bags across the street to the flat made her want to cry.

Limbs aching, eyes heavy, Kazz was pooped. She'd have a little rest for a minute...

'You want to be careful, leaving your door unlocked like that. Anyone might walk in.'

The voice was far too loud and far too close, and Kazz's eyes flew open. 'What?'

Betty was standing in front of her, her hands on her hips, a stern expression on her face. 'I said ...' She raised her voice further. 'You don't want to leave—'

'Sorry,' Kazz interrupted, sitting up. She wasn't sure why she was apologising. 'What time is it?'

'Time you were in bed , by the look of you,' Betty retorted . 'It's seven o'clock.'

'Morning or evening?'

The old lad y tutted . 'Evening. Stevie told me you pulled an all-nighter. That's not wise at your age.'

At her age? She was barely thirty! But she was forced to ad mit that Betty had a point. There was a time when Kazz could party all night and stay awake all the following d ay. It seemed she had lost the ability somewhere along the line.

Betty was tapping her foot impatiently as she held her hand out, but Kazz was reluctant to take it, fearing she might pull the old lad y over. However, Betty's grip was surprisingly strong for a woman of her age and physique, and before Kazz could protest, she had been hauled unceremoniously to her feet.

She stood there, swaying slightly.

Betty gripped her elbow. 'Come on. Where are your keys? And what's the cod e for the alarm?'

'I can't, I've got to—'

'You've got to get some sleep, that's what you've got to d o,' Betty insisted .

'But all my stuff is here.' Kazz gazed forlornly at the bulging suitcase and the waist-high tower of black plastic bags. It was going to take her ages to ferry this lot to the flat above the tea shop. And she would have to go round the back of the build ing and into the little courtyard where the spiral staircase lead ing to the flat was located . There was an entrance via the shop, but Kazz only had a key to the external d oor.

'You need a toothbrush and a nightie,' Betty d eclared . 'Everything else can wait.' She eyed the pile. 'Which bag is your toothbrush in?'

'I d on't know,' Kazz wailed . She wanted to tell the old lad y to go away, but she d id n't have the heart. She was only trying to help. But Kazz had been perfectly happy in her chair, if somewhat chilly and stiff.

'Leave it to me,' Betty said . She took an ancient mobile phone out of her bag and flipped the lid . Her tongue poking out, she pressed several buttons, slowly and d eliberately. 'Hello? Yes, it's me… At the bookshop… *The bookshop!*' She put a hand over the screen and hissed to Kazz, 'She says she d oesn't know anything about a bookshop.' She tilted her head and removed her hand . 'Keep up, Agnes. I'm at the bookshop with Kazz, Stevie's friend … Well, it d oes now, so there.' A hand over the screen again. 'She says Tanglewood d oesn't have a bookshop.'

Directing her next comments to the person on the other end of the phone, Betty carried on. 'Where the stationery shop used to be… That's right, the empty one, only it's not empty now, it's got books in it.' She heaved a sigh. It was so loud that Agnes would n't have need ed a phone to hear it. Everyone in Tanglewood must have. 'No, it won't affect the library… Be quiet, Agnes, and listen. I need you to round everyone up—' Betty rolled her eyes. She d id n't bother putting her hand over the phone this time as she said , 'Agnes says they've just got a round in.' She mad e a face and spoke into the phone again. All Kazz could d o was listen and wond er what the hell was going on. 'Your sweet sherry can wait. I need you here… *at the bookshop!* Sheesh! It'll only take a couple of minutes. I need some bags shifting… to the flat above the tea shop…' Another loud sigh. 'Mrs George can sit this one out.' Betty said to Kazz, 'What that woman *hasn't* got wrong with her can be written on the back of a stamp.'

She turned her attention back to her phone call. 'No, I didn't mean you, I was talking about Mrs George... I don't care if she heard me, I'll say it to her face... Look, are you coming or not? Good. Two minutes.' She snapped the phone shut. 'Sorted.'

Kazz barely had time to process what had just happened, before the shop door banged open and five people poured in. Betty immediately took charge, issuing instructions with the vigour of a sergeant major facing a bunch of new recruits. Within fifteen minutes, the pile of bags had been relocated to the flat, and Kazz was sitting on the bed in the main bedroom while Betty rummaged through her suitcase, looking for a nightie Kazz didn't possess. Five minutes after that, she was tucked up in bed, teeth brushed, face washed and wearing an oversized T-shirt she had bought to cover a bikini when she holidayed in Greece several years ago.

Betty nodded at her once, a single decisive inclination of her head. Then she was gone, the door slamming shut behind her, and Kazz was left alone to finally drift into a deep, restful sleep, where she dreamt of handsome sexy farmers and bossy old ladies.

Chapter 11

Saul found his father in the pens behind the big barn, moving rails around. Murray was nowhere in sight.

'Where have you been?' Geoff demanded. 'I've been looking all over for you.'

'I've just got back,' Saul said, yawning.

His father sent him a cross look. 'I hope she was worth it, son, because we've got our hands full today, and I can't have you slacking because you've been awake all night.'

Saul's mouth dropped open. 'It's not what you think.'

He was about to explain that he had been helping Kazz move her stuff from London to Tanglewood, and then he'd had to go see a bloke about a ram, but he decided not to bother. He had arranged it ages ago, as the farm needed fresh breeding stock, but the ram was near Builth Wells and it had taken him an hour to get there and an hour to get back, and in the end it had been a wasted journey because the ram wasn't a particularly good specimen, so he hadn't bought it.

'Where's Murray?' he asked, rolling his head to ease the ache in his neck. He had been on the go since early yesterday morning, and he was so tired that he could sleep for a week. He must have been mad to drive to Builth Wells after unloading Kazz's stuff, but the trailer was hitched up to the Landy, so he'd thought he might as well.

His head had been full of Kazz as he'd d riven up the A470, and he had kept remembering her in the passenger seat, fast asleep. She had looked so sweet, with her mouth slightly open and her eyelid s fluttering, and now and again she would utter a cute little snore. Seeing her so vulnerable had mad e him want to go all manly by sweeping her into his arms and vowing to look after her and protect her.

He d id n't think she would appreciate it, though. Kazz, so Leanne had informed him, was a sparky, no-nonsense lad y, who was more than capable of looking after herself.

Yet… she had shown him her soft sid e yesterd ay, and his heart went out to her as he thought of the upheaval she was going through.

His d ad broke into his thoughts. 'Murray is getting the ewes in. The vet is coming out tod ay to scan them.'

Ah, *that* explained his d ad 's mood . Scanning the ewes to find out how many were in lamb was always a tense time. The results could mean a good financial year or a bad one.

Saul whistled for Tam, knowing that the d og would n't be far away. 'I'd better get a move on,' he said , ignoring his d ad 's grumbling as he head ed toward s the shed whe the quad bikes were kept.

He got on the nearest one and fired it up, Tam leaping onto the back, her tail wagging, her ears pricked . At least someone was happy to see him, he thought, wishing he had been able to stay to give Kazz a hand after they'd unload ed the trailer. He'd felt bad for having to aband o her to the mammoth task of getting the place shipshape, and he wond ered how she was getting on.

Should he give her a call and ask?

No, better not. His reason for phoning her would n't be purely platonic, and since he had mad e a promise to himself not to d ate for a while, he d id n't want to break it with the first pretty woman to cross his path.

There was another reason, and one he wasn't sure he wanted to ad mit: he d id n't want to risk hurting her. Because if they started d ating, he would d efinitely let her d own at some point. Usually at around d ate number four or five. And she d id n't d eserve that. None of his d ates d id if he was honest.

Feeling a bit of a heel, he d ragged his mind away from his love life, and turned his thoughts to his future. If he could stay awake long enough this evening, he would work out a business plan. Knowing how much he would need as a d eposit, and how much he would need to borrow, would give him a starting point.

As he aimed the quad through the gate lead ing onto the hillsid e above the farm, Saul wond ered how Murray and his d ad would cope without him. A twenty-four hours a d ay, seven d ays a week operation, farming was hard work, and he felt a prickle of guilt. He loved what he d id , but sometimes it was overwhelming.

'Stop whinging,' he said und er his breath, recognising he was find ing it hard tod ay because he was knackered . It was his own fault. He should never have agreed to take Kazz to Lond on, but he was glad he had , and Kazz's face floated into his mind and hovered there. He had enjoyed spend ing time with her. He was also full of ad miration for what she was d oing, although circumstances had kind of pushed her into it. OK, not pushed , because she could simply have d umped all her grand ad 's books in a skip and found another chef job in Lond on. But he guessed the time was right for her to take her career in another d irection.

A loud bang from the rear of the quad made him jump, and he braked hard. Thankfully, he hadn't been doing more than about five miles an hour, because the track was sorely rutted, but even at that slow speed, the underneath of the vehicle could be damaged if he hit a rock.

Saul hadn't hit a rock.

He had hit a sheep.

Or should he say, the *sheep* had hit *him*.

Donald, the lamb that Saul had hand-reared in the spring, had rammed him, and was backing up to have another go. Tam had wisely jumped off the quad and was eyeing the sheep warily, waiting for instructions.

Donald charged, his head down, his legs stiff, and collided with the back of the quad. The bang made Saul flinch as the quad juddered forward. The daft animal wasn't pulling his punches. Having been born in March, he was still technically a lamb, but today he was acting like a fully grown adult. It didn't help that he had no fear of dogs or humans. Or quad bikes, by the looks of it.

'Oi!' Saul yelled, waving his arms. 'Go find something else to head butt.'

Donald bleated loudly and trotted towards him, his head lowered again. But this time it wasn't a charge; Donald wanted his nose scratched.

Saul sighed. 'OK, you win.' He rubbed the animal's hairy nose, and Donald waggled his tail in bliss. 'I've a good mind to send you to market,' he threatened, as he examined the rear of the quad bike. There were so many dings and dents on it already that he couldn't tell whether any of them had been made by Donald.

Saul pushed the sheep away and climbed back on the bike, Tam leaping up behind him. Although it was only the ewes that were being rounded up, he knew Donald would follow. In fact, the batty creature would make a valiant attempt at doing the round ing up himself. The silly sod thought he was a dog, remind ing Saul of the film about a pig that thought it was a sheepdog. If Saul did happen to find a farm to rent, he vowed to take Donald with him. Despite his threats, this was one sheep that would never go to market.

–

Tanglewood might be small, but its proximity to the National Park, along with the pretty river running through it, meant that it had become a mecca for hikers, ramblers and cyclists. The lovely range of artisan shops and the prid e that the resid ents took in their village also helped to attract numerous visitors, hopefully some of whom would want to buy books on their way through, and this was Saul's first thought when he opened his eyes this morning, and he wond ered how Kazz was getting on.

She had been on his mind quite a bit since Wed nesd ay, and although his mum had been keeping him abreast of what was going on, he was nevertheless curious and wanted to see for himself, especially since the bookshop would be opening its d oors tomorrow. He would be shocked if she could manage to pull it all together in such a short amount of time. Not many people could go from concept to reality in just a few d ays, and her can-d o attitud e was impressive.

Armed with a list (his mother would n't let a shopping opportunity pass her by), Saul head ed into the village, parking in one of the sid e streets and walking the rest of the way.

Making a d etour to his sister's flower shop, he poked his head insid e.

'Morning, Lea,' he said , his eyes scanning the cheerful blooms as their sweet perfume wafted up his nose. Leanne had an instinct for which flowers went with which, and she had even come second in a national floristry competition, which led to her working part of each month in Lond on for an internationally renowned 'florist to the stars'. Saul was so proud of her, he could burst.

Leanne was frowning. 'What are you d oing here? Buying some flowers for another one of your d ates?'

'I'm going to the bookshop,' he said .

His sister's eyes narrowed . 'Ah, I see.'

Against his better jud gement, he asked somewhat d efensively, 'What d o you see?'

'Don't go there, Saul. Kazz has got enough going on without being messed about by you.'

Saul blinked . 'I've no intention of messing Kazz about. I'll have you know I've sworn off d ating.'

'Ha! That'll be the d ay!' Leanne looked remarkably unimpressed at his announcement. 'You will never give up d ating.'

He d ecid ed to ignore the comment. 'I like books, and I want to see what she's d one with the place,' he said .

'If you are that interested , you could help. The poor girl has been working all hours.'

'I d id n't think it my place to. Anyway, I've d one my bit.'

Leanne's tone was accusing. 'I d id hear that you refused to take any money, not even for d iesel. I thought you were supposed to be running a business?'

Saul had thought so too, but when the time came, he simply had n't been able to d o it. He said , 'Is that why you're assuming I'm trying to get her into bed ?'

'Aren't you?'

His hesitation was minuscule. 'No, I told you, I'm sworn off dating.'

But Leanne had put the image of him and Kazz in bed together into his mind and now he could n't shift it. Heat began to pool in his stomach at the thought, and he shifted from foot to foot, embarrassed at the abrupt surge of desire.

'I'd better get going,' he said . 'Mum has given me a list.'

It was a good distraction, and Leanne chuckled . 'Make sure you get exactly what's on it,' she remind ed him. 'No substitutes,' Saul and Leanne chorused together.

Iris had scold ed all of her kid s, at some time or another, for bringing back the wrong item. Their father had n't been immune to a telling-off, either.

As Saul turned to leave, Leanne called after him, 'Remember what I said : no trying to get into Kazz's knickers.'

Saul hurried away before his sister saw the flush on his face.

To give himself time to calm down and rein in his wayward imagination (Kazz in nothing but a scanty pair of panties had the starring role), Saul decid ed to duck into Peggy's Tea Shoppe for a cuppa before he saw Kazz in the flesh.

Argh! *No*, not the flesh! Anything but the flesh! He tried to rid himself of that image by replacing it with one of her slumped in the passenger seat of the Land y as he drove back from Lond on. But even fast asleep, she had looked ad orable. Her mouth had been open a fraction, her lips parted —

'Tea. A large one,' he stammered , as he approached the counter.

Betty snorted . 'You're not in the pub now, you know. You'll have a normal size cup and lump it.'

'A pot?'

The old lady put her hands on her hips. 'What is up with you, Saul Green? We only ever serve tea in pots. You've been coming here long enough to know that.' She squinted at him. 'What's got you all hot under the collar?'

'Nothing.' Betty was fast bringing him down to earth. She was very good at that.

'Have you been to see our Kazz yet?' she demanded .

Our Kazz? His face grew warm again. She might be Betty's Kazz, but she wasn't *his*.

But she *could* be…

'Shut up.' He could do without any little voices in his head making unseemly comments.

'Pard on!?'

Shit, he had said that out loud . 'I wasn't talking to you,' he said to Betty.

'Good , because you're not too old for a clip around the ear.'

Saul let the comment pass.

'Well?' she demanded . 'Have you been to the book-shop?'

'I'm going there after I've had my tea.' He stared at her pointed ly.

Betty did n't take the hint. Instead , she pulled out a chair and sat down at a newly vacated table. When she pointed to the seat next to her, Saul did as he was told . He sat.

Betty pursed her lips. 'You're not going to mess Kazz around .'

'Not you as well? I've just had an earbashing from Leanne. She warned me off too.'

'It's not a warning.' Betty's gaze was piercing.

'A threat, then,' he amended, wondering what Betty might do if he did 'mess Kazz around', and not sure he would want to find out. Betty might be old, but she was spiky.

'Not a threat. Just a simple observation.'

Saul had no idea what she was getting at. His bafflement must have shown.

'You are not going to mess Kazz around,' she repeated.

Running a weary hand across his face, Saul said, 'I heard you the first time, Betty.'

'No, you didn't. She's your *for-six*.'

'Excuse me?' *Please go away and fetch me my tea*, he begged silently. He wasn't in the mood for the old lady's eccentricities. He knew she could be a bit odd, but she was acting stranger than usual today. Had she been sniffing the marzipan?

Betty leant forward and grabbed his forearm. 'Remember me telling you that a girl would come along who would knock you for six?' Saul stared at her wordlessly, and when Betty said triumphantly, 'Well, Kazz is that girl,' words continued to fail him.

And neither did he say anything when his mum gave him an earbashing for forgetting to pick up her groceries after he'd decided against calling in to see Kazz and had slunk back to the farm, Betty's words ringing in his ears.

Chapter 12

Kazz glanced around her shop for about the seventeenth time that morning. She was sure she'd forgotten something, but she couldn't think what.

It was still dark out, but it wouldn't stay that way for much longer. In an hour, the day would begin, and so would the start of a whole new chapter in her life, because today she would open the doors to her very own bookshop. It was a momentous occasion, and also an incredibly scary one. What if she didn't get any customers? What if she did, but no one bought anything? Kazz didn't know which would be worse. But what she did know was that she had tried her best. The shop was looking exactly how she had pictured it when she'd first begun to believe it could be a possibility. It seemed as though weeks had passed since Tia had thrust the keys in her hand, but it was barely a week ago.

Just six days.

Six long and incredibly busy days.

If someone had told her when she'd got off the bus last Saturday that by the following weekend she would have taken up residence in the flat above the tea shop and would be about to open a shop of her own, stocked with her grandad's old books, she would have laughed in their face. Yet here she was, so nervous that she needed yet another wee, and wondering whether it was too late to back out.

Her phone pinged with a message from Stevie, wishing her luck and telling her she'd pop in later. Kazz had already received one from Leanne, who was usually up before the birds because she visited the wholesalers to buy the flowers before she opened her shop.

Tia had a wedding at the manor today and Kazz hadn't expected to hear from her, but she had sent her a silly gif and several kisses. Kazz had even had a call from Rossiter last night, after he'd finished his shift, and she'd been moved that he wanted to keep in touch. It had taken him no time at all to find another job, but he was still looking because – after being front-of-house staff in a trendy restaurant – waiting tables in a pub chain establishment wasn't his ideal position.

There was one person she hadn't heard from, though, and that was her mum. Kazz still hadn't told her what she'd done, and neither would she. Not yet. Not until she had something positive to report. She had spoken to her yesterday and Diana had sounded so incredibly happy that Kazz would cut off her right arm before she'd do anything to spoil it.

She paid another nervous visit to the loo, then made a cup of tea and took it onto the shop floor. Although that was technically what it was, Kazz secretly thought of it as 'the library'. The room looked so cosy with the lamps lit (she would turn on the main overhead lights when she opened up), and she even had a Christmas tree in the corner. Decorating it had been the final thing she'd done yesterday, and she had derived great enjoyment from it, even though she wished she'd had someone to share the moment with. Scoffing a mince pie and slurping hot chocolate on her own had felt a little pitiful.

However, she could hard ly expect Stevie or the others to give up their Frid ay night to wrap tinsel around a tree, especially since they had been so supportive over the past few d ays. Despite having their own businesses to run, Stevie, Leanne and Ed ie had all popped in to give her a hand , while Tia had sourced bags, organised for a sign to be painted above the shop and even persuad ed her father-in-law to spare the hand yman from the Manor to put up load s of shelves along the opposite wall to the bookcases, and along the available space on the back wall. Lord Tonbrid ge had even supplied the materials – old floorboard s – although his hand yman had mad e it clear he wanted them back at the end of the lease.

Everyone had been so lovely, and so kind , that more than once she had almost been red uced to tears. She felt a bit weepy now, if she was honest, which wasn't in the least bit like her. Up until the d ay she'd lost her job and her home, and her mother had told her she was leaving the country, Kazz had been the least weepy person she knew. Now she seemed to be fighting back tears all the time.

No more, she vowed . Tod ay was going to be just fine, she told herself. She would get to closing time and wond er what all the fuss had been about. Not wanting to tempt fate, she would wait until this evening before suggesting everyone go to the pub for a celebratory d rink – her treat. It was the least she could d o. And when she was more settled and had the chance to d raw breath, she would cook them a sumptuous meal to thank them.

A rap on the wind ow mad e her jump, and she smiled when she saw it was Betty.

While Kazz had been drinking her tea and musing, the village had begun to come alive, with lights on in the bakery and the butcher's. Kazz guessed Betty was on her way to the tea shop to put the first batch of cakes and pastries in the oven, if Stevie hadn't already done it.

'Good luck,' Betty said when Kazz unlocked the door, and she impulsively gave the old lady a hug. 'You won't need it, of course,' Betty assured her. 'I'm sure you'll do brilliantly. I'll try to pop in and see you later, but I'm not making any promises. Tanglewood is starting to ramp up for Christmas, and it's getting busy.'

Kazz hoped some of that busyness would rub off on her little shop. There were only five more Saturdays until Christmas, not including this one, and she had to make the most of them. She was also looking forward to the Christmas festival. Stevie had told her it was being held two weeks before Christmas, and the event attracted loads of visitors.

'How is the festival planning coming along?' she asked.

Betty pressed her lips together. 'It would be grand if it wasn't for Julia Ferris, more commonly known as Lady Tonbridge. She's a right pain in the arse. Can you believe she even suggested holding it at the Manor? I soon told her where she could stick that idea. It's always been held in the village itself.'

Kazz had yet to meet the Lord and Lady of Tonbridge Manor, but she had heard all about Lady Tonbridge's interference in William and Tia's wedding plans, the most significant of which had been her attempt to dictate the dress Tia wore. She had been having none of it, though, and had secretly arranged for Edie to design and make a very special dress indeed. Stevie had sent Kazz photos, and Tia had looked stunning. Now, Edie was also making

Stevie's d ress, as well as the brid esmaid s' ones, and Kazz could n't wait; she loved wed d ings, as they were an excuse to get d ressed up and have some fun. And this one would be particularly special because it was her best and old est friend who would be tying the knot. However, that was months and months away yet; Kazz had a shop to open first.

As she said good bye to Betty, she waved to Ed ie, who was hurrying along the street toward s the pretty cobbled courtyard , where the brid al shop was located , and she noticed that a few more shops and businesses had come to life.

Taking a d eep breath and squaring her should ers, Kazz knew it was time her little shop d id the same.

–

A few hours later, Kazz would n't exactly d escribe the bookshop as buzzing, but there had been a stead y trickle not long after she had opened the d oor. And when she'd mad e her first sale – a first ed ition 1863 book on house-keeping – she had been over the moon, and it had taken every inch of self-control not to d o a jig on the spot. With her heart in her mouth, she'd keyed the amount into the card machine, and had held her breath until the sale had been processed .

The next one had been a little less fraught, and five sales later (five! Eek!) she was feeling marginally more confid ent.

'There you go,' she said , hand ing a paper bag with a copy of *Locomotive Cyclopedia* insid e to the woman who had just purchased it. 'I'm sure your nephew will love it.'

'He d efinitely will,' the woman said . 'He lives and breathes mod el trains. That's another Christmas present to tick off the list. I'm so glad I found you. I've been saying for ages that Tanglewood need s a bookshop.'

The customer's word s mad e Kazz's heart sing. Comments like this were exactly what she need ed to hear.

'Please tell your friend s about it,' she urged , hoping she sound ed upbeat and not d esperate.

'Oh, I will,' the woman said . 'Merry Christmas.'

Kazz repeated the sentiment back to her, thinking it was maybe a tad early to be wishing people a merry Christmas. But she was starting to get in the mood , and she put it d own to having a Christmas tree in the shop. Usually, she would be in a hectic kitchen, with steam and swear word s floating on the air, and not a hint of anything festive in sight.

This was certainly less frantic, although it was more nerve-racking, because at least she knew what she was d oing in a kitchen. She d id n't have a clue what she was d oing in a bookshop.

But, if she was honest, that wasn't strictly true: she d id have *some* id ea. Subconsciously, she must have absorbed more than she'd thought from all those hours and hours she'd spent with Grand ad , because she soon began to realise she was conversing somewhat knowled geably with her customers. Or at least, she wasn't making a total arse of herself.

Another customer claimed her attention, and when she next turned around , her pulse leapt and she faltered , because stand ing insid e the d oor was Saul.

Their eyes locked and her heart stuttered , missing a beat. Hastily, she cast her gaze d ownward s, her mouth d ry, d ismay coursing through her.*Oh no, you don't*, she told herself. Saul was not the kind of man to have palpitations over. Surges of lust? Yes. A crush? No. But, flipping heck, he was so d amned sexy that she d efied any woman not to react to him the way she had .

No wond er he had a reputation as the local Lothario.

When she managed to gather her wits and risked looking at him again, she almost yelped as she realised that he was close enough to touch.

'Looks good ,' he said , scanning the shelves. 'I can't believe you've managed to get it d one so fast.'

'I had a lot of help,' she said .

'Yeah, I heard .' He pulled a face. 'I should have... you know... given you a hand .'

'You d id more than your share,' she said . 'Thanks again for hauling this lot back. I would n't have been able to d o it, if not for you.'

'You would have found a way,' he said . 'I mean it. You d on't strike me as the type of person to give up easily if you want something bad ly enough. How's it been so far? Sold many books?'

'A few. I'm hoping to sell a few more before the d ay is out. Excuse me.' She hurried to see to a customer, leaving him free to wand er.

But she could n't prevent herself from glancing at him every so often out of the corner of her eye and when he went to the counter, she hurried over.

He was grinning. 'When I was load ing your books onto the trailer, I d id n't get a chance to have a proper look. I can't believe what an eclectic and rand om range you've got: fiction, and child ren's books, poetry, cooking... Aren't you tempted to hang on to any of those, consid - ering your profession?'

'Believe me, I have picked out a few.' She laughed . 'But I can't keep them all.'

His gaze swept over the nearest shelves. 'Some of those travel guid es are for countries that no longer exist. They must be real collectors' items.'

'Possibly.' Kazz d id n't know whether they were or weren't.

'And I love your Christmas table.'

Kazz noticed that he'd spent some time looking at the selection of Christmas-themed books that she had placed on a table near the d oor.

'Look at this,' he said . He was hold ing up a beautifully illustrated ed ition of *Christmas Carol*. 'I've got to have it.'

There was no way she was taking money from Saul – not after he refused any payment for d riving her to Lond on and back. 'It's on the house.'

Saul shook his head . 'I'm not having it if I can't pay for it.'

'I insist. You would n't take any money from me when you d rove me to Lond on.'

'That was d ifferent.'

Kazz put her hand s on her hips and her eyes flashed . 'How?'

'It just was. Anyway, if you start giving stock away, you'll never make any money.'

Betty's voice interrupted their argument. 'See, Agnes, I told you this shop won't affect the library. Hello, Saul.' Betty smirked at him.

Kazz was amused to see him cringe, and she wond ered why.

He turned his attention back to her. 'Please let me pay for it and I'll be out of your hair.'

'Seen something you like?' Betty asked , coming to stand next to him and jabbing him in the ribs with a bony elbow.

Saul shuffled a few steps to the left.

The woman who was accompanying Betty was standing in the middle of the shop. She had her eyes closed and was breathing deeply. Kazz wondered if she was OK.

Betty said to Kazz, 'This is Agnes, Tanglewood 's chief – and only – librarian. You have met, but you were half-asleep, so I doubt you remember. She's twenty years younger than me but acts ten years older.'

'Don't you love that smell?' Agnes said dreamily.

Ah, so that was what she had been doing: book sniffing.

'And for your information,' Agnes said haughtily, opening her eyes, 'I only act older than you because you behave like a teenager.'

Kazz had to agree. At this very moment Betty was singing the lyrics to 'Love Is in the Air' and winking at Saul.

'What did you say?' Agnes demanded . 'What's in the air? All I can smell are old books.' She inhaled again, drawing the air in through her sharp nose and letting it out in a whoosh.

Saul was slowly shaking his head , looking mortified . Quickly, without saying anything to Kazz or Betty, he took his wallet out of his pocket, threw several notes onto the counter, picked up the book and dashed to the door, leaving Kazz staring at him in astonishment as Betty creased up with laughter.

What on earth had that been about!

–

It was coming toward s the end of the d ay and   Kazz slumped   against the counter, her bod y sagging in relief. She could n't believe it! She had   taken more than she'd thought. Much more.

She d ouble-checked the figure, ad d ing each ind ivid ual number up for a third   time.

Kazz had   religiously mad e a note of every single sale, and   she compared it to the end -of-d ay report that she had run on the card   machine, and   the amount of money in the till (that was actually a d rawer in the sid eboard , in which she had   slotted   a cutlery tray to hold   the various notes and coins).

The figure was correct.

Oh, boy. She had n't been expecting that, and   she hugged   herself, squealing softly at the realisation that she had   mad e a fair amount of money.

Gathering up most of the bank notes but making sure she left enough in the float, she stuffed   them in her bag and   locked   up the shop. It was time to celebrate, and   the d rinks were on her!

First, though, something to eat. She was starving, and she mad e a note to bring sand wiches with her on Mond ay. She simply had n't thought about food   this morning, having been too nervous; but she was thinking about it now all right.

She was making an omelette when she had   a message from Stevie.

How did it go?

Stevie had   briefly popped   into the bookshop after the lunchtime rush, but she had n't been able to stay long.

Kazz replied ,*Better than expected*, and   ad d ed   a smiley face, clapping hand s and   a blowing kisses face.*Let's celeb-rate. How about the pub?* She quickly put the suggestion in the 'Brid ezilla' group chat that Stevie had set up to keep in touch with her brid esmaid s.

Stevie's reply was a sad face. *Sorry, too knackered. Also, Nick is on his way back from a showjumping event and I promised I'd have a meal ready. Another time?*

Kazz felt a twinge of d isappointment. *No probs.* Heart emoji. *Speak later.*

That's a shame, she thought. She would have liked Stevie to be there this evening. She would have liked Leanne to be there too, but Kazz alread y knew that she and Rex were off to a show in Card iff. A reply from Tia that she was still up to her eyes with the wed d ing at the Manor (it was going brilliantly, and the newlywed s were having the time of their lives) meant that she could n't come, either. Kazz was thrilled for her, though, aware of how much work had gone into setting up the manor as a wed d ing venue.

As she hopped in the shower, she realised that it would just be her and Ed ie tonight. But that was OK; she liked Ed ie a lot and it would be fun getting to know her better.

Ed ie arrived at the pub a few second s after Kazz, her face glowing from the chill outsid e. They hugged briefly, before Ed ie shrugged off her coat and hung it on the back of a chair.

'What can I get you?' Kazz asked .

'Um, a virgin blood y Mary, please.'

'Are you sure you d on't want something with a bit more oomph? I'm buying.'

'Best not. I've got the car. I would have asked James to pick me up, but he's out all night with the beavers.'

James worked for Natural Resources Wales and was also part of the beaver reintrod uction project. Ed ie and

James lived on a smallhold ing on the hills above Tangle-wood , and although Kazz und erstood that Ed ie was being sensible, she was d isappointed to be d rinking alone.

She ord ered Ed ie's d rink plus an oak–aged single malt for herself, and took them back to the table.

The pub was about half-full, mostly with people enjoying a meal, although there were a couple of chaps propping up the bar with pints of real ale in front of them. One of them had brought his d og. Music played in the background , not so loud that it would imped e conversa-tion, and the log burner was lit. It was all rather genteel and a far cry from the places Kazz usually frequented on her rare Saturd ay nights off.

'How d id your first d ay go?' Ed ie asked .

'Really well. I sold more than I expected .'

'That's brilliant! Good for you. I d id try to pop in but I had appointments back-to-back. You'd be surprised how many people get married around Christmas. I'm going to be up to my eyes in alterations for the next month.'

'That's good , isn't it?' Kazz felt like knocking the whisky back, but she held the urge in check, sipping at the d rink instead .

'Very,' Ed ie agreed . 'Business is booming, and I'm sure yours will too. Cheers.' She tilted her glass toward s Kazz, who clinked it with her own.

'So, where d o you want to go after this?' Kazz asked .

'I d on't follow.'

'Once we've finished these,' Kazz clarified , lifting her glass. 'Is there somewhere a bit livelier?'

Ed ie laughed . 'The Hen and Duck is as lively as it gets. If you want a bit more life, you'll need to go to Abergavenny. I believe a couple of bars there have live music.'

'Abergavenny?' Kazz pulled a face. The town was only six miles away, but she had been hoping for something closer.

Ed ie continued , 'If you want clubs you'll have to go to Card iff.'

Kazz's spirits d ropped . Card iff wasn't the easiest place to get to from Tanglewood .

It looked like it was the Hen and Duck or nothing tonight.

Feeling a little d eflated , she tried to look on the positive sid e – it mightn't be the celebration she had envisaged , but she was probably too tired to enjoy it properly anyway.

'Perhaps we can arrange a night out, all of us?' Kazz suggested . 'I haven't been to a club for ages.'

'Me, neither. Not since before Sammy was born. That remind s me, I can't stay long. My mum's babysitting him, so I need to pick him up soon. He's another reason I'm not d rinking this evening,' she explained with a smile. 'Kid s and hangovers d on't mix.'

Kazz managed a second whisky before Ed ie announced she had to leave.

'I'm so glad the bookshop has got off to such a good start,' Ed ie said . 'I'll d efinitely pop in on Mond ay.'

Kazz watched her slip out of the d oor and d ebated whether to go for d rink number three. But sitting on her own in a pub looked a bit sad , so she finished her whisky and left.

The street was quiet, just two people strolling arm-in-arm along the opposite pavement, although the chippie at the top of the road had several customers, and she wond ered what people d id for fun around here.

Not a lot, it seemed , and a pang went through her as she realised the Saturd ay-night scene would only just be beginning in the capital. People would be piling into bars and restaurants, hurrying off to the theatre or to see a show. There would be buses and taxis, ped estrians and cyclists, and people hurrying here and there, the sound of laughter and shouting, planes overhead , and sirens in the d istance.

Living in Tanglewood was going to take a bit of getting used to.

Chapter 13

Bored om wasn't something Kazz was overly familiar with. She had always been far too busy to be bored .

Until now.

This past week, since the shop opened its d oors last Saturd ay, had been an unexpected mix of busyness d uring the d ay and crashing bored om in the evenings. And d on't get her started on the yawn-fest that last Sund ay had been. Tomorrow wasn't shaping up to be any better, and she had a feeling she might start to d read Sund ays if she could n't find anything to fill the d ay.

She was so used to being surround ed by people, both in the restaurant and in the Lond on flat, that the slower pace of life in the shop was a new experience, as was being on her own after she'd finished work for the d ay.

She had no id ea what to d o with herself in the hours between closing the shop for the evening and going to bed . She d id n't think she'd ever slept so much in her whole life, and there was a limit to the amount of cleaning and cooking she could d o.

There was one upsid e, though – she now had time to read , and she had taken to bringing a d ifferent book home with her at the end of the d ay. Tonight's choice was *Wuthering Heights*. Again. Not exactly riveting for a Saturd ay night, but as she d id n't fancy going to the pub on her own, it would have to d o.

After locking up and returning to her lonely little flat, Kazz had barely taken her coat off and popped her bag on the floor by the sofa, when there was a knock at the door.

Guessing who it might be, she went to answer it and saw Stevie standing on the little landing. She was holding a cardboard cake box.

'I've brought gifts,' she announced, giving her an awkward one-armed hug.

Kazz eyed the box eagerly, and her mouth watered.

As Stevie stepped inside, she said, 'It's only a few pastries, but you know how much I hate seeing food go to waste.'

'Believe me, they won't be going to waste,' Kazz vowed. She was sorely tempted to skip her planned main meal and go straight to dessert.

She had come to realise that since she didn't have to cook for a living, she rather enjoyed cooking for herself in the evenings. Besides, it also filled the time.

Stevie sank into one of the squishy armchairs and yawned. 'What a day. I'm pooped! If I see another ginger-bread man, I think I might cry. I baked around a hundred this morning, and I sold all of them except for two. They're in your goodie box. How has your day been?'

'Busy, thank goodness. Fancy a glass of wine?'

'I'd better not. I mightn't stop at one and I've got to drive home.'

Kazz wanted to suggest that Stevie could leave her little yellow Beetle in Tanglewood's car park and pick it up tomorrow, but she didn't want to appear desperate for company – even though she was.

Kazz poured herself a glass and sat on the sofa. 'Got any plans for this evening?'

'Food and a film. What about you?'

With her gaze on her drink, Kazz said, 'Same, I suppose.'

Stevie looked chastened. 'Sorry, Kazz, I'm a rubbish friend, aren't I? We'll have a night out soon, I promise. It's just that it's so hectic at the moment.'

'You're a brilliant friend,' Kazz said firmly. 'The best. You're letting me stay here for a start, and you helped me set up the bookshop.'

Stevie made a face. 'I didn't do much to help. Heck, I did hardly anything. The idea was Betty's, Saul provided the removal service, and Lord Tonbridge loaned you his handyman. I didn't do anything.'

'Now that you put it like that, you're the worst friend ever,' Kazz teased.

They beamed at each other, then Stevie sobered. 'Seriously, we'll have to have a girly night out soon.'

'We could go clubbing.' Kazz's tone was deadpan, and she burst out laughing when she saw the expression on Stevie's face. 'Joking,' she said. 'Edie has already filled me in on Tanglewood's nightlife situation.'

Stevie was gazing at her sympathetically. 'It's not exactly the West End, is it? I remember when I first moved here, it took me a while to get used to it, but I got there eventually.'

'Nick might have had something to do with that.' Kazz smiled.

'Why don't you come to lunch tomorrow? You're not planning on opening the shop, are you?'

'No, I need a day off,' Kazz said, although, when she came to think of it, she may as well open up; it would be better than sitting in the flat and staring at the walls.

While it was nice of Stevie to offer, Kazz didn't want to appear needy, the sort of friend who was invited out of pity. She didn't think she was at that point yet, but it mightn't be too long. And Stevie and Nick worked so hard, they deserved to spend their free time together, and not with a spare wheel like her rolling up.

She made a decision. 'I'm going to Hay-on-Wye,' she said.

'Checking out the competition?' Stevie heaved herself out of the chair. 'Well, enjoy. I'm off to put my feet up. And don't forget, you're here to sell books, not to buy loads more.'

Kazz chuckled. 'I'll bear that in mind. Thanks for the box of goodies.'

Stevie leant in for another hug, then pulled away abruptly. 'Hang on a sec – how are you planning on getting there?'

'Um, bus?'

'Hmm. The Sunday bus service isn't brilliant and you'll probably have to change a couple of times. It'll take ages. It's only half an hour by car, but I bet it'll be more like two on public transport.'

The thought of sitting on a bus for a couple of hours didn't fill Kazz with dismay because, let's face it, she didn't have anything else to do. However, she didn't fancy having to change a couple of times either; the chance of her getting lost in an unfamiliar place was too great.

Stevie said, 'Leave it with me, I'll sort something out.'

The 'something' turned out to be Saul.

–

Kazz was surprised at how much she was looking forward to today. She told herself that it was because she had hardly been anywhere, except for the shop and the flat, since she'd come back from London with a trailer full of stuff, and not because it meant she would be spending the day with Saul. She took her time over choosing what to wear, settling on a thick jumper, a pair of tight-fitting jeans and warm boots with only a small heel, because she guessed they might be doing some walking. Although she often wore eyeliner and mascara during the day, this morning she added a coat of lipstick and a thin covering of tinted moisturiser.

Ready well before she needed to be, she tried to read, but spent more time gazing out of the window than at the page, and in the end she gave up and put the book down. This time she told herself the reason she couldn't concentrate was because she had read *Wuthering Heights* too many times and the story had grown stale.

She was standing by the window and craning her neck to peer down the street when Saul's Land Rover chugged into view. Her breath caught in her throat as she saw him behind the wheel and her heart quickened its pace. Time seemed to slow as the car pulled into the kerb, and a rush of warmth spread through her, her cheeks flushing with a mix of excitement and nervousness.

Grabbing her bag and shrugging on her coat, she hurried into the street, coming to a breathless halt next to the car just as Saul was getting out of it.

When he saw her, his smile took her breath away. For a moment she couldn't speak, her senses filled by him, but thankfully he broke the spell.

'Hi, are you OK?' he asked.

'Yeah, thanks. You?'

'I'm good.'

The perfectly normal conversation served to balance her, and she took a deep breath as she got in his old Land

Rover. 'Thank you for offering to take me to Hay-on-Wye. It's very kind of you. I was going to catch the bus.'

He chuckled . 'So Stevie said . It would have taken you a good couple of hours and about three separate bus journeys.'

'I keep forgetting that if you live out in the sticks you're stuck if you d on't have transport. I'm so used to trains, buses and taxis running around the clock.' Living in Tanglewood was *definitely* taking some getting used to.

'You may want to think about buying a car,' he suggested . 'Can you d rive?'

'I can, but I d on't. There d id n't seem any point in Lond on.'

He shot her a look. 'Do you miss it?'

'I miss the convenience. I d on't miss the traffic or being squashed nose to armpit on the Tube.'

'Coming from a big city to a small village must be a bit of a shock. It was quite sud d en too, so it isn't as though you've had ages to think about it,' he said . 'I know I would find it hard if the shoe was on the other foot. Apart from public transport, what else d o you miss?'

'I miss having fun. I used to work hard – really hard – but I played hard too. I still work hard but I d on't get to play anymore. I know it's early d ays and I haven't been here five minutes, and I need to concentrate on the bookshop, but…'

'You want to have some fun, too,' he finished for her.

'Is that too much to ask? Am I being silly?' She worried at her lip; Saul was probably regretting asking.

'You're not being silly. "All work and no play…"' he quoted , letting her complete the proverb.

'I d on't think I'm cut out for living in the country,' she said . 'I think I'll be going back to Lond on after Christmas.

137

I'll sell as many books as I can between now and the New Year, then I'll start applying for jobs. I'm sure Rossiter will let me stay at his place for a couple of weeks until I sort something out. We used to work at the same restaurant. He persuaded me to go to bingo with him one night, and they were doing a buy-one-get-one-free on cocktails, so he owes me for the horrendous hangover I had the next day.' She smiled sadly. 'That was the same day I found out my mother was moving to Spain, that I'd lost my job, and that me and my flatmates had been given notice to quit by our landlord. I must admit, I've had better days.'

'Will you go back to working in a restaurant?' he asked. A small frown line had appeared between his brows.

Kazz shrugged. 'I love being a chef, but I don't like the hours, so perhaps not. I don't know what else I can do, though.'

'Do you like selling books more than you like being a chef?' he asked, pulling up to a junction and indicating to turn right.

She didn't answer immediately, and when she did, her reply was slow and considered. 'Do you know what... I think I do.'

'But you'd prefer not to do it in Tanglewood?'

If she was honest, she didn't know what she wanted.

She sat up straight and peered through the windscreen, as activity up ahead caught her attention. 'Is something going on?'

The Land Rover was crawling over the bridge spanning the River Wye, and there seemed to be an awful lot of traffic about, and loads of people too. She had checked Hay out and knew it was a small town, renowned for its second-hand bookshops and for the literary festival that took place in the spring. But she d id n't realise the town would be this busy on a chilly Sund ay in November.

'It's the Hay Winter Festival. I assumed this was why you wanted to come here tod ay,' Saul replied .

Kazz stared blankly at him. 'There's a festival on?'

He ind icated to turn into an alread y overflowing car park, and she wond ered how long it would take to find a parking space. If they ever d id .

The smile Saul gave her mad e her heart skip a beat. 'Oh, yeah, there's a festival, all right. You're going to love it, even though we d on't have tickets to any of the events. Just being here is enough to get your booky juices flowing.'

Booky juices? Hmm.

'Have you been here before?' she asked as he inched the vehicle forward another couple of metres.

'Once or twice. I prefer the summer one, though, but only because it's bigger.'

'I d id n't realise you were such a literary buff.'

She knew he enjoyed read ing, because he'd told her, and on the journey to Lond on they had d iscussed their favourite books and the stories they'd loved when they were kid s, but she had assumed he was just being polite and occasionally read a book or two. And when he'd bought the copy of *A Christmas Carol*, she'd thought he'd felt obliged to buy something, seeing as he was there. She'd never imagined he loved books and literature enough to attend a festival. She found it rather sexy: good looks, intelligence and a love of books was a d angerous combination.

I wonder what he's like in bed?

Kazz screwed up her face as the thought sent shock waves through her. *Oh no, don't go there*, she told herself.

139

'Are you OK? Do you need the loo?' he asked.

Kazz was mortified. Not only had she been wondering whether he was any good in the sack, but she must have given out 'I need a wee' vibes.

'No, I'm fine,' she squeaked. 'Just excited.'

'Me, too. When Stevie said you needed a lift to Hay and I remembered that the festival was on, I couldn't wait. It's a pity most of the talks and workshops are sold out, but at least we can go sniff some old books and soak up the atmosphere. And you never know, we might see a famous face or two.'

Kazz stamped down on her libido and subsequent embarrassment as Saul finally found a parking space, and she lifted her coat off the back seat. She couldn't wait to explore.

The town, situated between the Black Mountains on the one side and the River Wye on the other, dated back to medieval times and was particularly well known for its ruined castle, built over nine hundred years ago.

But what Kazz loved was the square, with its impressive clock tower, and the narrow streets filled with bookshops. Barely able to contain her excitement, she dived into the first, only surfacing when Saul pointed out that there were another twenty or so to go.

It took all her restraint not to buy an armful from every shop she went into, and if it hadn't been for Saul constantly reminding her that her mission was to sell books, not purchase more, she might have spent the whole week's profit in two hours.

'Stop,' he laughed when she tried to persuade him to enter yet another. 'I need some lunch.'

It was only then that Kazz realised she was hungry, and her stomach uttered a loud rumble. After a bit of a search and a small wait (every eatery was bursting at the seams), they were finally seated in a quaint pub not far from the river, with the enticing aroma of food wafting up their noses.

'My two favourite things,' Kazz beamed . 'Food and books. I d on't care whether I'm cooking it or eating it, read ing it or selling it – I just love food and books. Thank you so much for bringing me.'

'My pleasure. I'm having a great time.'

'It's all so Christmassy, too.' She eyed his jumper. It wasn't the nicest festive jumper she'd seen, but it wasn't the worst, either.

Kazz owned a couple of jumpers herself, and she d ebated whether to invest in a few more. Her shop was looking very festive (Ed ie had d onated some bunting mad e out of snippets of red , green and gold fabric that Kazz had d raped around the wind ows) and Kazz felt that continuing the Christmas theme might be good for busi-ness – kind of remind ing people that the big d ay was just around the corner and they had presents to buy. And what better gift than a book!

She had also seen a couple of things she wanted to purchase tod ay, and she vowed to go back for the pretty cotton scarf with Jane Austen books printed on it, and the bauble in the shape of a stack of books to go on the tree.

'What are you having?' Saul asked , bringing her atten-tion back to the menu she was hold ing.

'Sorry, I was thinking about Christmas jumpers. I would have worn mine if I'd known you were going to wear one. I'm starting to feel quite festive.'

'That's good to hear. I love Christmas.' He pointed through the pub's wind ow. 'You could always get your face painted instead of wearing a jumper.'

Kazz craned her neck, and on the opposite side of the street she spied a lady in a red and green plaid coat, with a queue of children in front of her who were hopping about impatiently as they waited for their turn.

'Yeah, right.' She laughed.

'I'm serious. Why don't you have your face painted?'

'It's for kids.'

'Who says?'

'Well, um, everyone knows that.'

'I don't.'

'You're not everyone,' Kazz pointed out.

'Are you saying my opinion isn't valid?'

'Of course not.' She began to bluster, as she tried to work out whether he was serious.

'Chicken,' he teased.

Kazz narrowed her eyes.

'You haven't got the guts,' he added.

'I have!' Face painting, eh? She'd show him. 'I'll have the roasted winter squash with goat's curd tart, and the wild mushroom ravioli.' She stood up and put her coat back on.

'Where are you going?'

'To get my face painted. If our meal arrives before I get to the beginning of the queue, at least I've tried.'

Saul grinned at her. 'You've got your fingers crossed.'

'Haven't.'

'Have. I can tell.'

Kazz uncrossed her fingers and waggled them at him. 'Haven't. See?'

His laughter followed her out of the pub, and she smiled to herself. The last laugh would be on him. There was no way she would reach the beginning of the line before their first course arrived. No way.

Once upon a time Saul had had a bit of a fling with Stevie. And it had just been a bit of one, because Stevie had only ever had eyes for Nick. When she and Nick had got together, he had been bristly toward s Saul for a while, but all that was water und er the brid ge now.

So when Saul had seen Stevie's name come up on his phone's screen yesterd ay evening, all he'd felt was mild curiosity, but after he had spoken to her, his curiosity had turned into unexpected excitement because he was going to be spend ing tod ay with Kazz.

This morning, he had d ressed with more care than usual. He wasn't a vain man and d id n't spend hours choosing his clothes or primping in front of the mirror, so he had been surprised to find himself rifling through his ward robe and d rawers in search of something to wear. Putting his inability to make a d ecision d own to the fact that he normally d id n't bother to d ress nicely d uring the d ay (neither the sheep nor the chickens cared what he wore), he settled on a pair of cargo trousers and a Christmas jumper. He could give Kazz a laugh, if nothing else.

Also, he was fairly certain that this wasn't a d ate, so he was anxious to make sure she d id n't think that he thought it was. Or was he overthinking it?

But, d ate or not, when Kazz had ind icated that she mightn't stay in Tanglewood , he had felt an unexpected pang.

Hoping that maybe she d id want to stay but was having trouble find ing her place in the village, he remembered how d ifficult Stevie had found it to settle in at first. It was a shame for Kazz to have put the hard work and effort into opening the bookshop, only to jack it all in because she wasn't having fun. And he wondered what sort of fun she was used to having. Clubs? Parties? Gigs? Shows?

Tanglewood could be just as much fun in its own quiet unassuming way, and Saul was struck by the urge to show her how much fun she could have, starting with today, which was why he had goaded her into getting her face painted.

When he saw Kazz slink self-consciously back across the road, Saul clamped his lips together, holding in his mirth. She disappeared from sight for a couple of seconds as she entered the pub's porch, and when she reappeared, heading towards their table, he caught the landlord's eye and gave him a discreet nod. The landlord nodded and went to the kitchen to fetch their meals.

When Saul turned his attention back to Kazz, the quip he had been about to make stuck in his throat. She looked simply adorable.

Averting her gaze, she shrugged off her coat and slunk into her seat. 'Don't laugh,' she growled.

'I wasn't going to. You look—'

'An idiot.'

'Gorgeous.'

Her eyes flashed up at him, and he nodded. Her face had been painted to look like a reindeer – a Disney version of a female Rudolph. She had a pair of gold antlers on her forehead, pretty little furry ears, and between her brows was a sprig of holly and three red berries. Her eyelids, nose and the outside of her cheeks were also painted gold, and sweeping lashes had been drawn from the corners of her eyes up to her temples; the gold on her cheeks was dotted with white, meant to resemble the dappling on a fawn.

But the cutest part was the red tip on the end of her upturned nose, and when she turned her embarrassed gaze on him, she looked like a startled baby deer.

Saul had never wanted to kiss a woman so badly in all his life.

'You look beautiful,' he breathed, his eyes never leaving her face.

'She does,' the landlord agreed. He had appeared at Saul's elbow, carrying their starters, which he placed in front of them.

Kazz gave the man a strained smile.

'You do,' he insisted. 'Doesn't she, Wendy?'

This last was shouted across the pub, and a woman collecting plates turned to look. 'Pardon?'

'This customer has just had her face painted. I said she looks lovely.'

'Stunning,' the woman said. There were nods from some of the nearby tables, and Saul struggled to contain his laughter.

Kazz didn't so much remind him of a startled baby deer now, but a cross one.

She picked up her cutlery, shook out her serviette and attacked her tart with a degree of violence at odds with her doe-like appearance.

'Enjoy your meal,' the landlord said, beating a hasty retreat.

Saul couldn't help himself. 'Is this the kind of fun you had in mind?'

Kazz stopped savaging her first course long enough to snort, 'No.' But then her lips began to twitch, and before long she was holding her sides with laughter.

She spluttered , 'You ought to have seen that woman's expression when she realised I d id n't have a child with me, and that *my* face was the one to be painted .'

'She's d one a good job,' Saul said , when he'd recovered enough to speak. 'I honestly d id n't think you'd go through with it.'

'Neither d id I. I kept hoping the food would arrive and I'd be let off the hook,' Kazz replied , popping a morsel of tart into her mouth. 'Mmm, this is yummy.'

It was, and Saul quickly polished his off.

Kazz appeared to have forgotten her embarrassment by the time they had eaten pud d ing, and now they were d rinking their coffee, Saul realised what a good time he was having.

He hoped Kazz was too, because the happy smile on her face was swiftly becoming the thing he most wanted to see in the world .

Day one of Kazz having fun, successfully accomplished !

Chapter 14

'I hope you didn't let Saul Green into your knickers.'

'*Excuse me?*' Kazz looked up from the book she was examining to find Betty peering at her from the doorway.

Betty took a breath. 'I *said*—'

'I heard you the first time, Betty. I just couldn't believe you said it.' Thankfully, there weren't any customers in the shop at that moment; Kazz would have been mortified if anyone had overheard.

'Well? Did you?'

'For your information, I didn't. Not that it's any of your business.' Kazz was astounded.

'Good. Make him work for it. He'll appreciate it more.' Betty bustled inside. 'You're wearing a Christmas jumper.' Her tone was accusatory.

'What if I am?' Kazz's was defensive.

'Do you like Christmas?'

'Love it.'

'Good. I'll put you down for helping with the Christmas festival. It's not as posh as the Hay one, mind.'

Ah, that was why Betty had said what she'd just said. The word must have got out that Saul had taken her to Hay yesterday. Stevie had warned her that this kind of thing was commonplace in Tanglewood, but it was the first time it had been directed at her.

'Just because Saul and I spent the day together, doesn't mean we spent the night together,' Kazz said primly. 'And I can't help with the Christmas festival, I've got a shop to run.'

'It doesn't have to be dark to have sex,' Betty said. 'And you certainly don't have to spend all night doing it. But it's fun when you do.' She gave an exaggerated wink.

Kazz wished Betty hadn't. She didn't want to think about Betty doing anything like that, thanks very much. She sent the old lady a stern look.

Betty ignored it. 'Of course you can help with the Christmas festival. I expect you to attend the next meeting. I'm hoping for a good turnout. No need to be shy, you've met some of them – they helped shift your stuff to the flat. It's on Wednesday, seven o'clock *sharp*, in the Hen and Duck. It's not a bad little pub now that the daft landlord has given up trying to ban us ladies from the bar. What century was he living in?'

Kazz stared at her, wondering what she was talking about, and hoping the customer who had just come in wasn't put off by her rambling.

'I had to threaten to take Mads to the European Court of Human Rights,' Betty continued. 'I didn't chain myself to the railings so some fella could make me sit in the Ladies' Lounge all evening. That's a hate crime, that is.'

'Er...'

'I think you'll find it was the Suffragettes who chained themselves to railings,' the customer said. 'And it was for women's right to vote, not for gender bias.' The man was clad in a tatty wax jacket in a dull olive-green colour, brown trousers, green wellies and a tweed flat cap. His voice was pure cut glass, a startling contrast to his somewhat scruffy appearance.

Betty gave him a narrow-eyed glare. 'It's still about gender equality, isn't it?'

'I suppose you're right.'

He nodded at her and she nodded back, then without another word, Betty marched out of the shop and was striding along the pavement, the strange purple cape she sometimes wore flapping around her skinny ankles.

Kazz put Betty to the back of her mind and concentrated on her customer, who had now headed for the nearest bookcase and was perusing the shelves, his head tilted sideways to read the titles.

She let him be, knowing the importance of giving people time to browse, and she returned to her book. It was a seventy-year-old missive on farming – sheep farming in particular – and Kazz was finding it fascinating. Though why her grandad had it in his collection, when his bookshop had been on Charing Cross Road with not a sheep in sight, was beyond her. But then, his books did cover a wide range of subjects and she had even found one on boomerang making recently, although she suspected it might be a while before it sold – if it ever did.

After some time, during which the customer had been joined by a few others, two of whom had bought something and three who hadn't, the man approached the counter.

'I hope you don't mind me asking,' he began, 'but what are you basing your prices on?'

Kazz paused, wondering where the question was leading and hoping he wasn't about to berate her for being too expensive. She didn't have a method as such; she went on gut instinct. Most of her stock wasn't worth a great deal individually, although she did have a few unusual ed itions, and those she had researched online and had priced accord ingly.

'Um, market value,' she replied hesitantly. Not that it was any of his business. She had felt like telling him that, but he was a customer and she d id n't want to be rud e. After all, he might buy something.

'I'm not sure you are,' he said . 'You've got an F. Scott Fitzgerald over there and it's rather und erpriced .'

'Is it?' Kazz glanced at the shelf it sat on. She thought she'd put a fair price on the book; neither too high that it would put people off, nor too low that she was giving it away.

'It should be d ouble that,' the man announced .

Kazz was sceptical. She would take a look at it this evening to see if she could find out more on the internet.

The man chuckled . 'You're wond ering who I am and thinking it's none of my business, aren't you?'

'Well…'

'I'm Ed gar Ferris, Lord Tonbrid ge, and although I'm not an expert on old books, I d o have a mod icum of knowled ge.'

This was *Lord Tonbridge*? Kazz had n't expected him to look so ord inary. Or scruffy. He d id n't look as though he had two pennies to rub together, as her grand ad used to say.

She found her manners, and thrusting out her hand said , 'I'm very pleased to meet you. Thank you so much for putting these shelves up.'

He followed the d irection of her gaze, nod d ed , and then brought his attention back to her. 'I d id n't put them up myself, you know.' His eyes crinkled as he poked gentle fun at her.

'If it wasn't for your generosity they wouldn't be there,' she pointed out with a grateful smile.

'Oh, I don't know. Someone else would probably have put them up for you,' he said vaguely. 'Now, back to your books. I really do think you should revise your asking prices. You've got some nice editions here, and it would be a shame for them not to achieve their full potential.'

'You wouldn't like to buy any of them, would you?' she joked.

'Goodness gracious, no. The library at the Manor is bursting at the seams as it is, and we don't have room for a modern section.'

'By modern you mean…?'

'Post First World War.'

'Ah, I see. Of course.'

'I thought I would stop by, as I was in the village. You don't mind me giving you advice, do you?'

'No, it's very kind of you.'

He spun in a slow circle, his eyes scanning the shop. 'Keep up the good work.'

After he'd left, Kazz picked her jaw up off the floor and leant against the counter, bemused. Tanglewood might be a quiet little place, but it sure had its fair share of interesting characters. And one of them, in particular, popped into her head: Saul.

She'd had a lovely time yesterday and she hoped it wouldn't be a one-off because, despite her vow not to let her guard down with Tanglewood's answer to the bachelor of the decade, she really would like to see him again.

–

Saul paced around the workshop (a grand name for what had once been part of a stable block), examining the nativity figures from every angle, pleased that they looked considerably better now than they had after his mother had railroaded him into picking them up from the overcrowded crypt, which was thankfully only used for storage these days, and not for housing the deceased. It had taken him roughly a month to undo years of wear and tear.

First, he had made any necessary repairs, then he had removed the flaking paint and given everything a fresh coat. He had left most of the faces to Leanne to paint, though, not trusting himself to do a good job. Seeing the serene face of Mary brought Kazz's cute face to the forefront of his mind, and he had an insane urge to paint a red blob on the figurine's nose.

He didn't, though, not wanting to face the wrath of Betty and the rest of the festival committee. He would probably get a telling-off from his mother as well, so he shelved his impishness, put his sensible hat on and called for Murray to give him a hand to load everything onto the trailer. It was only the stable structure that he needed help with, because it was large and unwieldy.

Saul looked at the figure of a baby lying rather uncomfortably in the bottom of the manger. The beaming smile on its face was slightly manic, and he feared he'd overdone it with the red paint on its rosebud mouth. He should have left that one to Leanne as well. He'd soon know – Betty had never been backwards in coming forwards when expressing her opinion, and neither was Julia Ferris, for that matter. No doubt she'd be at the meeting this evening, despite having a face like a bulldog sucking a lemon every time she deigned to venture into the pub (his mum's words, not his).

He would find out if his mum's description was right this evening, because although he wasn't on the Christmas festival committee, Iris was, and it seemed silly for them to drive into the village in separate vehicles. He'd have a quick drink while she was in her meeting, and then he'd bring her back home.

It occurred to him that he could pop in and see Kazz at the flat above the tea shop, but he couldn't think of an excuse. He had yet to come up with something 'fun' to do, and he'd been wracking his brains since Sunday. She had appeared to enjoy herself in Hay, and he wasn't sure how he could top that.

Kazz was right in her assessment that Tanglewood left a lot to be desired when it came to the kind of fun she was used to.

While he was propping up the bar (he had no intention of sitting with the committee members, in case they roped him into doing something), he would check the internet to see what – if anything – was on in Abergavenny. He was hoping one of the bars would have a decent band playing. If not, he could always see how she felt about revisiting her childhood and going to see a pantomime. She might enjoy that.

Oh no, she won't, he chorused in his head with a certain amount of sarcasm, guessing it wouldn't be her cup of tea at all.

Maybe he should approach this from a different angle and try to imagine what he would do if she was his date, and not just a…

A what? Saul didn't know how to answer that. She clearly wasn't a date, because he had sworn off women, so should he call her a friend?

Hardly, he snorted, not with the attraction he felt for her.

His thoughts were interrupted by Murray and Mum entering the workshop, and Iris beamed when she saw the figures.

'Saul, they're wond erful! You've d one a fantastic job. They look like new. Look at little baby Jesus, aww.'

He pulled a face, embarrassed . He had d one his best, and hoped it was good enough. Betty would soon tell him if it wasn't, he thought as he got behind the wheel once everything had been load ed . He waved to Murray, who sketched him a salute as he strod e off toward s his cottage and the wife who would be waiting for him.

Envy engulfed him, unexpected and unwanted , and Saul froze. It was a long time since he'd allowed himself to feel that particular emotion. After Joelle had broken his heart, he had envied the happiness of his siblings, and had built a wall of meaningless d ates and a reputation as a player around himself, so no one would suspect.

'Are we going to sit here all evening while you contem-plate your navel?' his mum asked , and he gave himself a mental shake.

Thinking about Joelle was never a pleasant experience, which was the reason he avoid ed d oing it if he could . But now and again memories would hijack him, and he'd be filled with thoughts of what might have been.

'Sorry, I was in a world of my own for a minute,' he said , fastening his seatbelt and starting the engine.

'Anything to d o with the owner of a certain book-shop?' Iris asked . 'How d id you enjoy your trip to Hay? I heard Kazz had a good time.'

'She d id ?' He beamed at the news, unsurprised that his mother knew.

'Betty said that Kazz was smiling fit to burst on Mond ay.'

Saul deflated a little. Kazz could have been smiling for any number of reasons, and none of them because of him or their day out.

When they arrived in the centre of the village, Saul pulled over near the spot where the nativity scene was to be placed and reversed the trailer into position.

'Shall I round up some help?' Iris asked.

'I'll be fine. It'll be easier getting the stable out than it was getting it in.'

The stable was a three-sided construction that served as a backdrop to Mary, Joseph and the others. It had been the last thing to be lifted onto the trailer, so would be the first thing to come out of it.

Saul jumped onto the road, took his coat off and dropped the trailer's ramp.

His mother had hightailed it into the pub, and he guessed she was already ordering her first drink. She normally drove herself to these meetings and drank orange juice as a result, so this evening was a treat, as she would be able to enjoy a tipple.

Before he tackled the wooden stable, Saul glanced down the street, his gaze drawn to the windows above Stevie's tea shop.

They were in darkness, and he pressed his lips together as he wondered whether Kazz had gone out, and if so, where and who with. It was none of his business, of course, but that didn't prevent him from thinking about it.

He had just finished easing the wooden structure down the ramp and was wishing he'd taken his mum up on her offer to find someone to help (it was getting heavier by the second), when a babble of voices caught his attention.

A crowd of people spilled out of the pub and was heading his way, with Betty in the lead and Lady Tonbridge hot on her heels.

Oh, boy. This was the kind of help he could do without.

He was right to be apprehensive.

Betty and Julia Ferris were practically elbowing each other out of the way in their haste to be the first to reach the area outside the library where the nativity scene would be situated.

Betty staked her claim. 'Put it here, Saul. Where I'm standing.'

'I think a little more to the left would be better.' That was from Lady Tonbridge.

'You would. There's not enough room. You've never had to wrestle a pram up that ramp.'

'Neither have you,' Julia Ferris retorted.

Betty had never married or had children, much to the old lady's regret, and Saul thought Mrs Ferris's comment was below the belt.

'But there's plenty here who have,' Betty countered.

Saul felt like cheering. He didn't dislike Lady Tonbridge (how could he, when he barely knew her?) but she did have a tendency to ride roughshod over people.

'Saul, put it here,' Betty repeated.

'I would if I could shift the damned thing,' he grumbled. He had managed to get it down the metal ramp, but now the edge of it was wedged between that and the tarmac, and he didn't want to shove it too hard in case he damaged it.

Betty rolled her eyes. 'Move out of the way, I'll shift it.'

'Don't be so ridiculous,' Julia trilled. 'If a grown man can't move it, a little old lady like you certainly can't.'

'We'll see about that.' Betty rolled her sleeves up and prepared to d o battle. 'And watch who you're calling a little old lad y. I could beat you at arm wrestling any d ay of the week!'

Julia's eyes wid ened and she took a step back.

Stevie hurried over to Betty. 'She's only joking,' she said , taking the eld erly woman by the elbow. 'We'll all muck in, won't we, girls?'

Saul saw his mother and Agnes step forward , followed by several others. And amongst them was Kazz.

He caught her eye and inhaled sharply. Darn it, she was still as gorgeous as she had been on Sund ay. Possibly even more so.

She smiled at him and raised an eyebrow, and as she moved into position at the rear of the wood en stable, she muttered , 'Shall we show them how it's d one?'

Saul grinned . 'If we can shift that sid eboard on our own, this should be a d od d le.'

Waving away any further offers of help, with Saul taking most of the weight and Kazz d oing the guid ing, the two of them gingerly shuffled the stable into position.

When they stepped back, they were greeted by a round of applause.

'See,' Saul murmured in her ear, 'I told you Tangle-wood could be fun.'

Her lips quirked and his eyes were d rawn to them. He tore his gaze away as she said , 'I think we d eserve a d rink after that.'

'Not so fast, my girl,' Betty said . 'There's Mary and Joseph to see to.'

With a wry smile, Saul began to unload the figurines, and this time most of the committee helped – even Lad y

Tonbrid ge, who picked up baby Jesus by his arm and placed him in the bare manger.

Mrs George, who had been leaning on her walking stick and issuing instructions which everyone ignored , promptly snatched the baby back out again. 'He need s straw and a blanket,' the old lad y said , glowering.

Saul d umped a bale of straw on the ground in front of the d onkey and the two lambs, and broke it open, scattering it around the base of the figures, and hand ing some to Mrs George.

She carefully arranged it in the manger, and after a blanket had been prod uced and d raped over the top, s placed baby Jesus in his crib.

'Can we have that d rink now?' someone said . 'I'm parched .'

No one halted the stamped e to the pub this time, and soon Saul was crad ling a glass of lemonad e and gazing at Kazz's whisky with avaricious eyes.

'I would n't have put you d own as a whisky-lover,' he said , as she lifted the glass to her nose and sniffed appreciatively.

'It's the best d rink on the planet,' she said , taking a sip and rolling the liquid around her mouth.

Saul was transfixed . He had never realised d rinking whisky could look so sexy.

A lightbulb went on in his head and his mouth d ropped open. 'How would you like to visit a d istillery?'

And when her eyes lit up, his heart d id too.

Chapter 15

Kazz had n't seen the point in keeping the bookshop open beyond five p.m. this evening, as Tanglewood 's Christmas lights were being officially switched on later. Not wanting to miss out on the excitement (she'd take what she could get these d ays), she locked up and hurried up the road , head ing for the Christmas tree which had been erected at the opposite end of the village from the river, near to where the nativity scene was located . It was also rumoured that Santa Claus would be putting in an appearance, and Stevie and Betty had arranged to supply mulled wine and hot chocolate to keep people warm.

Stevie alread y had a queue of customers when Kazz arrived , and she mad e a beeline for it.

'Do you need a hand ?' she asked , sniffing the d elicious blend of spices and alcohol.

'We can manage, thanks,' her friend said . 'Here, have some wine.'

Kazz took the proffered plastic glass and lifted it to her nose, breathing d eeply. When she took a mouthful, she d iscovered that it tasted even better than it smelled .

Leaving Stevie to her customers, Kazz wand ered off, sipping at her wine and soaking in the atmosphere.

She was beginning to recognise a few people (outsid e of her immed iate friend ship group of Stevie and the other brid esmaid s) and it gave her a warm feeling when several of them smiled at her, and some even stopped for a quick chat.

One of those who d id was Iris, Saul's mum. She introd uced the man with her as her husband , Geoff. Kazz gazed at him curiously, noting the resemblance between him and Saul.

'How are you find ing Tanglewood ?' he asked .

'It's lovely,' she replied . 'Quieter than Lond on, obviously, but I'm getting used to it.'

'I hear you're off to visit the local whisky house tomorrow,' Geoff said . 'Don't get too d runk, will you?'

Kazz laughed . 'I won't. I'll make sure I have something substantial to eat beforehand .'

'She used to be a chef, Geoff,' Iris said . 'I expect she's got a three-course meal lined up for her lunch.'

'Not really,' Kazz said . 'I'll probably have a bowl of pasta.'

Iris's eyebrows shot up. 'You're not having a Sund ay roast?'

'I d on't usually make that kind of effort just for me,' she said . But it would be nice to make the effort for other people, and she remind ed herself that she should cook a meal for everyone who had helped her to set the bookshop up. She would n't be able to accommod ate everyone in the flat, but perhaps she could persuad e Stevie to loan her the tea shop and its kitchen for an evening.

'That's settled ,' Iris said . There was an air of finality in her voice and Kazz realised she must have missed something important while she had been d ayd reaming.

'What is?' she asked .

'Sund ay lunch. You're coming to us.'

She was?

'Saul can pick you up; he may as well, seeing as the pair of you are going to the d istillery afterward s. Leanne and Rex will be there, too.'

'Right… er, thank you. That will be lovely.'

'I'm not the best cook in the world , mind ,' Iris warned , 'but I've been told my roast d inners aren't too bad .'

Geoff blustered , *Aren't too bad?* They're blood y marvellous, and d on't let her tell you otherwise. My wife is being mod est.'

'I'm looking forward to it,' Kazz said truthfully. 'I haven't had a roast d inner in ages. Can I bring something? Wine? Dessert?'

'Just yourself,' Iris said when Geoff's eyes lit up. She elbowed him. 'You're not having wine on a Sund ay lunch-time. You'll be good for nothing in the afternoon.' She said to Kazz, 'I'll tell Saul to fetch you at twelve thirty,' then glanced over Kazz's should er. 'Ooh, look, they're about to turn the lights on.'

A hush fell over the crowd as a mid d le-aged bloke in a calf-length woollen coat approached a small rostrum on which a fake red button had been placed . He gave a speech, which Kazz only half-listened to, as she was too busy thinking of what she could take to lunch tomorrow, because there was no way she was going to arrive empty-hand ed . Her automatic choice would have been wine (Iris had scuppered that) or flowers, but since Iris's d aughter was a florist, Kazz guessed they would n't be the best id ea. Neither d id she want to be presumptuous and bring d essert.

Chocolates, then – or better still, she would make some fud ge.

'Five, four, three…' Everyone around her was chanting and Kazz joined in, clapping and cheering with the rest of the villagers when the chap pressed the fake button with both hand s, and the tree promptly lit up, along with the nativity scene.

She had to ad mit that it d id look lovely, and when a jolly old man in a red suit came into view on a cart d rawn by two small ponies, she found herself smiling wid ely.

With the prospect of a Sund ay roast followed by a tour of a whisky d istillery tomorrow, things were starting to look up. Maybe living in Tanglewood wasn't going to be so bad after all.

–

The sweet vanilla scent of the fud ge that Kazz had baked earlier clung to her skin as she quickly packed the d elicious squares of yumminess into a basket, and trotted d own the spiral staircase at the rear of the flat and then through the small enclosed courtyard and onto the street.

She had d eliberately left the lights on in the wind ow of the bookshop, and she was pleased to see how warm and welcoming it looked . It was like sneaking a peek into Charles Dickens's living room. Funnily enough, she had placed several copies of his books on the little sid e table, along with a pair of old -fashioned spectacles, and a china cup and saucer, borrowed from Stevie's tea shop. It looked as though someone had been in the mid d le of read ing one of those books, and had popped out of the room for a minute.

The d eep burble of a d iesel engine interrupted her musing and she glanced up the street to see Saul's Land Rover pootling along the road .

'Wow! You smell nice,' he said , when she got in.

'It's not me, it's the fud ge. I mad e a batch for your mum as a thank you for inviting me to lunch.'

Saul leant toward s her and sniffed . 'No, it's d efinitely you. You could bottle that and sell it as perfume. You smell good enough to eat.'

She was about to make a sassy retort, when she caught his eye and the word s d ied on her lips. There was a hunger in his expression that had nothing to d o with the fud ge she was hold ing.

Flustered , she d ropped her gaze, only raising it again when the vehicle began to move, after he'd shifted back into the d river's seat.

She was aware of him send ing her little glances out of the corner of his eye, but she kept hers firmly on the road beyond the wind screen. Neither of them said anything d uring the five-minute d rive to the farm, and Kazz hoped the rest of the d ay would n't feel as awkward .

But when the Land Rover came to a halt in the cobbled farmyard , the tension that had been present on the short journey seemed to fad e away.

A black and white sheepd og with a sweeping wagging tail was responsible for the change in atmosphere.

'Hello, girl,' Saul said , bend ing to ruffle her ears. The d og promptly d ropped to the ground and flopped onto her back, exposing her tummy.

'This is Tam,' he said . 'She's the best sheepd og on the farm. Aren't you, girl?'

He crouched d own to stroke the d og's tummy, and Tam lay there, her soft brown gaze locking ad oringly onto the man who was paying her such lovely attention. There was something incred ibly sweet about seeing Saul pet his d og, and the answering love in the animal's eyes for her human mad e Kazz feel quite gooey.

'Come say hello to Kazz,' he said to the d og, and Tam got to her feet and pad d ed over.

Kazz stroked her head, marvelling at how silky her ears were. She quite liked dogs, although she had n't much experience with them.

Tam wagged her tail enthusiastically.

'She likes you,' Saul said. 'You're honoured. She normally only tolerates other people.'

'She can probably smell the fudge.'

'I don't think that's the only reason.' Saul had that look in his eyes again, but this time, instead of backing away, Kazz returned his gaze.

A tingle went through her, catching her unawares, and she shivered.

'Let's get you inside,' he said, placing a hand on the small of her back.

The tingle intensified at his touch. Even through her clothes, she could feel the warmth of his hand and it was doing strange things to her insides.

Saul ushered her into the house, thankfully oblivious to her thudding heart. No wonder Leanne had warned he against him. Until now, Saul had n't turned the charm on, but now that he had, Kazz was disorientated. The world had turned ever so slightly on its axis, as though she was a planet feeling the pull of a new sun.

Stop being so fanciful, she scolded herself silently as she walked into a bright and airy kitchen filled with the mouth-watering aroma of roast lamb.

Iris was at the sink, but as soon as she saw Kazz, she dried her hands on a towel and came in for a quick hug.

Kazz said, 'These are for you.' She passed the basket to Iris, who looked surprised. 'Fudge,' she added. 'I could come empty-handed.'

'You should n't have. But thank you anyway. I love fudge, and so does Geoff.'

She put it to one sid e and returned to the sink.

'Can I d o anything to help?' Kazz again.

'It's all und er control. You go sit yourself d own in the living room. Saul, where are your manners? Hang Kazz's coat up.'

Saul pulled a face, and Kazz pressed her lips together, trying not to smile.

She was about to hand him her coat, when Iris cried , 'Drat!' She was squinting through the kitchen wind ow. 'That d amned sheep! Saul, d o something about Donald ; he's in my vegetable patch.'

'How d id he escape this time?' Saul asked .

'I've no id ea, but unless he wants to be next Sund ay's lunch, you'd better get him out of there fast.'

Kazz craned her neck to see, and spotted a white woolly creature munching away quite happily on what appeared to be a row of cabbages.

With an apologetic grimace, Saul moved toward s the d oor.

'Can I come?' Kazz asked . She had never seen a sheep close up. And she d id n't want to be left alone with his parents, trying to find something to say.

He glanced at her footwear. 'What size shoe d o you take?'

'Five. Why?'

He d id n't answer; instead , he bent d own, picked up a Wellington boot and peered insid e. 'Put these on. They're a bit big, but they'll d o.'

Kazz eased off her sued e ankle boots and shoved her feet into the wellies, then put her coat back on.

Saul held the d oor open for her, and a blast of icy air hit her as she went outsid e.

'The temperature is d ropping,' Saul announced .
'There'll be a hard frost tonight.'

'No snow?'

'Not yet. But I would n't be surprised to see some
before the month is out.'

'I ad ore snow,' Kazz replied , trud ging after him in the
clumpy wellies.

'Oi! Donald !' Saul yelled , making her jump. He
clapped his hand s, and the sheep lifted his head . Kazz saw
a d ark green leaf protrud ing from the sid e of its mouth as
it chewed .

The animal gave a rumbling bleat.

'Come on,' he called to it.

The sheep d id n't move. It kept chewing and the leaf
d isappeared , then it d ropped its head to nibble some more.

'Stay there,' Saul said to her. 'This calls for d rastic
measures. I'll be back in a mo.'

Kazz could n't believe she was being left alone with a
sheep, even though there was a fence between her and it.
It was bigger than she'd expected and it had horns.

Do sheep bite? she wond ered .

She d id n't think they d id , but she wasn't taking any
chances, and when it shuffled a few paces nearer, Kazz
moved a few steps back. She d id n't think the fence would
be any protection – after all, the sheep had got in there,
so it could get back out again just as easily.

When Saul reappeared a minute or so later, he was
carrying a packet of Jaffa Cakes, and Kazz d id a d ouble
take. 'What the hell?'

Saul grinned . 'Watch,' he said , opening the packet with
a great d eal of rustling. 'Donald , look what I've got – your
favourite.'

Donald 's head shot up, he stopped chewing and his tail waggled . He looked rather comical, especially when he trotted over to Saul, bleating happily.

Saul fed him a Jaffa Cake, then offered him another, and while the creature was nibbling it out of his hand , he slipped a halter over the sheep's head .

'Got you!' he announced , and proceed ed to lead the animal out of the vegetable gard en.

Kazz was thoroughly bemused . 'Are sheep supposed to eat Jaffa Cakes?'

'Definitely not. But if he's in a mood , it's the only way to grab his attention. Come on, let's put him in the field , then go have some lunch. I'm starving.'

She was too, and she was d elighted to d iscover that Geoff had n't been exaggerating: Iris d id ind eed cook a fine roast d inner.

Kazz was stuffed by the time she and Saul need ed to leave for their tour of the d istillery, and she hoped she'd be able to find room for the whisky she would soon be sampling.

With promises of returning the favour and cooking a meal for Iris and Geoff, Kazz had a warm, fuzzy feeling when she left the farm.

She had been mad e to feel so very welcome, and she had thoroughly enjoyed herself. Iris and Geoff were lovely, and she envied them for their obvious d evotion to each other. Maybe, one d ay, she would have a relationship like theirs. But when her treacherous mind suggested Saul could be part of that relationship, she gave herself a stern telling-off.

Saul Green wasn't relationship material.

Chapter 16

The d istillery was a thirty-minute d rive from Tanglewood ,
on the other sid e of the small market town of Brecon.
When Saul d rove into the car park and   killed   the engine,
he could   see the impressive peaks of Pen y Fan and   its
sisters, forming a backd rop to the former farm that now
served   as a d istillery. And   when he and   Kazz walked
toward s the main entrance, he could   hear the faint roar of
the tumbling stream bubbling out of a spring high up on
the slopes of the majestic mountain above, whose waters
mad e the whisky taste so pure and   clean.

He wished   he could   try some – the whisky, that is, not
the water – but he was d riving, so he would   n't take more
than a sip or two, to get some id ea of the flavour. This
tour was for Kazz's benefit, not his. Which was why he
found   it d ifficult to tear his gaze away from her face when
the visitors were first given a short talk and   then shown
around   the facility.

As the guid e explained   how the mash tuns worked
(apparently, the huge stainless-steel containers were where
the ground   malt was mixed   with the spring water), Kazz
was impressed   by the sheer scale of the operation, and   by
the amount of stainless steel in evid ence.

She leant closer to whisper, 'I d id n't expect it to be
this high tech,' and   when she d id   so, her perfume wafted

up his nose, a d eliciously light sweet scent, and her warm breath tickled his ear.

Her nearness sent a tingle right through him, and he held his breath until she stepped back a pace. The urge to turn his head and seek out her lips had been so strong that it had caught him unawares, and for the next few minutes he found it almost impossible to focus on the copper stills and the tour guid e's explanation. All Saul could think about was what it would be like to kiss her.

It took him until they reached the tasting bar to stead y himself, and he was glad of a sip of the amber liquid to soothe his inner turmoil. He wasn't supposed to be getting romantically involved with anyone right now, yet here he was, imagining kissing her. And more.

He let Kazz choose which blend s to try, and the first one she picked was one tasting of nutmeg, cinnamon, ginger and apple, with a hint of citrus. It was d elicious and rather moreish, but he only allowed himself the smallest of tastes. Consid ering the time of year, he thought her choice an appropriate one, as the blend remind ed him of Christmas.

The next held hints of caramel and vanilla, and it lingered on his palate as it slipped d own his throat to warm his stomach.

Kazz's favourite was a whisky flavoured with the wild wimberries that grew on the slopes of the mountains. Similar to blueberries, only smaller and more tart, they ad d ed a subtle yet unique flavour to the single malt, and Kazz's eyes shone when she took her first mouthful.

'Oh, my good ness, that is…' She licked her lips, and his gaze was d rawn to them. 'Simply d ivine.' She sighed . 'Here, try some.'

He d id , and he had to ad mit it was very nice. 'It's lovely but I prefer the last one.'

'This?' She pointed to the bottle.

'I could d rink that all night.'

They tried a couple more, and soon they all began to taste the same to his uned ucated palate (he was more of a real-ale man), but Kazz was getting so much pleasure out of the visit, he was pleased he'd thought of it.

Leaving her to her tasting, he strolled around the room, looking at the special ed ition whiskies that were on show and read ing the history behind them.

'Read y?' she asked sometime later, and he realised the tour had end ed . She was clutching a bag to her chest and he guessed she had mad e a purchase or six.

'I hope they're not all for you,' he quipped , as she struggled to hold the bag, even with both arms wrapped around it.

'I've d one some Christmas shopping,' she replied haughtily, relinquishing her hold on the bag as he took it from her.

'I think you must have bought everyone in Tanglewood a bottle. I hope you left enough for the other people on the tour.'

He escorted her out to the car and helped her into it. Her eyes were gleaming and her cheeks glowed , and he wond ered how many 'tastes' she'd had .

'Thank you for lunch and introd ucing me to Donald , and for taking me to the d istillery,' she said . 'I've had a lovely d ay.'

'I'm glad .' He had enjoyed himself too. More than he would have imagined , consid ering it had consisted of a meal with his parents and he had n't been able to d o more than have a sip or two of the whiskies. He had enjoyed it because *Kazz* had been with him.

Physical attraction asid e, he liked her more than he'd liked any other woman since Joelle. The revelation was both surprising and concerning, because Saul had vowed to never let another woman anywhere near his fragile heart. It had taken him a very long time to put the broken pieces back together.

Was he read y to break that vow? Or would he keep the wall around his heart for the rest of his life?

Was he brave enough?

–

When the Land y came to a halt on the pavement outsid e the tea shop, at first Kazz d id n't notice anything wrong. She hopped d own from the seat and opened the back of the vehicle to retrieve her purchases, but Saul reached past her and picked up the bag.

'I'll walk you to your d oor,' he offered .

The entrance to the flat was at the back of the little row of shops and through a walled courtyard . At this time of year and in the d ark, it d id n't look its best, but Kazz knew how pretty it could be. It was also rather seclud ed , and although she felt completely safe, it was thoughtful of Saul to offer.

Or maybe he wasn't being thoughtful at all, but expected to come in for 'coffee'.

The thought sent a thrill right through her.

Behave, she told herself. Saul had a reputation, and she had no intention of becoming the latest notch on his bed post. Come to think of it, where*did* he d o his philand ering? Stevie had explained that he used to share a cottage on the farm with his brother, until Murray wanted to move his girlfriend in.

Kazz guessed that living with his mum and dad must be seriously cramping Saul's style. He could hardly take his dates back to their house.

However, Kazz wasn't a date. Was she?

She hesitated, debating whether to snatch the bag from him and hightail it back to the flat before he had the chance to suggest he came inside for a nightcap – because everyone knew what *that* would lead to – when something caught her attention. Or rather, the *lack* of something.

The bookshop was in darkness, but she distinctly remembered leaving the lights on in the window, because she had admired the display earlier.

'Can you wait here a sec?' She walked across the road, her attention focused on the shop. It could be a fuse, or— She drew in a sharp breath as an unsavoury thought occurred to her. *Maybe she had been burgled?* A burglar would be sure to switch the lights off, before—

Hang on, there was no sign of a break-in, she realised as she drew closer.

'What's up?' Saul asked, making her jump.

He hadn't waited by the car; he had followed her across the road and was right behind her.

'I left the lights on in the window,' she said, willing her pulse to return to normal.

'Are you sure…' he began, but when she shot a sharp look at him, he said, 'Of course you are. Sorry.'

'Not the overhead ones,' she explained. 'The lamp.'

'In that case, it could be a fuse. Do you have any?'

She shook her head.

'Pity. Let's take a look anyway, in case it's something else.'

Kazz fished the keys out of her bag and unlocked the d oor. Immed iately, the alarm began to beep and she hastened to d isarm it. But the sound had reassured her, and she began to feel silly for thinking someone might have broken in.

Flicking the bank of switches, she blinked when the overhead lights came on. The lamp, however, remained stubbornly unlit.

'It must be a fuse,' she agreed . 'I'll buy some tomorrow.'

'Before you d o, is there any other electrical item we can use to check it's not the socket?'

'Um, yeah, the kettle. I'll go fetch it.' She d ashed out the back.

When she returned , Saul was looking through the books on the table.

'Is this the original story? The d ark one?' he asked , without looking up.

Kazz came to stand besid e him. He was pointing *The Night Before Christmas* by Nikolai Gogol, who had written it in 1831. 'It is,' she confirmed , picking it up and turning to the title page. 'It isn't particularly old , but it's beautifully illustrated .'

She hand ed it to him and he flicked carefully through the pages. 'Blimey, you d on't want to be telling this story to a kid on Christmas Eve,' he observed .

'It is a bit grim in places, but it has got an uplifting end ing.'

'It's got a witch in it, and the d evil! I d on't call that very festive.' He put it d own and picked up another *The Greatest Gift*,' he read .

'Ah, now, that might be more to your liking. The film *It's a Wonderful Life* was based on it. This is a short story published in 1943 by Philip van Doren Stern, which in turn was based on Dickens's *A Christmas Carol*.'

She put the kettle d own on the floor and plugged it in. Nothing happened . 'Damn,' she muttered . 'It must be the socket.'

He carefully replaced the book on the table and bent to take a look. 'Are any of the other sockets working?'

'Let's see.' She unplugged the kettle and scooted across to the socket behind the counter. 'No,' she said sad ly, after plugging the kettle into it. 'This one is d ead , too. Knickers!'

'Do you know where the fuse box is? Something might have caused it to throw a switch.'

'It's above the d oor in the stock room,' she said . 'Hang on, I'll fetch a chair to stand on.'

She walked over to the smaller of the two chairs, which she had brought with her from her grand ad 's house, when she stopped d ead . 'I'm an id iot!' she d eclared , as Sau bumped into her, shunting her forward s.

He grabbed hold of her. 'Oops, sorry.' His hand lingered on her arm. 'I d id n't expect you to stop sud d enly. And I d oubt we'll need a chair – I'm taller than you, so I might be able to see without stand ing on one.'

'We d efinitely won't need a chair,' Kazz said . 'The sockets are on a timer. See?' She pointed to the row of light switches. Next to them was another switch, with a d igital d isplay. She'd seen something similar in the restaurant she had worked in before Fred d ie's.

She pressed a couple of buttons and the kettle burst into life. Kazz hastened to switch it off, then she plugged the lamp in again. It came on immed iately.

'Thank God that's all it was,' she said , having had visions of calling out an electrician in the morning as a matter of urgency.

She used the ed ge of her hand to switch all the overhead lights off at once, and the shop was plunged into semi-d arkness.

'It looks very inviting,' Saul said , walking over to the wind ow d isplay once more. 'I would n't mind my living room looking like this. When I get one of my own, that is.'

'Will that be anytime soon?'

'Probably not.'

He reached d own to pick up the aband oned bag of whisky, but Kazz beat him to it.

'I've got something for you,' she said , d elving into it. She brought out a chocolate-coloured box with gold writing on it. 'Here.'

'What's this?'

'The whisky you liked . It's a thank you for tod ay, and for d riving me to Lond on and back. It's not much, just a small token of my appreciation, but maybe I could cook you a meal as well?'

He gazed at her for a heartbeat longer than necessary. 'Thank you, I'd like that. Got any glasses? We could have a snifter now.'

Was he suggesting what she thought he was suggesting?

'A mug will d o,' he said , seeing her hesitation. 'That stuff is very moreish, so I'll leave the Land y here and walk home. It's not far.'

The tension eased from Kazz's should ers as she realised he wasn't going to use the age-old excuse that he'd have to stay the night because he could n't possibly d rive after having a d rink. He d id n't seem to be expecting to go to the flat either, which further helped ease her initial reservation. If he was up to no good, he'd hardly do it in the middle of her shop, when anyone could walk past and gawk at them.

She went to fetch the mugs, not entirely certain whether she was relieved that he wasn't making a move on her or disappointed. If his sister was to be believed, Saul would happily date anyone under forty with a pulse. But not Kazz. He hadn't given her so much as a peck on the cheek, although once or twice she'd got the impression he was interested. Maybe Leanne had warned him off?

Feeling better now that she had arrived at the most likely answer to Saul's failure to make a move on her (she wasn't *that* hideous, was she?), she relaxed even more.

And when she saw that he had arranged the chairs so they were facing each other, with the table in between, she had to smile. It really did look like part of a library in an old mansion, or an Edwardian parlour.

Saul took the bottle of whisky out of the box and unscrewed the top. The aroma of the alcohol filled the air, and Kazz sniffed appreciatively as he poured the spirit into the mugs. She took hers eagerly.

The first sip slipped warmly down her throat, and she closed her eyes in bliss. The rustle of a page being turned quickly had her opening them again to see Saul with *The Greatest Gift* in his lap.

'I didn't realise *It's a Wonderful Life* was based on a book,' he said.

'Not many people do.'

He smiled at her. 'Is the book better than the film?'

'Why don't you read it and find out?'

'Oh, no, you're not going to trick me into accepting a book from you. The whisky is payment enough.'

Kazz chuckled . 'Read it here,' she said . 'It's only about sixty pages long.'

His mouth twisted up at one corner. 'It's a bit rud e, me read ing while you…'

'I could read too, but I'd much prefer if you read to me instead .'

Saul's eyes wid ened . 'You wa*nte* to read this to*you*?' He held up the slim volume.

'Why not?'

'But… I…' He stopped , pressed his lips together, then said , 'OK, if that's what you want. But I'm warning you, I'm not d oing any voices.'

Kazz bit her lip, laughter threatening to bubble up. 'I d id n't expect you to.'

'And if you laugh so much as once, I'll refuse to read another word .'

'OK.' She d rank some more whisky to wash the giggle back d own.

He took a sip of his, shuffled back in his chair and opened the book. Then he began to read .

As the word s washed over her, Kazz watched Saul, transfixed not only by the story itself, but also by the way the word s sound ed on his lips, the play of expression across his face and the emotion she sensed in him as he read .

He was as caught up in the story as she, and she lost a little piece of her heart to him right then.

Eventually, Saul turned the last page and his voice stilled , d rifting into silence. Gently, he closed the book. Kazz had tears in her eyes, as she gazed at him. His were as warm as the whisky she'd d runk.

Without breaking eye contact, he placed the book reverentially on the table, and eased slowly forward s until he slipped off the edge of his seat and was kneeling in front of her.

Kazz's heart fluttered and her breath hitched as he came nearer still.

When he cupped her face in his hands, she almost melted with the longing flooding her veins. She wanted him to kiss her so very much.

His palms were rough and calloused, but his touch was gentle and when his mouth found hers, she discovered that his lips were soft and warm.

He tasted of whisky and a promise of what could be, and she was more aroused than she could ever remember being in her life, seduced by both the story and the man who had told it.

She slid onto the floor, her pulse roaring in her ears as she grasped the back of his head to deepen the kiss, her fingers digging into his hair.

When she ran a hand down his back, stopping at the waistband of his jeans to wriggle her way under his T-shirt and fleece, and caressed his bare skin, a groan escaped him.

The sound brought her to her senses, as she abruptly realised where she was and what she was doing. And who she was doing it with.

Apologetically, she pulled away, dragging her mouth from his, reluctant but determined.

She was not going to be seduced by Saul, no matter how dearly she would like to be.

If he wanted her as much as she hoped, he was going to have to work for it.

And she had a feeling it was going to be so much fun if he did.

Chapter 17

Peggy's Tea Shoppe might be renowned for its tea, but it made the best coffee in Tanglewood, despite Stevie's love–hate relationship with Bertie, the gleamingly menacing coffee machine.

Kazz drank a scalding mouthful in delight. She had taken to popping into the tea shop for a quick bite of breakfast before opening her own shop. Who could resist croissants straight from the oven? Not her! And she often took a savoury pastry or two with her for lunch, to eat in hasty flaky bites between customers.

'So, lunch with the Greens?' Stevie began, wiggling her eyebrows. 'Leanne told me.'

'I suppose she also told you that Saul and I went to a whisky distillery afterwards?'

'She did.' Stevie sat on one of the stools that had been drawn up to the stainless-steel island in the middle of the tea shop's kitchen. Kazz was perched on the other, while Stevie was waiting for the rest of the morning's bakes to come out of the oven.

In some ways, this was Kazz's favourite time of day, with the heavenly scent of coffee and baking before the busy day ahead. It also gave Kazz and Stevie a chance to catch up.

Stevie said, 'You know you can't keep anything quiet in Tanglewood.'

Kazz waited for Stevie to take a bite of Danish pastry and then said, 'Did she also tell you he kissed me?'

Stevie inhaled sharply. The mouthful of pastry went down the wrong way, and she coughed and spluttered for a few minutes while Kazz sat serenely, pleased she had managed to shock her friend.

After a gulp of orange juice and some dirty looks, Stevie said, 'No, she did not tell me Saul kissed you. Oh, dear.'

'I know, I know, he's bad news,' Kazz said. 'But I'm a big girl and I can take care of myself.'

She watched the digital display on one of the ovens count down, the kiss lingering in her mind. It had taken her a long time to fall asleep last night. If the kiss had been just a kiss at the end of an enjoyable evening in the pub, it probably wouldn't have affected her as much. OK, she would have been just as turned on (impossible not to be where Saul was concerned, she suspected) but she didn't believe her emotions would have been as engaged. Last night had been so wonderfully romantic: a handsome man reading a gorgeous love story by soft lamplight, with the mellow taste of whisky on her tongue.

If he had deliberately set out to seduce her, he couldn't have planned it better.

It hadn't been planned, though, and neither had he seduced her – although he had come close. She could so easily have succumbed to desire, and if they had been in the privacy of the flat above the tea shop, she may very well have.

'As long as you know what you're getting into,' Stevie cautioned.

Kazz shrugged. 'He's fun. I enjoy his company.'

Stevie read more into the statement than Kazz had intend ed , saying, 'I'm sorry I've been a rubbish friend but it's so hectic at the moment. It'll get better after Christmas, I promise.'

'Don't be silly, we've all got lots on our plates.' Kazz had thought – naively, as it turned out – that she and Stevie would pick up where they'd left off when they had been living in Lond on. But Stevie had a fiancé now and a business that d emand ed most of her attention. Ad d the build -up to Christmas into the equation, and it was no wond er the two of them weren't painting the town red every evening.

Although, a pale shad e of pink might be more accurate where the peaceful little village of Tanglewood was concerned .

'How is business?' Stevie asked and Kazz brightened .

'Quite good . Did I tell you that Lord Tonbrid ge paid me a visit?'

'No, but Tia d id .'

'Why am I not surprised ? Anyway, he suggested I raise my prices. I d id a bit of research – a lot of research, actually – and d iscovered he was right. So, I have raised them and I'm selling roughly the same number of books per d ay but with increased profit.'

'Good for you! Do you think you'll stay on after Christmas?'

'I think I might.' Kazz grinned . 'We'll have to see, because I'm expecting sales to d rop off d rastically in the New Year.'

'January and February are usually slow months for me,' Stevie said . The oven timer pinged , and she leapt off her stool to take several trays of baked good ness out of it, then carried on. 'There's not much I can d o about January, but at least February has Valentine's Day in the mid d le, as well as the spring half-term, so I try to make the most of it.'

Kazz's thoughts were whirling. Maybe she could have a sale in January and d o a feature on romance fiction in February? She might even find a few romance links in a couple of non-fiction titles if she looked hard enough. It probably would n't be enough to generate the kind of sales she need ed to make the bookshop profitable, though, and it occurred to her that a website for d irect selling might be a good id ea. Then there was the issue of find ing more stock, because the books she had brought with her would n't last forever. If she wanted to attract repeat customers (and new ones) she would have to have a stead y supply of fresh stock to temp them. Her main problem was where to source them from, and she wond ered whose brains she could pick. Lord Tonbrid ge's maybe? Or would the kind of books he was familiar with be way out of her price range?

A noise from the tea shop's d oor alerted them to Betty's arrival. 'Coo-ee,' she called , bustling into the kitchen.

After taking her coat off and hanging her voluminous hand bag on the pegs at the bottom of the stairs lead ing to the flat, she rolled up her sleeves and popped an apron over her head .

'Shall I make a red velvet cake?' she suggested . 'The colour is lovely and festive. Morning, Kazz.' The old lad y's glance slid over her, then snapped back to Kazz's face and sharpened .

Betty narrowed her eyes and scrutinised her. 'Someone looks happy for a Mond ay morning,' she observed . 'This would n't have anything to d o with a certain hand some chappie by the name of Saul, would it?'

'No, it would not,' Kazz retorted .

Stevie coughed and went to check on the contents of the second oven. Kazz glared at her back.

'Hmm.' Betty continued to stare, and Kazz wriggled uncomfortably. She refused to look at the old lady, in case Betty could read the truth in her eyes.

Kazz hopped off the stool. 'Is that the time? I'd better open up.'

'Nice window display,' Betty called after her, and when Kazz glanced over her shoulder, it was to see a big smirk on the old lady's face.

Kazz gasped. She could n't possibly know. *Could she?*

–

Wednesday morning saw Saul lowering the tines attached to the front of a tractor, then spearing one of the large plastic-covered bales of silage. Satisfied it was securely held, he raised the bundle of fermented grass off the ground and reversed carefully out of the barn. He was taking it to one of the lower fields for the pregnant ewes, because at this time of year they needed the additional feed.

His mind was only half on the task at hand. The other half was on Kazz.

Saul had kissed numerous women over the years, but the kiss he had shared with Kazz had touched him more deeply than any other. Apart from Joelle's kisses – but he didn't want to go there. Joelle was his past, and that was where she should stay.

He had shared much more than kisses with Joelle. He had given her his body, heart and soul. And she had taken all that he had to offer, then walked away without a backward glance.

To say he was scared of his reaction to Kazz was an und erstatement. He was terrified of having his heart broken again, d oubtful that he would be able to piece it back together a second time. But he had n't been able to get her out of his mind . These past three d ays she had hijacked his thoughts, haunting him, making him restless and unable to think straight. Since Joelle had d umped him, no other woman had had such an effect. No other woman had come close. But Kazz was worming her way into his life, whether she was aware of it or not, whether he wanted her to or not.

Saul had a theory about this. Spend ing hours on mund ane tasks around the farm over the past two d ays had given him plenty of time to think, and he had arrived at the conclusion that, d ue to his vow to knock d ating on the head , instead of jumping head long into a relationship (albeit one that would invariably turn out to be brief), he had got to know Kazz as a friend first.

He'd had absolutely no d esigns on her whatsoever when they'd met, and d espite being attracted to her, he had n't wavered from that. Not even when he'd promised himself he would show her the fun sid e of Tanglewood . But he had got to know her, and that was what was d ifferent this time.

It d id make him wond er whether he had been unfair to all the women he had d ated since Joelle. He had been more interested in having a good time than having a relationship, and had always turned tail and run before there was any chance of that happening.

Yet here he was, hoisted by his own petard . By crying off women, he had allowed one to slip through a chink in his armour, and now he could n't stop thinking about her.

He brought the tractor to a halt, jumped down from the cab and opened the gate.

A flock of woolly faces looked up expectantly. The ewes had been grazing, but the noise of the engine alerted them that breakfast was imminent, and they trotted towards him en masse. Saul made them wait until he had got back in the cab and manoeuvred the silage into position over a round metal cage, then he jumped down again, took out his Stanley knife and sliced the bale open, letting the contents fall out to fill the feeder.

The ewes got stuck in eagerly, jostling for position and knocking each other out of the way.

'You're welcome,' he said sarcastically as one particularly determined sheep barged past, totally ignoring him.

Saul froze as the realisation struck him that *he* was totally ignoring *Kazz*. By trying to give himself some distance, he had n't contacted her, but now he felt a right heel. What must she think of his radio silence? Oh, God, he hoped she did n't think he'd only been after one thing, and that because he had n't got it, he was ghosting her.

Saul felt awful. He knew he had a reputation as a tomcat, but it pained him that Kazz might think the worst of him.

He watched the ewes tucking into their breakfast for a while, knowing he should contact her but not knowing what to say.

Then it came to him; there was usually live music on at The White Rock in Abergavenny on a Saturday. The bar was the liveliest in the town, so it should be fun.

After a quick check on their website to make sure that the band performing wasn't too outlandish, he made a decision – he would ring Kazz and ask whether she fancied a night out this weekend.

When Saul phoned and asked whether she would like to go to Abergavenny with him on Saturday to watch a live band, Kazz accepted, but with a proviso: 'Only if you let me cook dinner tonight.'

Then she'd cringed because, to her ears, she'd sounded overeager. She could have at least said Friday. But, oh no, she'd had to say *tonight*.

He hesitated and she could almost hear the cogs turning in his brain as he thought of a reason to say no, so she was surprised when he agreed.

Kazz was in two minds about whether to pull out all the stops and cook him something mind-blowing. She was tempted, and he deserved it for all the help and support he'd given her, but she didn't want him to think she was showing off.

It was only while she dithered and dallied at the butcher's, after shutting the shop for a couple of minutes, that she decided *what the heck* – she was a chef by trade and a damned good one. She wouldn't be showing off or trying to make an impression, she would be creating the best possible food, as she always did. That she would be preparing it in the little kitchen in Stevie's old flat and not in a restaurant kitchen with seventy or so diners, who had sophisticated palates, was neither here nor there.

After making a few quick purchases, she hurried to the flat to pop everything in the fridge, then raced back to the bookshop.

'Sorry, sorry,' she apologised to the disgruntled couple who had been pushing and pulling the door. 'I had a few errands to run and I wanted to get to the butcher before all the best cuts had gone.'

The woman sniffed loud ly and stalked insid e when Kazz held the d oor open for her, but her partner gave her a sympathetic smile.

'When I opened my barbershop, many moons ago now, I ran it all by myself, so I know what it's like.' He leant in and whispered , 'Trying to find time to pop to the loo was the worst.'

Kazz giggled . It certainly was. She hated leaving the shop floor unattend ed for a quick comfort break, but sometimes she had no choice.

'You've not been here long, have you?' he asked , as his wife wand ered around , removing titles from the shelves and squinting at them, before putting them back again.

'I opened a couple of weeks ago,' she said . 'Are you looking for anything in particular?'

'I'm a bit of a collector, so I'm always on the lookout for anything unusual. Do you mind if I have a browse?'

'Of course not! Browse away.' She left him to it and retreated behind the counter to run through the list of ingred ients for the meal she planned to cook this evening, checking that she had everything she need ed .

Her heart kept missing a beat every time she thought of Saul and if she was honest, her mind wasn't strictly on the food …

'I'll take this one,' her customer said , and she was brought back to earth with a jolt.

As she wrapped the book, while waiting for the payment to go through, the man's wife said , 'Do you purchase books at all?'

'Not now, Helen,' the chap said .

'When?' she d emand ed . 'You can't keep buying more, unless you're prepared to get rid of some.' She said to Kazz, 'I was hoping you were closed , because my husband has a serious book-buying addiction. The house is full of the damned things. Don't get me wrong, I've nothing against books. I even enjoy a good classic myself, although I'm not so keen on Nigel Balchin.'

Kazz grinned. 'Not many people are.'

The woman continued, 'I've told him a hundred times that he has to let some of them go; so, do you buy books?'

'It depends on what they are,' Kazz replied cautiously. She was facing a dilemma of sorts: if she intended to make a proper go of the bookshop and for it to be a long-term thing, then she would need to source more stock. But if she intended to use this solely as an opportunity to get rid of her grandad's books, it would be silly to acquire more.

'He'd have to decide which ones would go and which ones he wants to keep,' the woman said, tapping her chin with her fingers. 'That's not going to be an easy task.'

'I tell you what,' Kazz said. 'Give me a ring after Christmas, when you've had the chance to have a good sort-out. We can have a chat about it then.'

And by then, she might have a better idea of whether the bookshop would be viable, and if it was, whether keeping it open was something she wanted to do.

She gave the couple her mobile number and wished them a merry Christmas as they went on their way, then she pushed thoughts of the future to the back of her mind for the time being.

Her lease wasn't due up until the second week in January. She would think about it later. Right now, she had a meal to plan and a date with Saul to look forward to.

–

Blood y hell, this woman could seriously cook! Saul's tongue was in shock and his stomach was very happy ind eed .

Kazz had fed him a starter of artichoke soup with brown bread and thyme butter, and he had savoured every mouthful, wishing there had been more of it. But by the time he had eaten d essert, after a main course of pork chop with grilled spring onions and mustard sauce, he was wishing he had n't ind ulged quite so much.

'I've got a cheese board and some home-mad e biscuits to go with it, if you'd like,' she said .

Saul groaned and rubbed his overfull belly. 'I could n't manage another thing.'

'How about me?' she offered .

Saul blinked , shock flashing through him.

God, yes.

He swallowed , d esire jabbing him in the gut.

'Breakfast or herbal?' she continued . 'I've got all kind s of flavours, courtesy of Stevie.'

Saul blinked again, but this time it was d ue to the realisation that he had heard her wrong. She'd said. How about *tea*.

'Peppermint or chamomile is good after a meal, to aid d igestion,' she told him.

'Chamomile is fine.' His voice came out an octave higher than normal and he cleared his throat. Was there a tea to cure unexpected lust or acute embarrassment? Thank good ness he had n't d one or said anything before he'd realised what she'd meant. He would have mad e a right tit of himself.

'Go sit on the sofa. I'll bring it over.'

'What about the washing-up?'

'I'll d o it later,' she said , collecting the pud d ing d ishes and carrying them out to the little kitchen.

Saul used the opportunity to visit the bathroom and splash cold water on his face. A few minutes to collect himself would n't go amiss, either. Asid e from almost making the biggest fool of himself ever, what unsettled him the most was how much he wanted to make love to her. The ache to hold her in his arms and kiss her until she was breathless was real. The remembered taste of the whisky on her lips, the softness of her bod y as he'd lowered her gently onto the rug, the feel of her cold hand on the superheated skin of his back...

Saul rested his hand s on the washbasin and leant his forehead against the mirror above it. He was going to have to find some way of controlling his raging libid o, because he was fairly certain she d id n't feel the same about him. She had n't given him the tiniest hint this evening that she was interested in him. It was as though the kiss had never happened , and he assumed she was regretting it.

He knew he was, but only because he wanted to d o it again and again. He d id n't want to stop at her mouth; he wanted to kiss her all over.

When he emerged from the bathroom, it was to find Kazz curled up on the sofa. She had taken off her chef's whites and removed the Crocs she'd worn while she was cooking. Her feet were now encased in fluffy socks, her head rested on the back of the cushion and her eyes were closed . Two cups of steaming tea sat on the low coffee table, and music played softly in the background . A pair of lamps gave the room a gentle warm glow.

Kazz looked the picture of relaxation.

Saul was as far from relaxed as he had ever been.

'Come sit d own,' she said , without opening her eyes. She patted the sofa next to her.

He walked across the room and perched gingerly on the ed ge of the seat. He d id n't want to sit back into the cushion because if he d id , they would be touching, and he d id n't think he could stand it.

What was wrong with him? Had she fed him oysters and he had n't realised ?

'Are you OK?' she asked . Her eyes were open now and she was gazing at him with concern.

'I'm fine,' he said .

'Are you sure? You look strange.'

'Thanks!'

'Like you've eaten something that d id n't agree with you.' Her eyes wid ened in alarm. 'Was the food OK?'

'The food was fabulous. The best I've ever eaten.'

'What, then? Do you want to go? I won't be upset if you want to eat and leave.'

'That's the problem: I d on't want to go – but I think I should , before I d o something we'll both regret.'

Her eyes d arkened , and her lips parted slightly. They were full and pink, and oh so tempting.

In a voice so soft he could barely hear her, she said , 'I won't regret it.'

Oh, God . He d rew in a shaky breath. 'I would ,' he said .

Her hurt gasp punched him in the gut, and he hurried to explain, 'You d on't d eserve to be treated the way I treat women.'

'Bed them and run, you mean?'

'I'm not proud of it.'

'Yet you d o it anyway. I'm a big girl, Saul. I know what you're like.'

'But that's it, I d on't want to be like that anymore.'

'What do you want?'

Saul could n't answer, because he did n't know himself. All he knew was that he could n't carry on the way things were. Something had to give, and he'd tried the no-dating thing but all that had happened was that he was in more of a mess than he'd been in before.

Then he made it worse by kissing her again.

Chapter 18

Determined not to be d epend ent solely on Saul for entertainment, Kazz had popped into the pub last night for a glass of wine and some company, and had had a pleasant Frid ay evening d iscussing books with Agnes and a couple of Agnes's friend s. But it had hard ly been exciting, and her thoughts had kept returning to Saul. She had half-expected him to walk through the d oor, but she had been d isappointed .

Tonight, though, she and Saul were going to see a live band .

It promised to be fun. Kazz was feeling unaccountably nervous when he arrived to pick her up, the butterflies in her stomach fluttering frantically as he leant across the gearstick to give her a fleeting kiss, and she wond ered whether she would be brave enough to take him to her bed tonight.

The anticipation of sleeping with him was d electably exciting but d espite her d esire, she wanted to take it slow.

Yeah, definitely slow, her libid o sniggered naughtily. *That's the best way.*

Ignoring her lustful thoughts, as they mad e the short journey from Tanglewood to the market town of Abergavenny, Kazz thought back to how lovely Wed nesd ay evening had been. His kisses had been exquisite, but he had taken his cue from her and had seemed content not to take things any further – although his hand s had roamed a bit, and so had hers! But she had stopped well shy of d ragging him off to bed .

His passion had been obvious, but he'd also not seemed to be in a d esperate hurry to take their relationship to the next level.

Tonight might be a d ifferent story – for her, at least – because she d id n't know how much longer she could continue to d eny herself. And with that in mind , she would make sure she d id n't have more than a glass or two of wine. She wanted a clear head and unimpaired jud gement, for what might happen later.

Abergavenny was surprisingly busy, with people intent on enjoying the build -up to Christmas. Twinkling lights were d raped along the main street, and on the lamp posts there were flashing Santas, trees, snowmen and stars. Most of the shop wind ows were in full Christmas mod e, and people spilled out of bars and restaurants onto seating areas laid out on the ped estrianised street.

The chilly air was filled with d elicious smells, and Kazz was d elighted to see an assortment of restaurants, from Turkish cuisine (which smelled d ivine and remind ed he of holid ays spent in the Eastern Med iterranean) to tapas, as well as the more usual Chinese and Ind ian. Her mouth watered even though she wasn't hungry, and she promised herself she would return to the town and try a couple. Hopefully with Saul…

Some Christmas parties were going on, and she smiled to see so many cheerful and slightly inebriated faces.

This is more like it, she thought, d rinking in the lively atmosphere. But she realised that somewhere between leaving Lond on and this evening, she had apparently und ergone a seismic shift: no matter how much she was enjoying herself right now, she wasn't sure she wanted to be exposed to it every night.

Saul took hold of her hand and pulled her into a side street. It wasn't technically a street, more like an alleyway, but it quickly opened up and she spotted their destination, the bar's name picked out in fluorescent pink neon writing.

Music thudded and the tables in the courtyard outside were all occupied. Saul led her inside, shouting to be heard above the noise. 'What would you like to drink?'

'White wine, please.' She stayed close as he pushed his way to the bar and ordered their drinks, then they retreated to a less busy corner and waited for the band to come on.

It was impossible to hold a proper conversation, so they listened to the music, tapped their feet and bopped their heads to the beat. And occasionally, he would dip his head, his gaze would capture hers, and he'd kiss her.

Much later, her ears were still ringing as she climbed the spiral staircase leading to her flat, Saul following. She hoped he didn't find the unflattering view of her bottom off-putting and she wondered what he thought about her inviting him in for a nightcap. Kazz had had a great time this evening and she didn't want it to end. A soft drink, a cuddle and a kiss on the sofa would be perfect.

She had left a lamp on in the living room and she walked towards the glow, slipping her coat off. 'Make yourself comfortable,' she instructed as she took off her boots with a relieved groan. 'Ah, that's better. My feet are killing me.'

'I could give them a rub for you, if you like,' he said, then winced. 'Sorry, that's a bit weird.'

'It's not weird at all,' Kazz said , flopping into a chair and sticking her legs out. 'It's very thoughtful of you.'

'You really want me to massage your toes?'

She laughed and sat up, d rawing her legs in. 'Gotcha! Of course I d on't expect you to massage my feet. But if you're offering, you could give my should ers a rub. I kept having to crane my neck to see over the head of the guy stand ing in front of me.'

'You should have said . We could have moved nearer the front.'

'Do you want me to be d eaf for a week? It was loud enough where we were stand ing, I d on't think I could have hand led it any loud er.'

While she was speaking, Saul had removed his black woollen jacket and had thrown it on the back of one of the d ining-table chairs, then he moved into position behind her. He blew on his hand s to warm them, and for a shocked moment she wond ered whether he expected her to remove her red sparkly top, and she stiffened . Oh, God , was this it? Were they going to make love?

However, when he placed his palms on the top of her should ers and began to apply some pressure to the muscles on either sid e of her neck, pressing his thumbs d own with a circular motion, she relaxed a little.

'Ooh, that's nice,' she moaned , d ropping her head forward and uttering little murmurs of d elight as he worked on the knotted muscles between her should er blad es.

She could feel the tension d raining away, so when he stopped , removing his hand s from her back and resting them on the tops of her should ers, she let out a sigh of regret. It had been so nice that she would have happily let him rub her should ers all night.

Expecting him to move away, her heart fluttered when he leant forward and she felt his warm breath on her neck.

'Mmm, you smell wonderful,' he murmured, then his lips grazed the sensitive skin at the nape of her neck and she stiffened.

He immediately froze but she whispered, 'Don't stop,' and tilted her head to the side. When he nibbled her gently, his kisses working their way along the side of her jaw, she sighed.

Then, unable to bear it any longer, she shifted around, and his mouth was on hers and they were kissing frantically, desperately, and all her inhibitions were forgotten as she led him to the bedroom.

–

'It's been snowing,' Saul said.

Kazz was thankful the bedroom was at the rear of the building and not facing the street, because he was standing in front of the window, staring out of it, in all his naked glory.

Talking of rears, Saul had a very impressive backside, taut and nicely shaped.

'Come back to bed.' Kazz patted the mattress, where that backside should rightly be.

'Want to go play in it?' he asked.

'How deep is it?' Intrigued now, she pushed the duvet back and padded over to him, using his body to shield her in case anyone happened to be outside, looking up.

When she saw that there was only a faint white slush on the courtyard below, her disappointment was acute. 'It's hardly anything.'

'Not down in the valley – but look at the mountains.'

The upper slopes were white, their tops gleaming in the weak December sun.

'It probably won't last,' Saul said , 'so if we want to go for a walk in it, we'd better get our skates on.'

'Ice skates?'

'Ha ha.' He turned away from the wind ow and kissed her, then he slapped her on the bum and began to gather up his clothes. 'While you get read y, I'll make us some tea and toast. Dress warmly, and have you got any sturd y boots?'

'Will Doc Martens d o?' She had bought them to wear with thick tights and chunky knit d resses, but they were pretty good in the wet.

'Perfect.'

'What about you?' He had been wearing brogues last night, and she d id n't think his coat would be suitable either. She had a Parka, so she'd be all right, even though she'd bought it for its looks rather than its suitability on a snow-topped mountain.

'I always keep a Barbour jacket and a pair of wellies in the Land y,' he said . 'I never know when I'll need them.'

He left her to get read y, and when she emerged from the bed room, he presented her with two slices of buttered toast and a mug of coffee.

'Will we be going up Pen y Fan?' she asked . It was the most visited peak in the National Park and wasn't too far away.

'It'll be busier than a supermarket on Christmas Eve,' he said . 'Everyone will have mad e a beeline for it. I thought we'd hike up Skirrid Fawr, and afterward s I'll treat you to lunch in the old est pub in Wales.'

Lunch sound ed lovely. A hike up a mountain? Not so much.

'Is it as high as Pen y Fan?' she asked . She'd heard it was one hell of a trek to get to the top of the highest mountain in South Wales, and it was so gnarly that the army used it for their SAS training.

'Not by a long shot,' he assured her as they bund led themselves into their coats. 'Pen y Fan is nearly twice as high as Skirrid .' He grinned at her. 'I thought I'd break you in gently. It's steep, but the view from the top is fantastic.'

Kazz wasn't an outd oorsy person, so it was with some trepid ation that she got out of the car when they reached the base of the mountain. From this angle, it d id n't look too bad , and she breathed a sigh of relief.

'We'll go the long way round ,' he told her. 'It's less steep and very picturesque. Read y?'

She nod d ed and he shrugged his Barbour jacket on, then hefted a rucksack onto his should ers. 'Emergency rations,' he said , by way of explanation when he saw her looking. 'I always take it with me when I'm on a mountain. Better to have it and not need it, than not to have it and wish you had .'

That was cryptic, she thought, curious as to what was in it.

The climb began with a gentle incline up a lane, then a breathless stomp up through the wood land that cloaked the lower slopes of the mountain. But before they emerged from the treeline, Saul took a path to the left, and the going became less steep and more enjoyable – as far as Kazz was concerned .

With the branches bare of leaves, she could see tantalising glimpses of the view to the west and she was amazed at how high they had climbed in such a short amount of time. The ascent was grad ual, and soon the trees were left behind and they were walking on an open hillsid e, a patchwork of field s spread out below.

More climbing, as the mountain became steeper, left Kazz panting and breathless. Her legs were aching, but with Saul's urging, she finally mad e it to the top, and what she saw left her speechless.

A layer of snow coated the summit, a few centimetres d eep in places and so startlingly white in the December sun that it mad e her squint. The air was cold , crisp and incred ibly fresh, and she d rew d eep breaths into her lungs as she gazed around in wond er. Never had she seen such a view as this!

Turning in a slow circle, Kazz realised she could see a full 360 d egrees, from impressive mountains in one d irection, to rolling farmland in another.

'That's Abergavenny,' Saul said , pointing to a small town nestled in a valley below, and she marvelled to think she had been walking through its streets last night.

He pointed to a conical-shaped mountain. 'That's the Sugar Loaf. It looks like a volcano, but it isn't.'

She had wond ered about it, because it could be seen from Tanglewood , and she'd meant to ask.

'Over there is the Black Mountains range, and although you can't see it from here, Hay is somewhere beneath it.' He turned her bod y to face another d irection. 'See that? That's the Bristol Channel.' In the far d istance was a sliver of gleaming silver where the sky met the land . 'On a clear d ay, you might even see the Somerset coast.'

It took Kazz a long time to speak, and when she d id , she simply said , 'Thank you.' It would never have occurred to her to walk up a rud d y great big mountain, but she was so very pleased she had .

The beauty of the area astound ed her, and she could see why people came from miles around to appreciate it. Wild mountains, gentle valleys, cute villages – this part of Wales had it all, and she felt incred ibly privileged to be able to call it home. To her surprise and d elight, she realised she was beginning to fall in love with it, and Tanglewood especially. It was so d ifferent from the life she had led in Lond on, and any d oubts she had were fad ing faster than the haze shimmering in the d istance.

Grateful to Saul for showing her this remarkable view, she wrapped her arms around his waist and kissed him.

When she came up for air, there was such burning d esire in his eyes that she became breathless all over again.

Her rumbling tummy broke the mood , and he sniggered . 'I think someone could d o with a snack before we head back d own. Fancy a Welsh cake?' He tapped the rucksack.

She fancied Saul more, but her bed was several miles away, so a Welsh cake would have to d o. Besid es, she was looking forward to the promised lunch in Wales's old est pub.

–

'I've never been to the Skirrid Inn,' Stevie said on Mond ay morning, after Kazz had told her all about her lovely d ay out yesterd ay.

Kazz was perched in her usual spot in the tea shop's kitchen. 'It was gorgeous. I can't believe it's over nine hund red years old . They reckon it's haunted .' She'd had so much fun find ing out about it and had been absolutely fascinated . She had n't stopped talking about it all the way home, much to Saul's obvious amusement. Then he had given her something else to think about as he'd whisked her off to bed .

He d id n't stay last night, though – he had to be up early this morning – but he had promised to pop in to see her later.

'I've never seen you like this,' Stevie said , leaning against the island , a mug of coffee crad led in her hand s.

'Like what?' Kazz snapped out of her thoughts.

'Dreamy over a man.'

'I'm not d reamy! I had a good time, that's all.'

'I bet you d id .' Stevie chuckled . 'Leanne said that Saul d id n't go home on Saturd ay night.'

Kazz closed her eyes wearily. Those d ratted Tangle-wood gossip d rums. 'He stayed the night. So what?' Kazz went on the d efensive.

Stevie stud ied her, then said slowly, 'Just be careful.'

'I know what I'm d oing,' Kazz replied sulkily.

'Do you? As I said , I've never seen you like this about a man.'

'I like him, OK?'

'I think you more than like him,' Stevie pointed out.

Kazz hated to ad mit it, but her friend was right. She liked Saul a lot. She could even see herself falling for him.

'How many d ates have you been on?' Stevie asked .

'In my life? No id ea. I d on't keep count.'

'With Saul,' Stevie clarified .

'It d epend s on what you'd call a d ate. Two, or three if you count Saturd ay and Sund ay as separate ones.'

Stevie said quietly, 'He never makes it past five d ates.'

'What are you trying to say – that he'll d ump me on d ate number five?'

'I d on't know, Kazz. All I'm saying is that I d on't want to see you hurt.'

'Don't look, then,' Kazz shot back. Immed iately contrite, she d ropped her gaze and heaved a sigh. 'I'm sorry, I know you're only looking out for me.'

Stevie shrugged . There were spots of colour on her cheeks and Kazz knew she had upset her. 'It's just…' Kazz hunted around for the right word *really* like him.'

A small smile appeared on Stevie's face. 'I know you d o. I can tell. Just be careful, eh?'

'I'll try.' Kazz wasn't making any promises. How could she, when it was way too late to be careful?

Chapter 19

Kazz had never been ice skating, although she had owned a pair of roller skates when she was a kid . As far as she could recall, she had spent more time gripping onto the sid e for d ear life, than she had skating. She had n't been able to move more than a couple of centimetres without pinwheeling her arms and trying to take giant steps to keep her balance.

She d id n't expect this time to be any d ifferent.

'If I break something it'll be your fault,' she told Saul firmly. 'If I'm incapacitated , you'll have to man the shop.'

'It won't come to that,' he said , kneeling to help her put on her skates.

She flinched at the sight of the narrow blad es. If she had n't been able to stay upright with eight relatively wid e wheels und erneath her, she would n't stand a hope in hell when balancing on precarious strips of metal. She must have been mad to agree to this.

The ice rink, like her shop, was a pop-up one, in honour of the Christmas festival. It was located in the Hen and Duck's car park – with much grumbling from Mad s, the pub's grumpy land lord , after Betty had railroad ed him into it.

Although the festival technically d id n't start until tomorrow, there were plenty of activities taking place this evening and as soon as it had grown d ark, Kazz had closed the shop, guessing that people would be more interested in the little funfair that had come with the skating rink, than in buying old books.

Against her better judgement, she had allowed Saul to talk her into going ice skating.

The rink was small, with several surprisingly adept kids whirling around on it. The sight of their endless circles as they whizzed past made her feel quite dizzy. Saul encouraged her to get to her feet, which she only managed because she was clinging onto him so tightly, and she hadn't even left the matted area yet.

Walking on ice was a far more dangerous activity and Kazz let go of him only long enough to transfer her death grip to the barrier encircling the rink.

'Slide one foot forward, then the other,' he instructed.

Kazz lifted a foot, made heavy by the boot and the blade, and placed it down again. She did the same with the other. She managed to move a less than impressive ten centimetres.

'You have to glide, not walk,' Saul advised. 'Like this.'

He pushed off with one foot and flowed gracefully across the ice, then spun around so he was travelling backwards.

'Show off,' she muttered, then giggled when a boy of about eight sped past him at a rate of knots, passing so close that Saul did a speed wobble.

He flailed towards the barrier and grabbed it with a rueful smile. 'Looks like I'm not as good as I think I am,' he said.

Kazz bit her lip and peered at him from underneath her lashes. 'Oh, I don't know,' she murmured wickedly.

He sucked in a breath, and she giggled.

'Do you want to leave?' he asked , his expression hopeful.

'No, I d o not. You d ragged me onto this d amned ice so we're going to d amned well skate.'

'We are, are we? And how d o you propose to d o that, when you won't let go of the barrier?'

Kazz gritted her teeth, released her hold and mad e grab for Saul, clinging onto his coat with both hand s as she wobbled and tottered , her feet slid ing away from her.

Saul grasped her around the waist to stead y her. 'OK?'

She pressed her lips together and nod d ed *She*, but she d id n't want to let Saul see how nervous she was. It wasn't falling on her backsid e that worried her – it was falling and breaking an arm or a leg, or both.

Slowly, he guid ed her around the rink, close enough to the barrier so that she could grab it if she need ed , but she was d etermined not to. If Saul could d o this, then so could she.

'You're d oing great,' he enthused , 'but as much as I like you hold ing on to me, d o you mind not gripping so hard ?' He was skating backward s very slowly and Kazz was hold ing his hand s in a vice-like grip.

Her bod y was tenser than a tent pole, and she was so stiff that every muscle was rigid . She would ache like the d evil tomorrow and she could alread y feel a soreness d eveloping in her ankles.

After one slow tortuous circuit, Kazz was read y to call it a d ay. At least she had given it a go, she told herself.

'Hot chocolate?' he suggested , and Kazz read ily agreed . That was more like it and while they queued for the d rinks, she gazed around at what else was on offer at the festival.

The main street had been blocked off to traffic, and a mini fairground had been erected . The ice rink was just the start of it. There was also a mini helter-skelter, a pin-the-tail-on-Rud olf game, an inflatable Twister, plus load s of other things, as well as lots of food and d rink stalls. Kazz had worried that Stevie's tea shop might be affected tomorrow, but Stevie assured her it would n't be.

'Not everyone wants to eat food in their hand s,' Stevie had said . 'Many like to sit d own at a proper table ind oors. You'll see.'

Kazz was keeping her fingers crossed that she would see an upturn in sales, too. The bookshop had been d oing better than she had expected , and she was now quietly hopeful that she could make a success of it long term. She was still ad justing to the slower pace of life in Tanglewood , but Saul was helping with that, even though they d id n't see each other every evening, so some d ays after work she was at a loose end .

But she was getting used to living on her own. It had been somewhat of a roller-coaster (the Christmas festival d id n't sport one of those, thankfully, else Saul might have wanted a go) and at first, she had relished having a place all to herself, had revelled in the peace and solitud e of the flat above the tea shop. Then she had come to d read it, feeling lonely and restless, unused to not having people around her. But now, she was beginning to appreciate it. Most of the time, that is; more and more she had found herself wanting to be with Saul.

Unbid d en, Stevie's warning that Saul rarely mad e it past a fifth d ate forced itself into her mind , and she flinched . Was tonight d ate number four or five? And were they still at the d ating stage, or d id she and Saul have an actual relationship? It felt like a relationship to her, but she couldn't be certain that he felt the same way, and she didn't feel confident enough to ask.

'I love the Christmas festival,' Saul announced, licking cream from his lips. He had already eaten all the marshmallows on the top of his drink, and she saw him eyeing hers speculatively.

'Oh no, you don't,' she said. 'These are mine.' She scooped one up with her finger and popped it in her mouth, the gooey sweetness exploding on her tongue. The drink even had a red-and-white candy cane in it, which she was saving for last.

'This is the real start of Christmas, as far as I'm concerned,' he was saying. 'You should take some time out tomorrow to enjoy it.'

'I can't. There's no one to mind the shop and I don't want to close, even for half an hour.'

'I'll mind it for you, if you like?' he suggested. 'I don't know a fraction of what you know, but I can ring sales through the till if you show me how to use that card machine of yours.'

That was so sweet of him. 'You might regret saying that,' she teased.

'Seriously, I won't. You'll be busy tomorrow and you're going to need a break at some point.'

'I admit, it does get a bit difficult sometimes. I hate leaving the shop floor unattended, even if I'm desperate for the loo.'

'In that case, you must let me give you a hand. You don't have to look around the festival if you don't want to, but at least it'll give you a chance to have a sandwich and a cup of tea in peace.'

'Are you sure I'm not putting you out?'

'Never,' he said . His gaze was intense, and Kazz felt a jolt go right through her.

She wasn't sure what to say to that, or whether she should say anything at all, because she had probably read too much into it.

He continued , 'I'm not sure what time I'll get to you because stuff will need d oing on the farm, but I promise I will see you before lunch. Heck, I'll even *bring* lunch. I'll pick something up from one of the food stalls. Got any preference?'

'Ooh, roast chestnuts.'

'For *lunch*?'

'No, there's a guy over there selling roast chestnuts.' Kazz pointed . 'I could eat a bag of them right now.'

Saul laughed and took her by the hand . 'Your wish is my command . If the lad y wants chestnuts, the lad y shall have chestnuts.'

'What if the lad y wants a kiss?' she asked archly.

'The lad y can have one of those too; she can have as many as she wants.'

'How about we skip the roast chestnuts?' she suggested . 'They'll still be here tomorrow. I've got something equally as toasty in mind .'

And when she d arted into the flat and d ragged him into the bed room, Kazz forgot about roast chestnuts and everything else to d o with the outsid e world , and she had the feeling that Saul d id , too.

–

Saul had n't entirely forgotten about the chestnuts, and when he presented Kazz with a brown paper bag as he walked into her bookshop on Saturd ay morning, she burst out laughing.

While she peered into the bag, Saul feasted his eyes on her. She was wearing a red knitted jumper with a reindeer on the front, had antlers on her head, and was wearing slim-fitting black jeans. She looked utterly gorgeous and incredibly cute, and he would dearly have loved to whisk her off to bed, the way she had done to him last night.

But obviously he couldn't – she had a shop to run and he had promised to help. He settled for a swift kiss instead, then wandered around the shop to familiarise himself with where everything was.

When his gaze fell on the window display with the padded wingback chair, heat flooded through him. That was where they had shared their first kiss – and what a kiss it had been.

He couldn't prevent a huge smile from spreading across his face and he hastily checked to see whether anyone had noticed that he was grinning like an idiot; he wanted to help customers, not put them off.

After having a quick scan around the shop, he returned to the counter, and Kazz showed him how to operate the card machine and where the wrapping materials were kept. He was eager to have a go, so he served the next customer by himself, even indulging in a bit of banter as he waited for the payment to go through.

'You're a natural at this,' Kazz said. 'You're wasted on sheep and tractors.'

'There you go,' he said to the customer. 'Don't forget to pop back in soon; new stock – or should I say old stock, ha ha – is coming in every day.'

When the customer was out of earshot, Kazz hissed, 'But it's not, is it? I've got no new stock at all.'

'Why not?' Saul was puzzled . He realised   the shop had   only been open a matter of weeks and   Kazz's main objective was to sell her grand ad 's books, but—

He froze as a realisation hit him. Kazz had   no intention of continuing with the bookshop after the lease ran out. She could n't have, otherwise she would   be making arrangements to acquire more stock.

Dismay filled   him, and   not because the bookshop would   be no more, but because without it to keep her here, Kazz would   have no reason to remain in Tanglewood .

An ache began in his chest, and   it quickly spread   to the rest of him at the thought that her time here might be limited . But wasn't *this*? He had   alread y d ecid ed   that remaining at the farm wasn't an option and   had   mad e a tentative attempt to look for a farm of his own to rent. However, the od d s of said   farm being anywhere near Tanglewood   were slim. Which meant that even if Kazz d id   make a permanent home for herself in the village, he would   probably be leaving it at some point.

If Kazz had   been any other woman, her leaving would n't have bothered   him in the slightest.

If Saul had   kept to his vow of giving up d ating for the foreseeable future, it would n't have mattered . But it d id   matter, and   that was because he felt more for Kazz than he'd   ever felt for anyone else – except Joelle.

But Joelle was in his past, and   he was floored   by the realisation that he wanted   Kazz to be in his future. The question he had   to ask himself, though, was… d *id she* want to be in *his*? Or was she treating him the same way he had   treated   numerous other women, as a bit of fun and someone to pass the time with. And   if she was, d id   it serve him right?

He concluded that it probably did. He mightn't have set out to deliberately hurt anyone, but he knew he had, nevertheless. In his defence, he had never let it go too far. He had always pulled away before the woman he was dating did anything silly, like fall in love with him, but that didn't make him feel any better about himself right now. He had been so intent on having a good time, without the commitment, that he hadn't properly stopped to consider anyone else's feelings.

Did that make him a jerk? He kind of thought it did, and he wasn't proud of it. But the irony was, he wasn't behaving like a jerk when it came to Kazz. He genuinely liked her more than was probably wise. Karma was getting her revenge because the way things were heading, he was about to be the one getting hurt.

He wished he had been able to keep to his vow to stay away from women, but how could he stay away from the only woman who had crept under his skin in years?

She said, 'Are you OK? You look a bit strange.'

He felt it, too. 'I'm fine, just wool-gathering. Do you trust me enough to leave me on my own in the shop?'

'I most definitely do!'

'Don't sound so surprised,' he said, with a chuckle to show he wasn't taking offence.

'Sorry, that came out wrong. I'm not surprised in the slightest. Not now.'

'But there was a time when you would have been?' He was still teasing, but he was also curious.

'There was, but that was before I got to know you. Do you mind if I go out for a bit? I won't be long, but I'd like to soak up some of the atmosphere.'

'Take as long as you want,' he said. 'If I get stuck, I can always ring you.'

'True. OK, if you're sure.' She gave him a quick kiss. 'I'll see you in a bit.'

She went out the back to fetch her coat and bag, and when she reached the shop door, she paused to give him a wave.

Saul raised his hand to wave back, and that was when he saw someone who made his stomach turn over.

Kazz was holding the door open for a woman who was about to enter the shop, a woman he knew only too well.

What the hell was *Joelle* doing here?!

Chapter 20

Saul's instinct was to leave, sharpish, and he did take a step towards the door. Kazz was still in sight and he could easily call her to come back. But he would have to explain why, and he didn't want to do that.

Joelle hadn't noticed him. Her gaze was drifting around the shop, although she didn't appear to be looking at the books themselves.

That didn't surprise him – Joelle hadn't been a reader, and she hadn't understood why he loved the pastime so much. Which made him question why she was here, if she didn't want to check out the books.

He took a moment to study her, his heart hammering. His mouth was dry and there was a distinctly unpleasant churning in his stomach. He felt shaky too, and he wished he could sit down.

His ex hadn't changed, not in any significant way. Her hair was shorter, a spiky blonde cut that showed off her cheekbones and the column of her neck. Her face was slimmer than he remembered, but her eyes and lips were the same.

A middle-aged couple briefly obscured his view and as he shifted position to try to see around them, he locked eyes with the woman who had broken his heart.

Saul froze. He stopped breathing, his heart stuttered and all coherent thought fled.

He continued to stare at her, transfixed. For the life of him, he could n't move. Seeing her again had opened a wound he'd hoped had long since healed, and he felt hollowed out and d rained.

'Saul?' Joelle had a tiny frown line between her eyes. 'Is that you? It is, isn't it? Gosh, what are you d oing here? You d on't work here, d o you?'

He swallowed and tried to find his voice. To his surprise, his reply was calm and controlled, with no hint of the turmoil insid e.

'No, just mind ing it for—' He stopped. He had been about to say 'a friend ' but Kazz was more than that.

Joelle laughed, the noise filling the space between them, vibrating through his mind. She had the same laugh – light, tinkling. Once upon a time, he had lived for that sound, had d one anything and everything to hear it.

'For a second I thought you had givcn up farming,' she said, catching her bottom lip between her teeth, her manner bord ering on sed uctive. His eyes were d rawn to her mouth; the mouth he had kissed more times than he could count.

He felt nothing.

She d id n't give him time to reflect on the surprising realisation. 'Come here, let me give you a hug. It's been so long, Saul.'

Saul d id n't move. He d id n't think he could, but when she threw her arms around him, his own automatically came up to embrace her.

She hugged him tightly for several second s before releasing him, and when she stepped back, she took hold of his hand s. 'It's so good to see you again.'

'Is it?' His reply was bleak. She had d umped him without a second thought and now she was telling him it was good to see him again? Rigid ly, he asked , 'Is there anything I can help you with tod ay?'

Joelle's laugh tinkled again. 'Don't be like that. You sound like one of those people on a help d esk.'

'Well, is there?'

'Not really.'

'Why are you here, Joelle?'

'For the festival. I thought it would be nice to visit the old place.'

'*The old place* is less than an hour's d rive from Hereford . You could have come back any time.'

'How d o you know I haven't?' she countered .

He d id n't, but he assumed that somehow, if she had returned , he would have sensed her presence.

There was a time when he used to be able to d o that. He could be in a room full of people, with his back to the d oor, yet he would know when she entered it.

'Someone would have mentioned seeing you.'

'Ah, yes, the Tanglewood gossip mill. It's still alive and kicking, then? That's one thing I d efinitely d on't miss about living here.'

'What d o you miss?'

Her lips twisted into a wry smile. 'Is there a Mrs Saul and lots of little Sauls running around ?'

The question took him aback. 'No, there isn't.'

'I'm surprised . I thought you would have been snapped up by now.'

'*You* d id n't think I was that great a catch.' His reply was bitter.

Joelle tilted her head to the sid e and pouted at him. 'Don't be like that. We weren't right for each other, surely you saw that?'

216

Saul had   seen no such thing. He had   thought they were perfect together.

'Anyway, it was such a long time ago. We've both moved   on since then,' she ad d ed .

She might have; Saul wasn't as sure. He'd   thought he had , but the way he had   hard ened   his heart against love since she'd   walked   out on him told   a d ifferent story.

Kazz's sweet face leapt into his mind , and   he inhaled sharply. Maybe his heart had n't been   as hard   as he'd thought, because since he'd   met Kazz, it had   begun to soften.

'Yes, we have moved   on,' he said . Joelle more than him. His life was more or less the same as when she'd   left. Scrap that. He'd   gone backward s now that he had   moved   back into the farmhouse with his parents. However, Saul had plans to rectify that, by way of obtaining the tenancy on a farm – when he found   one that was suitable.

Joelle, on the other hand , appeared   to have sped   ahead . She had   more than moved   on, if her outfit was any ind ication. She looked   incred ibly well put-together and expensive. He was no fashion aficionad o, but he knew d esigner gear when he saw it. Thread s like hers d id n't come cheap.

She said , 'How's your mum and   d ad ?'

'Good .'

'Leanne?'

'She's good .'

'I saw her on TV. She was in that floristry show… What was it called ?'

'*Budding Stars*.'

'That's right. It was a shame she d id n't win. I thought she was brilliant. I hear she's now working for one of the

217

jud ges, as well as running her own business in Tanglewood . She must be busy.'

'You hear a lot.'

Joelle shrugged . 'I like to keep up with the local news.'

'Your local news is in Hereford . Or d on't you live there
anymore?'

'I still live there.' She glanced at her watch. It was a
Rolex, and he wond ered whether he was supposed to be
impressed . 'We should have a proper catch-up. How are
you fixed for lunch?'

'Lunch?' Saul was d umbfound ed . 'Tod ay?'

'Well, yes, that was the id ea.'

'I can't, I'm—'

'Mind ing the shop,' she finished with a smile. 'Another
time, perhaps?'

'Yeah, another time.'

She took out her phone. 'Let's set a d ate. It would
probably be better if you came to Hereford , there's so
much more choice there and , let's be honest, Tanglewood
d oesn't have a great d eal to offer. There's not a restaurant
in sight. The twenty-seventh is good for me. Shall we say
one o'clock? I'll message you the name of the restaurant.
I take it you haven't changed your number?'

'No, I—'

'Good . The twenty-seventh, at one. I'm looking
forward to it.' She put a hand on his bicep and moved
closer to kiss him on the sid e of his mouth. 'We've got a
lot to catch up on.'

'But I—'

'You're looking good , Saul. But then, you always d id .'
She raised her eyebrows and her lips twisted into a wry
smile. 'It really is good to see you again. It's been far too
long.'

Her hand lingered on his arm for a moment, then she slowly lowered it and walked toward s the d oor. As she reached it, she gave him a long look, then she was gone, leaving him with an ache in his chest and a head full of confusion.

–

The Tanglewood Christmas festival had bags of festive atmosphere, but Kazz could n't bring herself to be away from the bookshop for long. She had a brief scurry around , absorbing as many sights as she could , noticing with pleasure the queue in Peggy's Tea Shoppe, pleased for Stevie to see it so busy.

Kazz's thoughts kept returning to Saul, and she hoped he was getting on OK. He had n't phoned her yet, so that was a good sign.

Another reason why she d id n't want to d ally was that she would have liked to have had him by her sid e; it wasn't the same on her own. So as soon as she'd bought herself some lunch, she thread ed her way along the high street back to the bookshop, while munching on a turkey, cran-berry and stuffing roll. It was still only half-eaten when she got there and she took a moment to finish it outsid e, not wanting to waft the smell of her lunch through the shop.

In ord er for Saul not to think that she was checking up on him, she d id n't stand d irectly in front of the wind ow, but off to one sid e. She still had a view of the insid e, and she was pleased to see several customers perusing the shelves.

One of them, a well-d ressed , attractive woman in her early thirties, was stand ing near the counter, talking to Saul. She appeared to know him rather well, and Kazz watched in d isbelief as the woman moved in for a kiss. It wasn't a full-on snog, but her lips grazed Saul's mouth, so it was no maid en-aunt peck on the cheek. And now she was stroking his arm!

Kazz shrank back as the woman head ed for the d oor.

Thankfully, Saul had n't noticed her. How could he when he only had eyes for that woman? His gaze followed her as she left the shop and tracked her as she crossed the road .

Who was she? And why was she being so familiar with him? The woman had d efinitely been flirting – Kazz knew a flirt when she saw one. And Saul had n't d one anything to d iscourage it.

A thought occurred to her – one that squeezed her heart uncomfortably.

Was Saul setting this woman up to be his next conquest?

Four d ates, five d ates… Kazz thought they had moved on from d ating and were head ing toward s a more solid relationship, girlfriend –boyfriend stuff. But had he been planning on d umping her all along, and was even now lining up the next unfortunate woman who thought she had a chance with him?

Kazz had let him into her knickers and now that she had , had he lost interest?

Betty had warned her, but she'd ignored it. More fool her!

Saul was now talking to a man and his d aughter. The little girl was hopping from foot to foot, either from bored om or excitement, Kazz could n't tell, and she wond ered whether she should give him the benefit of the d oubt, or whether to ask him outright.

The unfinished turkey roll was still in her hand , and she turned away to find the nearest bin, her eyes scanning the crowd .

There was no sign of the woman who had been in her shop.

Saul's eyebrows rose as she walked in. 'You weren't gone long.'

'Long enough,' she said .

'It's busy out there, isn't it?'

'Have you been busy in here?'

'Give us a chance! You've only been gone ten minutes. I d id sell a book on 1950s rail networks, though. The chap was telling me all about the mod el railway he's got in his attic.'

'Did anyone else buy anything? How about the lad y who just left?'

'What lad y?' Both his tone and his expression were blank, but Kazz wasn't fooled . He knew which lad y she meant, she was certain of it.

'Never mind ,' she said , and walked toward s the storeroom to stow her bag and coat, pinpricks of hurt, like little need les, jabbing at her heart.

It wasn't a pleasant feeling, and she only had herself to blame. She had been warned often enough, but she had been so sure she would be the one to tame him.

The irony was that Saul wasn't a bad boy as such, in that he wasn't wild or irresponsible. He seemed perfectly respectable, almost boy-next-d oor. He was a farmer, for God 's sake. He still lived at home with his mum and d ad . His was a far cry from a Lothario lifestyle, and Kazz supposed that was part of his charm – and that she, like the others who had gone before her, had fallen into the trap of believing she stood a chance with him.

When Kazz returned to the shop floor, Saul was chatting to a pair of eld erly lad ies, and she observed him quietly, noticing how he exud ed charm and friend liness. The women were lapping it up. She watched him close the sale, then mad e her presence known.

'Thanks for helping out,' she said . 'I can take it from here.'

'Are you sure? I d on't mind staying to help. It's quite good fun, and it makes a change from sheep. You can't have a proper conversation with a ewe.'

'Yeah, I noticed you like to chat.'

'You have to, d on't you? Customer service and all that.'

Did his customer service involve offering one of those customers an entirely d ifferent kind of service, she wond ered archly. 'What d id she want, anyway?'

'Who?'

'The woman in the white coat.'

There was that carefully blank expression again.

Kazz continued , 'If I haven't got the book she wanted , maybe I can track one d own.'

'Oh, her. She d id n't want to buy anything. She popped in to say hello. She used to live in Tanglewood .'

Some of Kazz's tension eased . So that's who she was, an ex. 'Back for the festival, is she?'

'Yeah.'

'Staying long?'

'Just here for the d ay.'

On hearing that, the rest of her tension d issipated . If the woman wasn't from around here, she d id n't pose a threat.

Then Kazz immed iately hated herself for the thought. She was acting like a jealous harpy, even if it was in her head . Saul had every right to speak to whomever he pleased , ex or not, without being subjected to her version of the Spanish Inquisition. How would *she* like it if he questioned her about Rossiter? Which remind ed her: she wanted to post a Christmas card to Rossiter, and she had n't d one it yet. She'd alread y received one from him, and with only two weeks to Christmas, she had better get a move on before she missed the final posting d ay. Send ing a text wasn't the same.

However, she would have to be satisfied with that and a phone call when it came to her mum. Kazz had missed the last d ay for posting overseas because she had n't known where to post anything. Now that her mum and Vince had an apartment (they were moving in at the end of the week) she could always send them a belated gift.

Her mum had told her that she had popped something in the mail for her, but it had n't arrived yet, and Kazz guessed that having arranged for her post to be red irected might cause a d elay. It's not like her mum knew of her relocation yet, and moving to Tanglewood had been such a hurried affair that using a postal red irection service had seemed logical, especially as she was waiting for news about her final salary payment from Fred d ie. She was owed a month's wages, and she need ed her P45, even if she probably would n't be using it.

'You're looking glum,' Saul said , putting an arm around her. 'Is everything OK? I d id n't make a boo-boo, d id I?'

'Sorry, just thinking about Christmas.'

He gave her a squeeze. 'It's going to be hard for you, with your mum in Spain,' he sympathised . 'Don't you want to take a couple of d ays off and go join her?'

'I'd love to, but I can't afford it.'

The possibility of flying out on Christmas Eve had crossed her mind , but she wanted to open the shop on the twenty-eighth. People may well be in January sales mod e and she d id n't want to lose a d ay's trad e. If she w serious about making a go of the bookshop (and she most d efinitely was) she had to make the most of each and every d ay.

'I could lend you—' Saul began, but Kazz stopped him.

'That's very sweet of you, but I meant I can't afford the *time.*'

'Ah, I see. What you need is an assistant.'

'I've been thinking the very same thing.'

She stepped away to serve a customer, relieved that her fears about the woman were ground less, and that Saul was acting no d ifferently toward s her.

When she returned to his sid e, she continued the conversation. 'I'm not going to make any d ecisions this sid e of Christmas,' she said , 'although I will need another person in the shop going forward . I'll have a good think about it in the New Year.'

Saul was beaming. 'Does that mean you're going to stay in Tanglewood ?'

'I think it d oes.' She beamed back.

'You've mad e my d ay. How about we go out for a d rink next weekend to celebrate? I would suggest this evening, but everywhere will be so crowd ed .' A shad ow passed across his face but before she could ask him what was wrong, it was gone and he carried on, 'We could ask Stevie and Nick, and the others.'

'Better still, how about I cook everyone a meal as a thank you for all their help and support?'

'What a lovely id ea. I'm no cook, but I'll happily give you a hand .'

'No need ,' she said . 'I mightn't know much about running a bookshop, but I d o know how to cook for a crowd .'

'OK, but if you need anything, ask.' He captured her gaze and stared intently into her eyes. 'Anything at all. I'm here for you.'

Kazz had the d elicious feeling he wasn't referring to chopping veg.

Chapter 21

When Kazz gave the tea shop a final once-over, she had a tear in her eye. It looked absolutely gorgeous, even if she did say so herself, and she hoped her guests would be equally as impressed.

Stevie had loaned Kazz the use of the kitchen and the tea shop itself for the thank-you meal she had invited everyone to, because the flat was far too small to cater for eleven people. The table only fitted four chairs around it and there wasn't enough space in the flat's little kitchen to prepare such a large meal. Even with the use of the tea shop's facilities, Kazz had felt a bit stretched, but that was due to being so busy in the bookshop (she must look into acquiring more stock as a matter of urgency in January).

She had prepared as much as she could ahead of this evening, but with the tea shop also running at full capacity, it hadn't been easy. Aware that everyone would be tucking into a traditional Christmas lunch this time next week, and with mince pies and turkey at every turn, she opted for a less festive but equally mouth-watering menu: feta and spinach tartlets to start, beef tenderloin for main, followed by a pumpkin and pecan cheesecake pie.

As soon as the beef was in the oven, she turned her attention to the tables and the place settings. It had only taken her a few minutes to push four tables together and rearrange the chairs, and then she had put pristine white cloths on each one and laid them with gleaming cutlery and sparkling glasses. Stevie had alread y d ecorated the place and it looked lovely and festive, so all Kazz need ed to d o was to d rape white fairy lights d own the length of the pushed -together tables and light the cand les in the gold lanterns.

She just had enough time, before Saul and the first of her guests arrived , to nip up to the flat to change. Although why she bothered , when she would be wearing her chef's whites over the top, she d id n't know.

A knock at the d oor had her hurrying to answer it, and she was pleased to see Saul. He scooped her into an embrace, kissing her d eeply.

'Ooh, what was that for?' she asked when he released her.

'No reason,' he said . 'Something smells nice.'

She grinned . 'I'm assuming you're referring to the food and not me?'

'You smell nice too,' he said . 'Mm, garlic, onions…'

Kazz swiped him on the arm. 'If you're not careful you'll be paying the chip shop a visit.'

'They d o a lush curry sauce,' he began, subsid ing when she raised an eyebrow. 'I'll shut up, shall I?'

'I think you better had .'

'Is there anything I can d o to help?'

'That's more like it. Thanks for the offer but everything is und er control. Look, here's Stevie and Nick.'

Her friend and her fiancé hurried insid e. 'Damn, it's cold !' Stevie exclaimed , with a shiver. She gazed around her tea shop. 'The tables look lovely, very festive. What can I d o to help?'

'Nothing, thanks. Saul, would you like to be barman and open the wine?' Kazz had placed several bottles of

Malbec and Riesling on the table, and there were more in the kitchen. It was a shame some of her guests were driving and could n't indulge. If she had a car, she would have offered to take everyone home.

That was something else to add to her to-do list for after Christmas. She would need her own transport for viewing and collecting new stock, and that was just for starters. Tanglewood was so rural that even a trip to the nearest supermarket was a major undertaking without a car. Despite being able to pick up most of the groceries she needed in the village, she could do with a major stock-up.

There was a muted pop as Saul eased the cork out of a bottle of red, and she left him to pour while she went to check on the oven.

When she emerged from the kitchen, it was to discover that everyone else had arrived, including Betty, who had already taken a seat at the table. She had tucked her napkin into the neck of her jumper and had a knife in one hand and a fork in the other.

'Someone's hungry,' Leanne murmured as she came in for a hug with Kazz.

'Bless her,' Stevie said, passing Leanne a glass of wine. 'She was so pleased to be invited, she's been looking forward to it all week.'

Kazz had feared that Betty might feel like a spare wheel, considering everyone else was part of a couple, but she need n't have worried. The old lady looked very much at home, and she was slurping wine like it was going out of fashion.

Kazz could n't not have invited her. She was the very reason Kazz was in Tanglewood. Without Betty putting the idea in her head, Kazz would never have thought of opening a bookshop. She had a lot to thank the old lady for.

Tia had wheeled herself into position, with Will by her side. Sitting next to her was Rex, then Leanne, with Betty at the end. On the opposite side were Saul, Nick, Stevie, Ed ie and James, with Kazz at the other end. She had also invited Lord and Lad y Tonbrid ge, because it was a friend of Lord Tonbrid ge's who owned the build ing her shop was in. Ed gar had also been such a great help, organising one of his employees to put the shelves up, and he'd given her ad vice on the prices she had been charging for her books. But he had sent his apologies, and Kazz was secretly relieved. She thought Lord Tonbrid ge was a lovely chap, but he would have cramped everyone's style. Tia was also pleased her in-laws would n't be here this evening, claiming she saw enough of Julia at home.

Now that everyone was seated, Kazz proceed ed to serve the first course. Let the merriment begin.

–

'That was d elicious,' Stevie said later in the kitchen. She was helping Kazz clear up, load ing the d ishwater while Kazz rinsed off the pots and pans. 'You haven't lost your touch.'

'I should hope not. It's only been a few weeks since I stopped working in Fred d ie's kitchen.' Kazz was buzzing, the high of people enjoying the food she had cooked surging through her veins.

She smiled at Saul as he came into the kitchen with the tablecloths.

'Do you miss it?' Stevie asked.

'Nights like this make me remember why I wanted to become a chef in the first place – to create an experience,

229

not just a meal, and to see people having fun partly because of the food I've mad e them. I'm not sure I'll ever completely stop being a chef, to be honest. Oh, let me help.'

Saul had d ropped the tablecloths and Kazz bent to pick them up, opening the washing machine d oor and shoving them in. 'Where d o you keep your d etergent, Stevie?'

'In that cupboard , there. Are you OK, Saul? You look a bit pale.'

Kazz shot him a glance. Saul d id look peaky. 'You're not coming d own with anything, are you?'

'I'm fine. Tired , that's all.' His smile seemed strained . 'I've offered to walk Betty home, if that's OK?'

'Of course it is,' Kazz said . 'See you in a bit?' She waited until he was out of earshot, then said , 'He can be very sweet.'

'So, I see. You've got it bad , haven't you? I think he has, too.'

'I hope so.'

'I never thought I'd see Saul settle d own.'

'You're jumping the gun. It's early d ays yet.'

'But you like him a lot.' It wasn't a question.

'Yes.' Kazz's reply was short.

She had n't fully explored in her own mind what her and Saul's relationship was, or how she felt about him. She knew she was falling in love and , if she was honest, the d epth of her feelings scared her. The last thing she need ed right now was Stevie asking her questions she d id n't have answers to.

'I'd better go say good bye to Betty,' she ad d ed , anxiou to escape and worried that Stevie would continue her line of questioning.

'I've had a lovely, lovely time!' Betty cried expansively.

The old lad y was a little worse for wear. Her face was flushed , and she was slurring her word s. 'You cook like an angel, my d ear.' She gripped Kazz's forearm and leant toward s her. 'You can cook me d inner anytime.'

Stevie, who had followed Kazz into the cafe area, said , 'That's praise, coming from Betty.'

Betty turned her attention to Stevie and said in a conciliatory tone, 'She d oesn't bake as well as you.'

Kazz laughed . 'Too right, I d on't. Or you, Betty. You've got a magic touch when it comes to pastry.'

'Aw.' Betty's eyes glistened , and Kazz hoped the old lad y wasn't about to burst into tears.

For all her bristly exterior and tough-as-old -boots persona, Kazz knew Betty had a heart of gold .

'Before I go,' Betty said , 'there's something that's been playing on my mind – what are you d oing for Christmas?'

'As in…?'

'Christmas d inner. You won't be spend ing it on your own, will you?'

'Um…'

'She's coming to us,' Stevie announced . 'So is Betty.'

That was the first Kazz had heard of it. She had been wond ering what she would d o, but she had no intention of inviting herself anywhere.

'Did n't I say?' Stevie's brow furrowed .

'Er, guys, I was hoping she'd come to the farm for Christmas lunch,' Saul said , and all head s turned to look at him.

Kazz was torn.

'Ooh, Iris d oes a wond erful Christmas d inner,' Betty d eclared . 'Not that you d on't,' she said to Stevie. 'Your Yorkshire pud d ings are better than hers, but I think she's got the ed ge when it comes to the gravy.'

Stevie burst out laughing. 'I love you, Betty.' She was shaking her head as she reached for the old lady to give her a hug.

Betty's eyes were suspiciously bright as she hugged her back. 'And I love you, dear girl. You're the grand daughter I never had. Right, young man.' She cleared her throat and marched up to Saul. A swift poke in his side with a bony finger made him wince. 'Take me home before I make a fool of myself.' She glanced back at Kazz. 'Go to Iris's for dinner; you'll have more fun at the Greens.'

Stevie's mouth dropped open. 'Are you saying I'm no fun?' she demanded.

'Every time I've been to yours for Sunday lunch, you fall asleep.' Betty chortled. 'I don't see Christmas dinner being any different, do you? See you on Monday.'

Kazz watched Betty and Saul leave, and she hugged herself. It looked like she was spending Christmas Day with Saul.

The Christmas she had been dreading was now something she was quite looking forward to. Could life get any better?

–

'I've had such a lovely time,' Betty sang, as she staggered down the road, hanging on to Saul's arm.

'It was nice,' Saul agreed. The meal had been outstanding, the company wonderful and the ambience festive. What he hadn't enjoyed quite as much was hearing the happiness in Kazz's voice when she'd mentioned how much fun she'd had cooking. Her wanting to return to being a chef wasn't the issue. What worried Saul was the likelihood of her returning to London because she wouldn't be able to find a suitable job as a chef locally.

'She thinks the world of you, does Kazz,' Betty announced. 'I'm glad she'll be spending Christmas with you. It can be a lonely time of year, and she's got no family around her.'

'She can borrow mine,' Saul joked. 'I've got enough to spare.'

'Have you told her about Joelle?' Abruptly, Betty appeared considerably less inebriated than she had when she'd been in the tea shop.

Saul stumbled. The last thing he expected to hear tonight was Joelle's name, and definitely not from Betty's lips.

'Joelle?' he repeated.

'I saw her.'

'So?' He knew he was being belligerent, but this was none of Betty's business. And what did she know anyway? That he and Joelle had once been an item? That could be said of him and quite a few other women.

'It won't be the same this time,' Betty said. 'Kazz isn't Joelle.'

'I know that.'

Betty cackled. 'You're dying to tell me to mind my own business, aren't you?'

'No comment.'

She cackled again. 'I won't take offence. I never do. Bigger fish than you have told me to keep my nose out.'

Saul rallied. 'I'm sure that's not the case.'

The snort Betty uttered wasn't at all ladylike. 'We'll leave it there, shall we?'

'That's a good idea.'

'I'm full of 'em, my lovely. Now, here's my key. Open my front door for me, there's a good boy.'

Saul did as he was told and saw Betty safely inside, waiting until he heard her lock the door and slide the safety chain on, before walking away.

He didn't immediately head back to the tea shop, though. After the bizarre conversation with Betty, he needed a minute or so to himself.

Betty's cottage was one of a row of similar houses, a stone's throw from the river. It was a picturesque location, but also a precarious one, as the river had been known to flood. He distinctly remembered helping the residents evacuate their houses the last time the river had broken its banks. He and Nick had had a hell's job trying to persuade Betty to leave. The stubborn old biddy had been determined to remain – until Stevie had persuaded her to go and stay with her in the flat above the tea shop until the flood waters had receded.

He'd helped with the clean-up operation afterwards, too.

Saul had a lot of time for Betty, but he wished she had kept her nose out this evening. Seeing Joelle last weekend had shaken him, and it had taken him a few days to regain his equilibrium.

He had been shocked more than anything, but once he had recovered from the surprise, he had been relieved and very thankful to discover he hadn't been as upset as he thought he would be. So many times over the years, Saul had played out the scenario in his mind of how he would act, what he would say, how he would feel if ever he saw her again.

Considering he'd had so much practice (in his head, at least), when he had finally come face to face with the woman who had broken his heart, he had been a wooden, bumbling mess. She had dominated the meeting straight from the off and had even bulld ozed him into agreeing to have lunch with her.

He d id n't have to ask himself how he could have allowed that to happen, because she had always been able to get him to d o exactly what she wanted .

He probably would n't go.

What was the point? It wasn't as though he would get anything out of it, apart from a resurgence of memories he had spent years trying to repress and a lingering 'what if things had been d ifferent' sad ness. He d id n't feel the urge to catch up. What he *did* feel was the urge to let sleeping d ogs lie. What was the point in raking it up again?

Saul mad e a d ecision. He would message Joelle and tell her he d id n't want to meet up after all. It was time to let go of the past and concentrate on the future.

Chapter 22

Kazz could n't d ecid e whether she was exhausted or relieved . A bit of both, probably. She was exhausted because the shop had experienced its busiest week since it had opened , and she was relieved because it was finally Christmas Eve and she had three glorious, wond erful d ays off to look forward to.

Like most of the other shop owners in Tanglewood , Kazz had d ecid ed to close at three p.m. tod ay, and shutti the shop earlier than normal mad e her feel as though she was a teenager skipping school.

Hurrying back to the flat, she planned on having a long soak in the bath, with plenty of bubbles, both the foaming kind and the variety that came in a bottle with a cork, and after that she would d ig out her sparkliest d ress, style her hair and put some slap on.

She was meeting Saul and load s of others outsid e the Hen and Duck for a carolling session around the village, before piling into the pub for some festive cheer. But before any of that took place, there was something Kazz had to d o. She d id open the wine, though, because she had a feeling she might need a d rink.

'Kazz, my gorgeous girl! How lovely! I thought you were going to call me tomorrow. Is everything OK?'

'Hi, Mum, everything is great.'

'Are you at work? I suppose it's going to be a busy couple of d ays for you.' Her mother's tone was sympathetic.

'I've just finished work and I've got the next three d ays off.'

Silence.

'Mum, are you still there?'

'Sorry, I'm gobsmacked . Fred d ie never gives you time off over Christmas – the miserable sod . When d id he tell you? Too late to get a flight to Spain, I'll wager. One d ay that man will get his comeuppance.'

'He alread y has. Have you got time for a chat? I've got something to tell you.'

'Is it bad news? Oh, please tell me it isn't.'

'It's not. But you might want to sit d own.'

'Hang on, let me go into the kitchen. I think I might need a gin.'

Kazz heard a frid ge opening, a bottle cap being twisted off, the chink of ice in a glass and then the unmissable sound of a bottle of tonic being opened .

'There, that's better. I'm all ears.'

Kazz slugged her wine, then plunged right in. 'Fred d ie has been arrested for fraud , and the restaurant is shut for the foreseeable future.'

'*What!* Oh, my poor girl. Just before Christmas, too. That's heartless, that is. I'll catch the next available flight—'

'Mum—'

'I d oubt if I'll get one before Boxing Day, but you never know.'

'Mum!'

'Get off the phone and I'll check and let you know. Don't worry, you'll—'

'*Mum!* Can you listen for a second ?'

'Don't tell me there's more.'

'You won't believe how much more there is.' Kazz d rank another mouthful of wine. 'You know you wanted me to clear Grand ad 's house? I kind of d id , but not in the way you meant. I moved to Tanglewood and opened a bookshop.'

There was silence for a moment, then her mother said , 'Sorry, love, this line is d read ful, I could have sworn you said you've moved to Tanglewood .'

'I have. And I've opened a bookshop.'

'But what about your job? What about the restaurant? I'm sure all this nonsense about Fred d ie will be sorted once Christmas is out of the way. It's probably some silly mistake.'

'He was arrested at the beginning of November. It's no flash in the pan.'

'I d on't und erstand . Did you try to get another job? A talented chef like you should n't have had any trouble. Oh!' There was a gasp. 'You've not been implicated , have you?'

'No, Mum, I haven't.' This conversation was going as bad ly as Kazz had feared .

'What on earth mad e you d ecid e to move halfway across the country and open a bookshop?'

'I was about to be mad e homeless and —'

'*What?!*'

Kazz winced as her mum screeched d own the phone.

'Homeless? When? Was this in November too? Why d id n't you say anything? I would never have gone to Spain if I'd known.'

'That's exactly why I d id n't say anything,' Kazz replied with a sigh. 'Anyway, when I found out, it was too late;

you'd alread y given up Grand ad 's house. We were all given notice on the d ay you told me you were going to live in Spain.'

Her mother was quiet for so long that Kazz wond ered whether she'd been cut off. 'Mum? Are you there?'

'I'm still here. I'm trying to process it, that's all.' Her voice was small. 'You found out I was aband oning you and that you were being thrown out of your flat on the same d ay?'

And that I no longer had a job, she thought, but there was no point in ad d ing to the guilt her mum was feeling. See, this is why she had n't told her before now, because she knew what her reaction would be.

'You d id n't aband on me. It's not like I'm seventeen. I had a d ecision to make and when Betty suggested I open a bookshop—'

'Who is Betty?' her mother interrupted .

'She's an old lad y who works for Stevie.'

'Why would she tell you to open a bookshop? I'm confused .'

'It d oesn't matter who suggested it,' Kazz said hastily. 'The id ea was a good one.'

'Was it?' Diana's d oubt was plain.

'It was. The shop is d oing brilliantly, Mum. Much better than I expected . It was only going to be for a couple of months, until I had got rid of most of the books, but I've d ecid ed to keep it on. I'm going to stay in Tanglewood .' There, she'd said it.

'I think I need another gin. I've d runk this one.'

Kazz listened as her mother mad e another.

'My good ness,' Diana said , picking up her phone again. 'It's such a lot to take in. Are you living above the book-shop?'

'No, I'm staying in Stevie's flat, but if I'm going to stay here permanently, I'll have to find somewhere else. A nice little cottage perhaps.'

It was going to cost her, but she couldn't rely on Stevie's generosity forever. Stevie would need her flat back come the spring, because she let it out to holidaymakers. It was very convenient, though, being opposite the shop, so maybe Kazz could negotiate a rent that would suit her and Stevie. She had grown quite fond of the little flat.

'It sounds like you've got it all worked out,' her mother said. Her voice sounded lifeless and weary.

'I have, Mum.' Kazz was keen to assure her. But her mother could be a little more enthusiastic. She sounded as though she couldn't care less. Then Kazz found out why.

With a hitch in her voice, Diana said, 'I can't believe you kept all this to yourself. Why didn't you tell me sooner?' She sounded hurt and close to tears.

'I didn't want to worry you. You had only just gone to Spain, and if I'd told you, you would have been on the next flight back.'

'Bloody right I would have!'

'There was nothing you could have done, Mum.'

'I could have helped you find another job and I could have begged Grandad's landlord to let me keep the house on, and you could have moved in with me.'

'What about Vince? What about your new life in Spain?'

'Vince would have understood.'

'I'm sure he would. But you were so happy, Mum. I couldn't take that away from you. And everything has worked out fine in the end.'

'But you've had to carry all that worry by yourself.'

'Not all of it. I've had load s of support.'

'Stevie's a good friend,' Diana said .

Kazz had n't been referring to Stevie. Her thoughts were on Saul. 'She is.'

'We'll have to come visit you in the New Year,' her mum said . 'I can't wait to see it.'

'Tanglewood is lovely – so quaint, and the people are so friend ly. And you'll love the bookshop. I hope you d on't mind but I brought some of Grand ad 's furniture with me to use in the shop. I'm using the sid eboard as a counter.'

'That old thing? However d id you get it out of the house?'

'With a lot of swearing and a great d eal of help. I've also got Grand ad 's sid e table and chair, and the lamp from the sitting room. Oh, and his rug. And the bookcases.'

'It sound s like you've recreated his living room.'

Kazz replied softly, 'I've recreated his bookshop.'

She heard her mum sniffle d own the phone. 'He'd have been thrilled . And so proud of you. I'm d ying to see it.'

'You will,' Kazz promised .

'I'm d ying to see you, too. I can't wait to give you a cud d le.'

Kazz's eyes prickled and her chin began to wobble. She was also d esperate for a cud d le.

'Oh, no!' Diana cried . 'Your Christmas present! I sent it to your flat in Lond on.'

Kazz laughed , her cheeks d amp. 'It arrived a couple of d ays ago. I arranged to have my post red irected for a few months.'

At that, Diana burst into tears. 'I'm so blood y proud of you and I love you so much.'

'Love you too, Mum,' Kazz sobbed , relieved that her mother had taken it so well.

She had been d read ing telling her, but she was right to have waited until now. Everything had worked out for the best.

–

Saul let out a low whistle. 'You look stunning.'

Kazz d id a twirl. 'I'm glad you approve.'

He more than approved . He wanted to unzip that gorgeous d ress and carry her off to bed . The stilettos could stay on. For a while, at least.

'Let me grab my coat and we can get going,' she said .

'We could have a night in, instead ?'

The pub d id n't seem half as appealing as it had a couple of minutes ago. He had been looking forward to a lively evening in the Hen and Duck, but after seeing how gorgeous Kazz looked …

'Behave,' she told him. 'There'll be plenty of time for that later.'

'Promise?'

'Oh, yes.' She gave him a coquettish look, and he groaned .

'Stop being such a tease.'

'That's not teasing.' She moved closer and trailed her fingers along the waistband of his jeans. *This* is teasing.' The hand d ropped lower for a second before she snatched it away.

Saul groaned again. The woman was d riving him wild and she knew it. How was he supposed to get through an evening of carousing when all he wanted to d o was make love to her?

She put her coat on and picked up her bag, saying casually, 'I phoned my mum earlier. I told her about the bookshop.'

Knowing how worried she had been, he stud ied Kazz's face for clues. She was beaming, so he guessed it had gone well. 'What d id she say?'

'She can't wait to see it. She said Grand ad would be proud of me. She is, too. You would n't believe how many times I almost gave in and told her, but I'm glad I waited , otherwise there would be two of us living in this flat, and I'm not talking about you.'

'I d on't live here,' Saul pointed out.

'You practically d o. You're here almost as much as me.'

It was true. He'd only spent one night in his own bed this week.

'I'm beginning to think you may as well move in,' she said , walking toward s the d oor. Then she halted and turned a horrified face toward s him. 'I d id n't mean— I'm not suggesting—' she stammered .

He took her in his arms, not sure how to hand le this. He supposed it d epend ed on whether it had been a slip of the tongue on Kazz's part – that is, she would like him to move in but d id n't think he would go for it – or whether it had been a turn of phrase and she was mortified in case he thought she was serious.

'I know what you meant,' he said , not knowing at all.

'Thank good ness for that. I thought you'd think…' She trailed off and laughed nervously, leaving him none the wiser.

As she locked up the flat and they negotiated the spiral staircase, Saul wond ered whether it would be such a bad thing if he d id move in. He loved being with her. He could n't think of anything nicer than waking up next to her, or cud d ling together on the sofa in the evening, knowing he d id n't have to leave when the film end ed . But it would be a commitment, one he wasn't sure either of them was read y for yet.

Now wasn't the time to be consid ering such momentous and potentially life-changing things. It was Christmas Eve and he wanted to celebrate the festive season with the woman he loved .

Saul's shoe slipped on the bottom step and he had to grab the hand rail to prevent himself from falling backward s.

'Are you OK?' Kazz asked . 'Those stairs can be lethal if you're not careful.'

'I'm fine.' He slipped a hand into hers. 'That'll teach me to pay attention.'

'Ogling my bum again?' she teased . 'I'm surprised you can see it with this coat on.'

Saul d id n't like to tell her that the reason he had n't been paying attention was because the notion had popped into his head that he was in love with her.

Ad mitted ly, he liked her one hell of a lot. But? Was it possible to fall in love without realising it? And was it possible to fall in love with someone after just a few weeks?

Might he just be in lust?

As they strolled up the high street, Kazz chatting about her d ay, Saul tried to analyse his feelings, asking himself what his reaction would be if she was to end it now.

The resulting bolt of pain in his heart at the mere thought of such a thing was all the answer he need ed . He would be heartbroken.

'Hmm, that's nice,' he murmured absently, in response to something she said .

Kazz huffed . 'You're not listening, are you?'

'What?' He forced himself to concentrate. 'Sorry, I was thinking about what I'd like to d o to you later.' He gave her what he hoped was a sexy, suggestive smile.

'Your mind is only ever on one thing,' she grumbled good -natured ly. 'Don't you ever think of anything else?'

'Food ?'

'Typical! Food and sex. You're such a bloke!'

'Guilty as charged .'

'I suppose you're into football as well.'

'Rugby.'

'Same d ifference.'

'It most d efinitely is not!' Saul objected . 'Would you like me to explain?'

'God , no!' Kazz shud d ered .

Saul was happy that she had n't d elved any d eeper into why he had n't been paying attention and the conversation had moved on. He wanted to keep the knowled ge that he had fallen in love with her to himself for a while. Maybe forever. He'd have to see how it went. He could n't assume she loved him in return, and there was no way he would tell her, not without some certainty that Kazz felt the same.

Then again, Joelle had professed to love him, and look how that had turned out. He still could n't believe she'd wanted to have lunch with him for old times' sake. He guessed she d id n't have the slightest inkling how bad ly she had hurt him.

It was a good thing he had messaged her to tell her that he could n't meet her for lunch after all. He'd said he was too busy right now. Her reaction had been a sad face emoji, but as she had left it at that, he was hopeful it was the end of the matter.

There was one thing he was grateful for, however: seeing her again had made him realise he was over her. And falling in love with someone else had confirmed it.

Determined to enjoy this evening, Saul shoved all thoughts of love and relationships to the back of his mind. There would be time enough to decide what he was going to do about this new complication in his life. For now, he was going to enjoy Christmas.

Chapter 23

Kazz stared at the presents sitting und erneath her tree on Christmas morning and prayed that Saul's family would like them. She had alread y swapped gifts with Stevie and Ed ie, and knowing that Stevie would be seeing Tia at some point tod ay, she had given her Tia's present to pass on. Which left Leanne, Saul's parents and Saul himself.

She had n't been sure whether to get Saul anything, not entirely certain what their relationship was. They simply had n't spoken about it.

In the end , she had chosen something personal – but not too personal: an engraved flask for when he was out and about on the farm, plus a new beanie. The d ecision to give his parents a gift had been easier to make, consid ering she was spend ing Christmas Day with them. But it had also been hard er to choose something because she wasn't sure what they liked .

She had settled on a bottle of the wimberry whisky for Geoff, which she had bought on the visit to the d istillery, and a bottle of blackberry brand y for Iris, after Saul had mentioned that his mother sometimes liked a brand y after a meal if they went out to eat. Kazz had also bought a huge selection of cheeses and biscuits to go with it.

Saul was rooting around in the kitchen and had been for the past half an hour, and she wond ered what he was d oing. He'd informed her he intend ed to make them both a special Christmas Day breakfast, but it sounded as though he was raiding her cupboards and throwing everything on the floor.

'Are you OK in there?' she called. He had expressly told her not to come in, but she was starting to get a little concerned.

'Yeah, I'm good. Give me two seconds.'

Kazz perched on the sofa and turned the TV on, finding a festive film to watch while she waited for her breakfast.

True to his word, Saul emerged shortly after, bearing a tray. On it sat what looked like a pancake in the shape of Rudolph's head. It even had antlers, with raisins for its eyes and a strawberry for its nose. The tray also held a cup of tea and a present.

The gift was beautifully wrapped, and she wondered whether he had done it himself. She also wondered what was in it.

'Breakfast first,' Saul warned as she reached for the present.

He popped back into the kitchen and emerged with a second tray, and Kazz began to eat, hardly taking her eyes off the present, except for shooting Saul quick glances.

Curiosity gnawed at her. The present was small, about the size of a square Post-it note, and about three centimetres high.

Might it contain a piece of jewellery?

When she'd eaten the last morsel of pancake, Saul finally relented, although he insisted on taking their breakfast things back into the kitchen first, before coming back in and settling down next to her.

'Go on, open it,' he urged.

Carefully, Kazz removed the ribbon and put it to one side. Then she unpicked one end of a piece of Sellotape and eased the paper open to reveal a white box with silver writing.

Recognising it as the name of a jewellery shop in Abergavenny, Kazz became apprehensive. What if he'd bought her something expensive, and all she was giving him was a flask?

Her worry faded when she saw what lay inside. A silver necklace, the pendant in the shape of an open book, gleamed up at her.

'It's lovely!' she cried, taking it out and turning it over in her hands. 'Whenever I wear it, I shall think of you.'

'In that case, I hope you never take it off,' Saul murmured, taking the necklace out of her hands.

Kazz swivelled around to offer the back of her neck for him to put it on her.

A kiss on the soft skin underneath her ear made her squirm, but she was determined not to give in to his unspoken suggestion they return to bed. His parents were expecting them in a couple of hours, and she wanted to shower and take her time getting ready.

As it turned out, she did end up having to hurry if they didn't want to be late...

–

Christmas was a time for families, and although Saul guessed Kazz must miss spending it with her mum, she seemed to be having a nice time with him and his family. At least, he hoped she was.

Leanne, Rex, Murray and Ashley had joined them for lunch, and the eight of them had enjoyed an incredibly lovely meal. Kazz had also met his old er brother Stuart and his wife Lisa, and their three child ren (whom Saul ad ored), when they called in later, and everyone had a fun afternoon playing charad es and other games. His other brother Martin and his wife, Janine, were absent because they were spend ing the d ay with Janine's mum, but he guessed that Kazz would probably meet them at some point, and it d id mean that she had n't had to contend with all the Greens at once. Saul knew it could get a bit rowd y when all five siblings, plus their respective partners and kid s, were in the same room.

When it grew d ark, Saul's d ad levered himself out of the chair and announced that he was going for a final check around the farm. It was a routine that was d one every evening, ensuring that shed s were locked , gates were closed and the animals were where they should be. The d ogs also need ed feed ing and a poorly sheep could d o wi fresh bed d ing.

Saul helped his d ad prepare the food for the d ogs, slipping some morsels of the d arker turkey meat into his pocket as a treat for them when his father's back was turned .

He left Kazz in the living room, d iscussing fashion with Leanne, Lisa and his mum, and he could hear Leanne busily arranging for her and Kazz to go to the January sales on the d ay after Boxing Day.

Good luck, he thought; he would n't be caught d ead near any shops d uring sale time. He heard Card iff mentioned and shud d ered . The city would be heaving and there probably would n't be much worth buying anyway.

Rex and Stuart had retreated to the kitchen with a couple of bottles of pale ale, a pack of card s and a determination not to lose, while keeping an eye on the kids who were starting to flag after the ungodly hour they'd forced their parents to get up.

Saul was no stranger to early mornings, but he didn't fancy being railroaded out of bed by three excited children and a snowstorm of wrapping paper.

Talking of snowstorms, flakes were drifting lazily from a full sky and seemed to be sticking.

'Stuart and Lisa had better make a move soon,' Saul pointed out. 'So had I, unless you fancy putting Kazz up for the night?'

'You and she seem pretty close,' his dad said, as they let the dogs out for a final run around after they had scoffed their suppers. 'Are you serious about this one?'

Saul considered his response. 'I think I am.'

'Good. It's about time. Your mother and I were beginning to think you'd never settle down.'

Saul chuckled. 'Hang on, Dad, it's early days yet. We've only known each other a couple of months.' It wasn't even that.

'So? I knew I wanted to marry your mother within the first five minutes of meeting her.'

Saul was incredulous. 'You fell in love that fast?'

'No, her dad had a brand-new Massey Ferguson. All shiny and red, it was. If I wanted that tractor, I was going to have to marry her to get my hands on it. Oh, and he had a farm, of course.'

Saul rolled his eyes. 'I don't for one minute believe you married Mum because her parents owned a farm.' Saul's maternal grandparents had two children, a boy and a girl, but the boy, Saul's uncle, had died before Mum and Dad met, so Mum had stood to inherit the farm when Granny and Gramps passed on.

For many years the two generations had lived in this very house and farmed the land together. And two generations had become three when the kids had come along. Saul, his brothers and his sister had been devastated when Gramps died, then Granny a couple of years later.

'If I didn't marry your mother for the farm, then what else could it be but love at first sight?' Geoff countered. 'Because it's true: I did know I was going to marry your mother the first time we met, if she'd have me. I left it a while before I proposed, though, as I didn't want her to think I was a total nutcase.'

'She knows now, though, right?'

'Cheeky bugger.' Geoff scowled. 'What I'm trying to say is, love doesn't have a set of rules. If you love her, it doesn't matter whether you fall in love the minute you clap eyes on her, or whether it takes years to grow. Love is love.'

Saul was astounded. He didn't think he had ever heard his dad speak like that before. He wasn't a chat-about-emotions man. He tended to be gruff and rather reserved, although he did call a spade a spade.

'Bloody hell, Dad, that's profound.'

'I can be serious when I need to be,' Geoff replied.

'You're jumping the gun a bit. We're not at the love-declaration stage yet.'

'You don't have to *say* something for it to be true.'

Wow, that had got heavy fast. Saul whistled to the dogs. It was time to head back inside. The conversation was making him feel uncomfortable, so to cover his embarrassment (and the fact that his dad was right), he said, 'Who are you and what have you done with my dad?'

'Just speaking the truth, boy,' Geoff said. 'It's as plain as day that you think the world of her.'

'But does she think the world of me?' Saul countered.

'You're going to have to work that one out for yourself. Women baffle me.'

'You're not the only one.'

'Speaking of women, we'd better get back indoors before your mother sends out a search party.'

With the outbuildings checked and the snow now falling more heavily, Saul and his dad made their way back to the house.

They entered the warmth of the kitchen, stamping their feet and blowing on their hands. Iris was making sandwiches, and her eyes widened when she saw the snowflakes daubing their shoulders.

'Don't tell me it's snowing,' she said. 'I'm making tea for everyone. Is it coming down heavily?'

Saul hung up his and his father's coats as Geoff said, 'Not yet, but the sky looks full of it. We'll have time for a bit of tea, but after that everyone should get off home.'

Iris squared her shoulders and Saul smiled. His mum was a farmer's wife through and through – she would n't let a bit of weather prevent her from feeding her family. 'I'd better get a move on, then. Geoff, butter that lot. Saul, get the sausage rolls out of the fridge. And don't forget the pickles and chutney.'

He did as instructed, but he could n't help saying, 'You do realise we're all still stuffed from lunch?'

'Nonsense. There's always room for a turkey, cranberry and stuffing sandwich, and a slice of yule log.'

Now she came to mention it, he could probably manage a mouthful or two...

The food was laid out on the kitchen table for everyone to help themselves, while his mum was on tea, coffee and squash duty (the squash was for the children), and his dad was told to make alcoholic d rinks for those who weren't d riving.

'I feel so guilty about you not being able to have a d rink,' Kazz said , sid ling up to him and slipping her hand around his waist.

He shrugged . 'I can have one when we get back to yours.' He reached for a sand wich and said casually, 'I assume I'm staying the night?'

'I would be d isappointed if you d id n't.'

Either his mum had been listening or she had been thinking along the same lines, because she said , 'Why d oesn't Kazz stay here tonight? It'll save you having to d rive in the snow, and you can have a beer or two.'

Saul was happy enough for Kazz to stay, but would she want to? He raised a questioning eyebrow.

Kazz's expression was one of faint alarm. 'I haven't got any night things, or a change of clothes for the morning.'

Iris said , 'I'm sure we can d ig out some PJs of Leanne's, and a pair of leggings and a jumper for you to wear tomorrow. I'll leave it to you, no obligation, but Geoff and I would love for you to stay.'

Saul waited until his mum was in conversation with Lisa before he said , 'Sorry she hijacked you like that. Please d on't feel obliged to stay. We can eat this and go back to yours before the weather gets any worse.' Bend ing his head , he whispered in her ear, 'We could watch a film and cud d le on the sofa.'

'What d o you usually d o on Christmas night?' she asked .

'I d on't cud d le on the sofa, although we usually watch a film. Mum has got load s of Christmas ones record ed , *Home Alone*, and so on.'

'So you spend it here, with your family?'

'Er, yeah, I suppose I d o.'

'Then that's what we'll d o tonight,' she said firmly, then hesitated . 'Will I be sleeping in your bed ?'

Saul's gaze met hers and he bit his lip to keep the teasing smile in. 'I think you should , d on't you? Otherwise Mum will think I'm twelve years old and I'm having a sleepover.'

Her eyes wid ened . 'But she'll think—'

'That we're a couple?'

She nod d ed , uncertainty on her face.

Saul took a breath to stead y himself. Stand ing in the mid d le of his parents' kitchen, next to a table lad en with food and surround ed by his family, who kept jostling them as they reached for a pork pie, was not how he'd imagined this conversation to take place.

'Isn't that what we are?' he asked her gently.

Her expression was solemn. 'I'd hoped we are.'

'Then we are,' he confirmed , his relief acute. For a moment he had been worried she d id n't think so.

A slow smile spread across her lips, lighting up her face with such rad iance that it took his breath away.

If they had been alone, he might have been tempted to utter those three little word s. But they weren't, so he'd save them for another d ay. Anyway, it was probably sensible to take it one step at a time – because telling Kazz he loved her would be a very big step ind eed .

Chapter 24

When Kazz woke on Boxing Day morning, she kept her eyelids closed and snuggled deeper under the covers, revelling in the warmth. Her bed was super comfy and —

Her eyes shot open as the realisation she had spent the night in Saul's parents' house flooded through her. She had expected it to be rather awkward, but it had been anything but.

After Leanne, Rex, Stuart, Lisa and the children had gone home, Iris had made deliciously creamy hot chocolates, plonked a bowl of nuts on a side table within easy reach, and put on one of the films she had recorded. When Kazz saw that it was *It's a Wonderful Life*, she smiled at Saul, blushing as she recalled their first kiss.

Soon after the film ended, Iris and Geoff went to bed, leaving Kazz and Saul snuggling on the sofa. Saul had poured them both a whisky, then he'd turned off the lamp and opened the curtains, and they had watched the steadily falling snow until tiredness had overcome them and they'd gone to bed.

She had fallen asleep in his arms and woke up in them this morning, thinking how lucky she was. Yesterday had been almost perfect. The only way it could have been better was if her mum had been there, but Iris and Geoff had made her feel so incredibly welcome that she almost felt part of the family.

As she lay there, enjoying the lie-in, Kazz gazed through the open curtains out onto the hillside above the farm.

The world outside was white.

She tried not to disturb Saul as she extricated herself from his embrace, but it was impossible. His arms tightened around her as he opened his eyes and smiled.

'Stay here,' he said, nuzzling her neck.

'It's been snowing!' She wriggled out of bed. 'Can we go play in it?' She didn't care that she sounded like a big kid. She didn't get to see snow like this very often, if ever. And as she pressed her nose against the glass, she marvelled at how pristine everything looked. The snow was so white that it hurt her eyes.

Abruptly, Saul sat up. 'Bugger. What's the time?' He didn't wait for an answer, scrambling out of bed instead, and feeling on the floor for his phone.

'What's wrong?' Kazz asked, beginning to feel alarmed.

'I'm late. There are animals to feed and jobs to be done.' He grabbed a pair of overalls and gave her a kiss. 'Sorry, I've got to love you and leave you; work on a farm doesn't stop because it's a bank holiday. I'll try to be as quick as I can.'

'No need to rush,' she said as he hurried towards the door. 'Can I do anything to help?'

'You go have some breakfast and stay warm. We'll play in the snow later.' He closed the door behind him, and she heard him head towards the bathroom.

A short while later, Kazz self-consciously wandered into the kitchen, following the smell of coffee. She was dressed in an oversized jumper that reached to her thighs and a pair of thick black leggings. Iris had even given her a brand -new packet of knickers and a pair of fluffy socks. The socks had Christmas pud d ings on them.

'Morning, sleepyhead ,' Iris said , on seeing her.

Kazz immed iately felt guilty. Iris had probably been up for hours. 'I d id n't mean to stay in bed this long,' she apologised .

It was only eight fifty-five, but since Kazz had opened the bookshop, lazing around in bed in the mornings had n't been an option, except on Sund ays. And not even then, if Saul spent the Saturd ay night with her, as he had to be out early to start his chores on the farm.

'Nonsense,' Iris said . 'It's your d ay off. You are entitled to get up late. Tea or coffee?'

'Coffee, please. I'm assuming you've been up for ages.'

'I always get up when Geoff d oes. The bed is too lonely without him in it.'

Kazz d id n't know where to put herself; she d id n't want to imagine Iris and Geoff in bed , thanks! On the other hand , it was rather sweet. Despite being married for God knows how many years, they were still in love.

'Anyway,' Iris continued , putting a mug of black coffee on the table next to a bowl of sugar and a small jug of milk that she'd taken out of the frid ge. 'I've always got jobs of my own to get on with – a never-end ing list of them.'

Kazz said , 'I asked Saul if I could d o anything to help, but he told me to stay ind oors.'

'He was right to, it's bitter out there. It might be pretty to look at, but it's harsh up on the mountain.'

'Is that where Saul and Geoff have gone?'

'Not to the top, because we've brought the sheep into the field s for the winter, but it's higher up than the farm.'

Kazz sipped her coffee and thought about Saul. He was far more complex than she had realised when she first met him all those weeks ago, and over this past d ay or so she had seen a d ifferent sid e to him again. Lothario or not, he was hard -working, thoughtful and ad ored his family. He was also practical and good with his hand s (she steered away from *just* how good he was), yet he enjoyed read ing and loved nothing more than to lose himself in a book.

The more she got to know him, the hard er she was falling for him.

Kazz sighed ruefully*Falling?* She had alread y fallen.

Despite her best intentions, she had fallen in love with Saul Green. She might have known that once she let him into her bed , she would invariably let him into her heart.

And it felt fantastic!

Kazz became aware that Saul's mum was stud ying her, and she squirmed in her seat.

Iris pulled out a chair and sat d own, clasping her hand s on the table in front of her. 'Do you mind if I'm frank with you?'

'Not at all,' Kazz replied , wond ering what she was about to say.

'You're the first girl he's brought home to meet us, but before I read anything into that, I wanted to check it's not just because you're a friend of Leanne's.'

Gosh, how was she supposed to answer that? 'I think he might have felt sorry for me, being on my own at Christmas,' she said .

'It's not that. You could have gone to Stevie and Nick's, but Saul wanted you to have d inner with us. And we're d elighted you d id . It's been lovely having you.'

'Thanks. I've enjoyed it, too.' She wasn't enjoying this part quite as much, though. What was Iris getting at? Was she warning her off her son, or welcoming her into the family?

Iris rubbed her hand s together, the knuckles turning white. 'I wanted to ask if it's serious between the pair of you. And before you answer, let me say I will be d elighted if it is.' Her face turned pink and she d ropped her gaze.

Kazz felt flushed too, and it had nothing to d o with the heat belting out of the Aga. 'We've not known each other long,' she hed ged .

'But you d o like him?' Iris persisted , looking up.

'I d o.'

'Good .' Saul's mum blew out her cheeks. 'I was beginning to worry. You see, he can't keep a girlfriend for love nor money. He's always out on a d ate with this one or that one, but they never seem to come to anything. Leanne says he's nothing more than a tomcat, picking them up and d ropping them just as quick, but I can't see it myself. I reckon he gets d umped as much as he d umps – if you know what I mean. He can get girls easily enough, he just can't hang on to them.' Iris paused , her eyes bright. 'I'm hoping he'll hang on to you. Geoff and I both are.'

Kazz was d umbstruck. Iris clearly d id n't have a clue about Saul's reputation and Kazz d id n't intend to be the one to enlighten her. And neither d id she want to d iscuss how she felt about Saul with his mother! Still, it was nice to be given the seal of approval. She had heard so many tales of mothers-in-law from hell. Take Tia, for instance… Although her friend had finally seemed to have reached an und erstand ing with Lad y Tonbrid ge. It was nice to know Kazz would be accepted by Iris and Geoff, if it ever came to it.

And perhaps it might, because if she was the only woman he had taken to meet his parents, then he must feel something for her.

Mustn't he?

'Is that what I think it is?' Kazz demanded later that morning. She was staring incredulously at the wooden contraption that Saul was holding.

'We're going sledging,' he announced grandly.

The sledge looked like it had been made out of old pallets. A slatted seat was attached to a pair of carved runners. Saul held a rope that was secured to the front. The sledge didn't look particularly safe, or fast – although it was probably a good thing if it was slower than a slug crossing a road.

'There's only one sledge,' she pointed out.

'We only need one.'

'I'm not going to go down the Cresta Run on my own, even if you are waiting to catch me at the bottom,' she warned.

'You won't be going down on your own. We'll be going down together.'

'On the same sledge? We both won't fit on.'

'We will. You sit in front, and I'll sit at the back and steer.'

'You can steer this thing?' She stared doubtfully at the rope.

Saul followed her gaze. 'That's not for steering,' he said. 'That's for dragging it up the hill.'

'Which hill?'

Saul pointed to the slope above the farm. He was grinning like an idiot.

'We're going up *there*?'

'Not too far, only a hundred metres or so.'

'That's far enough.' A lot could happen in a hundred metres. They could fall off, for a start.

261

'It's just about right,' he said . 'The slope is steep enough to build up a good head of steam, but it levels off so the sledge can slow down before it goes into the fence.'

'What if it doesn't slow down enough and *does* go into the fence?'

'We'll have jumped clear before then. But don't worry, that's never happened .'

'There's always a first time,' she muttered , not relishing the thought of flinging herself off a moving object to land in wet snow. 'How *do* you steer this thing?'

'Come on, I'll show you.' Saul took her mittened hand and began to tow her, and the sledge, up the snow-covered hill.

Kazz had borrowed a thick puffer jacket from Iris (her coat having been deemed unsuitable for traipsing around in the snow on a Welsh hillside), and she was sweating when she reached what Saul alarmingly referred to as the 'jump-off point'. Kazz had no intention of jumping off anywhere.

She was seriously considering telling him to go ahead and that she would walk down and meet him at the bottom, when Saul lined up the sledge so it faced down the hill and straddled it with both legs, holding it in place. She noticed he kept a firm grip on the rope.

'You get on first and I'll get on behind you,' he said . 'Don't worry, I won't let you fall off.'

She wasn't worried he would let her. She was worried that falling off would be an inevitability, no matter what he did .

Gingerly, she clambered onto the death-trap (sorry, *sledge*) and lowered her bottom slowly onto the seat. The wood was cold , and she winced . Now that she had stopped walking, she was starting to chill.

She felt Saul get into position behind her and his arms came around her waist to grip her tight. But d espite his solid , strong presence at her back, Kazz wasn't convinced this could end in anything other than traged y.

'Read y?' he asked .

Her 'No!' turned into a shriek as he pushed off and the sled ge began to move.

This isn't so bad, she thought as it slid slowly d own the hill, but even as the thought went through her mind , the horrid contraption began to pick up speed and within second s it was hurtling d own the slope faster than a boy racer on a d ual carriageway.

The speed of the wind in her face nearly tore the bobble hat from her head , and the sled ge's runners sent flurries of snow into the air to wet her cheeks and land in her open, screaming, terrified mouth.

'Argh!' she yelled as the fence rapid ly grew nearer and nearer, and —

Without warning, Saul threw his bod y to the sid e, taking Kazz with him, and the sled ge kinked to the left.

She thought they were going to come off, but instead the sled ge began to slow.

But it d id n't slow enough. The fence was still rushing toward s them and she simply knew they were going to hit it.

Kazz closed her eyes and prayed *Please, please, please…*

They'd stopped . The sled ge had come to a halt about ten metres short of the fence.

'Whoop! Whoop!' Saul yelled .

In d isbelief, Kazz sat there. They had n't crashed head - long into the fence. They were alive and unhurt.

'I want to go again,' she announced , and she scooted around to kiss Saul sound ly on the lips.

When she finally released him, he said, 'I told you it would be fun, did n't I?'

After a couple more goes, they returned to the house, cold but happy. Then his mum insisted on Saul and Kazz staying for lunch – which consisted of bubble and squeak, and leftover turkey, with a huge slice of Christmas cake for afters – before they eventually made their way back to the village and Kazz's flat.

After a hot bath (it had been a bit of a squeeze with both of them in the tub, not to mention the watery mess on the floor) they wrapped themselves in fluffy towels, and Kazz curled up on the sofa, tucking her feet underneath her. She'd had such a lovely day, and although it was still early, she was ready to cuddle with Saul in front of the TV and vegetate until bed time.

'It's been a great Christmas,' Saul said, sitting next to her. His hair was damp and he smelled of soap.

He lifted his arm up and she shuffled across to snuggle into his side, putting her head on his shoulder and letting out a contented sigh.

'It has,' she agreed. 'I've had a lovely time. Thank you so much for inviting me.'

'You're welcome.' He kissed the top of her head.

'I don't think I'll be long out of bed tonight,' she said, and he sniggered.

'That's good. Being in bed with you is my favourite pastime.'

'I'll have to get *some* sleep,' she warned. 'I'm going to Cardiff with your sister tomorrow.'

'I don't envy you. I'd prefer to muck out the sheep shed than go anywhere near a shop on the first day of the sales.'

'It's lucky you aren't coming with us, then, isn't it?' She laughed and snuggled d eeper into his sid e. 'I'm sure me and Leanne will have a lovely d ay.'

Chapter 25

The last thing Saul wanted was to meet Joelle for lunch today, but when she'd sent him a message this morning, she had n't been wishing him a happy Christmas. She wanted to see him today, as planned , because she had something important to tell him.

So it appeared that Saul *would* be going near some shops after all, in the centre of Hereford , having lunch with Joelle. It d id cross his mind to refuse, because what could she possibly have to say that was so important? And why would she imagine he would be interested ? She was hard ly going to announce that she had mad e a mistake all those years ago and that seeing him on the d ay of the Christmas festival had mad e her realise she still loved him. And even if she d id , Saul now knew he was over her. He suspected that he had been over her for a while, but had n't realised it because he had mad e his mind up that his heart had been broken and he had been d etermined never to allow it to happen again by keeping every woman he had d ated at arm's length.

Find ing the restaurant where they were to have lunch, he hesitated outsid e. It wasn't too late to abort the meeting. There was nothing Joelle could say to him that he might consid er important, but his curiosity overcame his reluctance. He would hear what she had to say, and then he'd leave, after making it clear there would n't be another meeting.

Although he arrived d ead on time, Joelle, typically, was late. It had been an annoying trait of hers, and he had forgotten how much it used to irritate him. He had been so besotted with her that he invariably used to cast his irritation asid e.

Looking back, he und erstood he had allowed her to walk all over him.

He would wait ten minutes, he d ecid ed , as he was shown to a table near the wind ow, and if she had n't arrived by then, he would leave. Her tard iness implied that her time was more valuable than his, and he resented that. It was bad enough that she had d ragged him all this way without telling him why, and now she had the temerity to keep him waiting.

A frisson in the air alerted him to her presence as she breezed into the restaurant, and he smiled ruefully at her ability to turn male head s. She had n't lost her magnetism, which was a combination of attractiveness plus haughty self-confid ence. Immaculately d ressed in a red pantsuit and high-heeled boots, she shucked off her coat and hand ed it to a hovering waiter without looking at the poor man, who took it, open-mouthed .

Joelle had always been a bit of a d iva, but she was even more of one now, Saul realised .

He remained seated at the table, not rising when she moved in for a d ouble-cheeked kiss.

His lack of manners d id n't appear to bother her.

'Have you been here long?' she asked , snapping her fingers to attract the waiter's attention. She need n't have d one so, because the poor bloke had n't been able to take his eyes off her.

'Long enough.' Saul's reply was gruff.

'Don't be grumpy, Saul. I wasn't late on purpose. What would you like to d rink? Have whatever you fancy – my treat. I'll put it on expenses.'

'Water, please,' he said to the waiter.

Joelle arched a perfectly shaped eyebrow at him. 'Really?' She shrugged . 'Make that two. Bottled . With bubbles.' When the waiter left, she said , 'If it's fizzy I can at least pretend it's something more exciting.'

'What is it you want to tell me?' Saul asked . He wasn't in the mood for small talk.

'Let's ord er first, shall we? I'm starving. I've been on the shop floor all morning.'

'The shop floor?'

'Yes. Don't you know? I'm the area manager for Rosy Glow, and with the January sales starting tod ay, the store is incred ibly busy.'

'Rosy Glow?'

'Cosmetics? You must have heard of it.' She narrowed her eyes. 'Maybe not. Never mind , you soon will. We're opening a branch in Tanglewood .' Joelle seemed very pleased with herself.

'Is that what you wanted to tell me?'

The waiter appeared with their d rinks.

'I think I'll have the baked celeriac.' Joelle had n't bothered to look at the menu and Saul guessed she had eaten here before.

Saul d id n't care what he ate, so he d id n't bother looking at the menu either. 'I'll have the same,' he said .

Ord er placed , Saul was keen to return to the d iscussion. 'Is that what you wanted to tell me?' he repeated .

'Not all of it, no. How is Leanne?'

'You asked me that the last time we spoke, and I told you she was fine.'

'I meant personally, not professionally. Is she married or seeing someone?'

'She lives with her boyfriend , Rex.'

'Child ren?'

'Not yet.'

'How about your brothers?'

'What's with the twenty questions?'

'Just trying to make conversation. I must say, Saul, you never used to be this rud e.'

'That was before you—' He broke off, aghast at how close he'd come to letting her know she had broken his heart.

She reached across the table and Saul snatched his hand away.

Her expression was sympathetic. 'I'm sorry I hurt you so bad ly.'

'You d id n't.' The lie was stiff and wood en.

She wasn't fooled ; her gaze was full of contrition.

Neither of them acknowled ged the waiter as he placed their meals on the table.

'It's good to see you again, Saul. I could n't believe my eyes when I walked into that bookshop. For a minute there, I thought you'd taken up a new career.'

Saul gritted his teeth. Why would n't she get to the point and tell him what she thought was so important that she had to tell him to his face. 'Say what you've got to say.' He had no id ea what game she was playing, but his patience was growing thin.

'I d id care about you…' Joelle's voice was soft.

'Not enough.'

'No, not enough,' she agreed . 'But I hope we can move past that. I d on't want there to be any awkward ness between us because I'm going to be in Tanglewood a fair bit soon. As I said , Rosy Glow is opening a new branch in the village and I'll be supervising the refit, recruitment, and so on. I wanted to tell you in person.' She pulled a face. 'I know things end ed bad ly between us and I know you were more invested in the relationship than me. I'm sorry for that, but I could n't help how I felt. I was ambitious… Tanglewood was too small. It wasn't enough.'

Just like I hadn't been enough, he thought. 'You moved to Hereford , not Milan or New York. You could have commuted .'

'It would n't have worked , Saul.' She reached across the table again, and this time he let her place her hand over his. She was right, it would n't have worked . She had n't loved him enough to make their relationship work.

'It's a sixty-minute commute each way,' she was saying. 'And I was working long hours. We would have hard ly seen one another. It wasn't practical. Which is the reason I'm moving back to Tanglewood for the next three months, so I can oversee the new shop opening properly, without spend ing a rid iculous amount of time on the road . We're going to be seeing quite a bit more of each other, Saul.' She stared d eep into his eyes as she ad d ed , 'How much, is up to you.'

–

'Blood y trains,' Leanne muttered for what seemed like the twenty-sixth time.

'It d oesn't matter,' Kazz soothed . 'We can still have a fun d ay out.'

Leaves on the line, a mouse on the track, an impassable snowflake – the rail service had n't given a reason for the trains from Abergavenny to Card iff being cancelled , and when Leanne had enquired at the tiny ticket office, the lad y had n't had any id ea when they would start running again. Faced with the choice of aband oning their shopping trip, d riving to Card iff or changing d estination, they had opted to hop on the next train to Hereford instead , consid ering it was d ue in five minutes and would take less than half an hour to get there.

Kazz had been expecting a town similar in size to Abergavenny, but she was surprised at how much larger Hereford was. It even had a cathed ral. And from what she could see, the ped estrianised main street had a fair number of popular chain stores, where everything was very samey. After living in Tanglewood , with its small, quirky, privately owned shops, Kazz wasn't as interested in the big retailers as she used to be.

'I'm surprised you wanted to go shopping at all, consid ering you spend a couple of d ays a month in Lond on,' Kazz joked . 'Could n't you find what you wanted there?'

'I could , but it's no fun shopping on my own.' Leanne linked her arm through Kazz's. 'Let's go try some stuff on, then have lunch. I'm after a new d ress for Hogmanay.'

'Oh yes, you're off up to Scotland for New Year.' Iris had mentioned it on Christmas Day. Rex was Scottish and they were visiting his parents for New Year.

'We're flying,' Leanne said excited ly. 'I haven't flown anywhere for ages. And they've got *snow*.'

'*We've* got snow,' Kazz pointed out.

'Not like Scotland has. We've got a couple of centi-metres at most in the village, although I know the hillsid es have more. Where Rex's parents live, they've got a couple of feet! Ooh, let's go in here.' She steered Kazz into a clothes shop and started going through the racks of dresses.

Kazz thought she might as well have a look, considering she was here, and it wasn't long before the pair of them had taken an armful of clothes into the fitting room.

'I like this one,' Leanne said, emerging from the cubicle and doing a twirl. The dress was electric blue, with a fitted waist and an A-line skirt reaching to below her knees. She looked lovely.

'Buy it,' Kazz urged. 'It looks good on you.'

'But what if I see something else I like?'

'You might not, though. If you don't buy it and then decide to come back for it, Sod's Law it'll be gone.'

'You're right. And if I do see something else, I might treat myself to that as well. I haven't bought anything new in ages. Are you getting any of the ones you tried on?'

Kazz wanted to, but she thought it best to save her money. If she was going to start looking for a more permanent place to live, she would need money for furniture. Thankfully, the deposit she had paid for her share of the flat in London had gone back into her bank account, so that would hopefully cover a deposit on a new place, plus the first month's rent.

Maybe she and Saul could have a look at some properties online this evening? Or maybe not. She didn't want him to think she was hinting at them moving in together.

'I need shoes to go with this dress,' Leanne declared, after she'd paid for it and they'd left the shop. 'I can't believe how painless that was. I normally go in every shop at least once, and never find anything. I'll go shopping with you again! You must be my lucky charm.'

Several shops and a great many pairs of shoes later, Leanne was starting to flag. 'I take back what I said about you being lucky.' She gave Kazz a friend ly elbow in the ribs.

Kazz elbowed her back. 'I bet you wish you'd come on your own now.'

'Definitely not. Shall we have a spot of lunch? I could d o with a sit-d own.'

'What d o you mean?' Kazz chuckled . 'You've been sitting d own trying shoes on for the past hour.'

'My feet hurt.'

'I'm not surprised . Those last ones you tried on were rather high,' Kazz pointed out. 'I've seen less tall skyscrapers. What were they? Four inches?'

'Five, I think.'

'No wond er your feet hurt! Are you thinking of a proper restaurant or a cafe for lunch?'

'Don't mind . You choose. You're the chef.'

'Not anymore – I'm a bookseller now. Cafe, I think. What about d own there?' The sid e street boasted at least two that Kazz could see, and a restaurant.

She had her sights set on a place on the opposite pavement, and as they head ed toward s the zebra crossing, Kazz automatically glanced into the restaurant on the other sid e of the road . It was rather bougie and was about two-third s full, so the food must be OK.

She was about to change her mind and suggest they eat there instead of at the cafe, when she saw a familiar face.

No, it couldn't be.

Saul was in Tanglewood . He had told her he would be busy repairing a something or other. He'd mentioned a piece of machinery, but she could n't remember what it was called or what it was supposed to d o.

And why the hell was she thinking about bloody machinery when Saul was having lunch with the woman she had seen talking to him in the bookshop on the day of the Christmas festival?

'Come on,' Leanne urged. The traffic had stopped to allow them to cross, but Kazz couldn't move.

Her feet were glued to the pavement in shock, and she couldn't take her eyes off Saul and the woman.

'Are you OK?' Leanne asked. 'We're holding people up.' She pulled Kazz back from the kerb, calling, 'Sorry!' to the cars that were waiting. Then she said to her, 'What's wrong? Why did n't you—?'

Kazz pointed, and Leanne stopped talking and followed the direction of her finger.

'Is that…?' Leanne moved a step closer to the kerb. 'It can't be.' She gasped. *It is!* And that's…*Oh, shit. He's with Joelle Lawson.*'

Kazz dragged her gaze away from Saul and the woman. They were staring lovingly at each other across the table. He had n't looked away from her face once, and he seemed oblivious to anyone else's existence.

Kazz found her voice. *Who* is Joelle Lawson?'

She was aware Leanne was staring at her, and when she looked at her friend, there was pity in her eyes as she said, 'Joelle is the woman who broke Saul's heart.'

–

'Tell me everything,' Kazz demanded.

They had given the cafe a miss and found a pub, Leanne insisting Kazz had a brandy for the shock.

Kazz had asked for a whisky instead and sat nursing it, not able to bring herself to taste it now that it was in her hands because it reminded her of Saul.

Leanne was on orange juice and tonic water because she would be driving them back to Tanglewood from Abergavenny station later.

'I have a good mind to march in there and ask him what he thinks he's doing,' Leanne growled. 'The stupid f—'

'Can you please tell me?' Kazz was trying not to cry, and so far, she was succeeding but it was a close-run thing, and not knowing was tearing her apart.

'I thought he was over her,' Leanne began, 'but I'm afraid I might be wrong.'

Kazz's eyes bored into her friend, willing her to carry on and, after downing half her orange juice as if it contained something stronger, Leanne continued.

'Her father was in the army. The family moved to Tanglewood because he was based near Brecon. Believe it or not, my brother hadn't had many girlfriends before her. Don't get me wrong, he liked girls but he was more interested in sport – rugby especially – and having a laugh with his mates. Joelle swept him off his feet. He's never admitted it, but I think she was his first love.'

'Great.' Kazz knocked back the whisky, slamming the tumbler onto the table. 'I think I'm going to need another.' Shaking, she went to the bar and ordered a double. When she sat down again, she asked, 'Why did they split up?'

'I don't know. All I heard was that she had been offered a job for some up-and-coming cosmetics company and the next thing she had moved to Hereford.'

'But that doesn't explain why they split up,' Kazz said, picking up her drink. The second whisky slipped down as easily as the first, and as the alcohol hit her stomach, she began to feel light-headed.

275

Leanne sighed . 'If you want my opinion, I think she was using him for a good time and she d ropped him when it suited her. Who wants a boyfriend an hour's d rive away if you're not that into him? All I know is, it changed him. *She* changed him. It was subtle and if you d id n't know him really, really well, you probably would n't have noticed , but he kind of withd rew into himself emotionally. He d ated load s of women, but never allowed himself to get close to any of them. He never went out with anyone for long – five d ates maximum. Most d id n't even get that far.'

Leanne placed a hand on Kazz's arm when she rose to buy another whisky. 'Don't have any more, Kazz, wait until you're home.'

Kazz flinched . She had been starting to think of Tanglewood as home; she had certainly felt more at home in the flat above the tea shop than anywhere else she had lived since she'd moved out of her mum's. But seeing Saul with another woman had rocked her to the core.

OK, so they had n't been snogging or anything, but there was more than one way to be intimate, and gazing lovingly into each other's eyes was one of them. And now, Tanglewood d id n't feel quite as homely anymore.

Mind ful that Leanne d id n't need to haul Kazz's inebriated corpse through the streets of Hereford , Kazz subsid ed .

Leanne went on, 'Most of his d ates d id n't get as far as d ate number five – until he met you. You're d ifferent.'

Kazz snorted . 'Not d ifferent enough. He's having an intimate lunch with his first love, if you remember?'

'You need to talk to him. I d on't know what he's playing at, and for what it's worth I think he's an id iot for giving her the time of d ay, but promise me you'll hear what he's got to say for himself before you d o anything d rastic.'

'Like telling him he's a lowlife scumbag and hoping he'll go to hell?'

Leanne's smile was sympathetic. 'Yeah, something like that. Look, why d on't you message him? Tell him that you saw him having lunch, and see what he says?'

'I'd prefer to speak to him face to face.'

'Fair enough. I expect he'll come to yours later.'

'Bugger, you're right. I d on't think I can face him yet.' Kazz need ed some time to process what she'd seen and to work out how she was going to play it.

'How about you message him and tell him we've d ecid ed to make a girls' night of it: wine, a takeaway, a romcom on the telly?' Leanne suggested . 'Hell, we can actually d o that, if you want. We can pick up a couple of bottles of wine on the way home – but no d runk texting. When you speak to Saul, you should d o it sober.'

As they got up to leave, Leanne pulled Kazz toward s her and gave her a hug. 'I'm positive there's a simple explanation,' she said . 'Are you sure you d on't want to speak to him now? It'll put you out of your misery.'

'I'm sure,' Kazz replied . And the reason for her reluctance was that she wasn't in the least bit sure his explanation *would* put her out of her misery. In fact, she had an awful feeling that it would make her feel more miserable than she had ever felt in her life.

Chapter 26

'You can stay the night, if you want.' Kazz leant across the sofa to top up Leanne's wine glass.

'I'd love to, but I can't. We're flying to Scotland tomorrow, remember? So I'd better try to get some sleep. If I stay here, I won't get a wink. We'll be too busy talking all night. Have you told Saul not to come over?'

'Not yet. I'll d o it now. Sorry to ruin your shopping trip.' They'd cut out after the pub and head ed straight back to Tanglewood and the comfort of Kazz's flat.

'You d id n't ruin it. I bought the most gorgeous d ress. And it's not your fault that Saul was lunching with Joelle.'

Kazz picked up her phone, wond ering where Saul was now. It was four thirty-six, so lunch was over long ago, but had he gone back to the farm, or was he still with Joelle? And if so, where were they and what were they d oing?

Unwilling to go any d eeper d own that particular rabbit hole, Kazz hastily began typing a message.

> Do you mind if we give this evening a miss? I'm going to have a girly night in with Leanne xxx

She thought long and hard about the kisses, before d ecid ing to leave them in. She usually end ed her texts with three kisses, and she didn't want to do anything to alert him.

Saul replied within a few seconds.

> No probs. Knackered anyway. Could do
> with a good kip in my own bed x

Kazz scrutinised the message. He sounded just as he always did, and she bit her lip.

> Did you fix the machine thingy?

> Yeah. Had to go to Hereford to buy a part
> tho.

Kazz's eyebrows shot up.

'What?' Leanne asked.

Kazz said, 'He's admitted to being in Hereford. Said he had to buy something.'

'There you go! I said there would be an innocent explanation, didn't I?'

Kazz didn't share her friend's relief. 'He might have an innocent explanation for being in Hereford, but it's one hell of a coincidence that he bumped into his ex while he was there.'

'Stranger things have happened,' Leanne argued, but she didn't sound convinced either.

'It doesn't explain the lunch or the hand-holding over the silverware.'

Leanne blew out her cheeks. 'Are you going to mention you saw him?'

'Not right now. I want to see how deep a hole he's going to dig for himself.'

'At least he told you he was in Hereford. He didn't lie about that.'

'True…' Kazz began to type.

> We went to Hereford too. Train to Cardiff cancelled. You could have given us a lift.

His response took longer to arrive this time.

> Did you buy anything nice?

> No. Didn't see anything I liked.

Leanne snatched the phone out of her hand, and her fingers flew across the screen.

'Hey!' Kazz cried. 'What did you say to him?'

'I told him you'd speak to him tomorrow, as I was sulking because you were ignoring me. You can't have that kind of conversation by text.'

Kazz sighed and picked up her wine glass. 'You're right, I can't. And I probably am reading too much into it.'

She didn't mean it, though. She had a feeling she was reading the situation exactly as it had been written. There was no plot twist, no red herring… Their romance had become a traged y and   she was pretty sure she had   reached the last page.

There would   be no happy-ever-after for her and   Saul.

–

Saul puffed   out his cheeks and   shoved   his phone back in his overalls pocket. Talk about a narrow escape! He could n't believe Kazz and   his sister had   gone shopping in Hereford   instead   of Card iff. What if he had   bumped into them? His story of popping to Hereford   for a part might have been believable to Kazz, but it would n't have washed   with Leanne. His sister would   have seen right through him. He would   never have changed   out of his work clothes to pick up a part, and   neither would   he have need ed   to go into Hereford   town centre. The spare parts place was on the outskirts, on an ind ustrial estate.

He should   never have agreed   to meet Joelle. He should have insisted   that she said   what she had   to say over the phone.

He had   been in two mind s whether to tell Kazz that he had   spent all d ay on the farm, but Mum, Dad   and Murray knew he'd   been out for a significant part of the d ay, and   they might mention something to her. At least by telling her that he'd   been in Hereford , he was covering his backsid e.

Saul heaved   a sigh. What a d ay. He wasn't used   to subterfuge and   he d id n't like lying, but until he'd   known what Joelle wanted , he had   thought it best not to mention it.

He still wasn't sure whether he should   mention Joelle to Kazz at all. Kazz was aware that he'd   had   quite a few girlfriend s over the years, so as far as she was concerned ,

Joelle was just a name on a fairly long list. No one knew what she had meant to him or the devastation she had caused to his heart. So there was no reason for him to tell Kazz right now. Maybe at some point in the future he would mention it, but he had n't asked her about her previous boyfriend s, and she had n't asked about his past relationships.

Joelle being in Tanglewood for a few months hopefully should n't prove to be too awkward, and maybe he would have to confess to Kazz that he had once been in love with the woman, but he would cross that brid ge when he came to it. Right now, his relationship with Kazz was going brilliantly and he d id n't want to d o or say anything that might rock the boat.

'Saul? *Saul!*' His mother was yelling for him as she hurried across the yard, her wellies sloshing through the d irty slushy pud d les that the melting snow had left behind. The flood lights placed strategically on the sid es of the barn and the house illuminated her face, and he wond ered why she looked so excited.

'What's up?' he asked as she d rew nearer. She was breathless and her cheeks were flushed. 'Please tell me you've won the lottery,' he joked.

'Better than that. You'll never guess!'

'What?' He began to chuckle. His mother looked like a kid on Christmas morning.

'Murray and Ashley are going to have a baby! Isn't that marvellous?' She clapped her hand s. 'Another grand child. Ooh, I can't wait!'

'That's wond erful news. I'll pop over to the cottage and congratulate them.'

'Don't leave it too late, because they are going to visit Ashley's parents tomorrow to tell them the news. They won't be back until after New Year's Day.' Ashley's parents had a d airy farm near Carmarthen.

Saul was d elighted for his brother. Murray would be a brilliant father.

His mum was saying, 'I thought she was looking a bit peaky but I d id n't like to say anything, and I had my suspicions when she d id n't d rink anything on Christmas Day.'

'Did n't she? I d id n't notice.'

'You would n't; you were too wrapped up in Kazz.' His mother beamed at him. 'It'll be your turn next.'

Saul burst out laughing. 'Slow d own, Mum, we've only been going out together for five minutes.'

She gave him a meaningful smile and tapped the sid e of her nose.

'Don't you turn into Betty,' he warned . 'One eccentric old bid d y in the village is enough.'

Iris clapped her hand s again and d id a jig of excitement. 'I'd better phone Leanne and tell her, and Martin and Stuart. Then there's—'

'Mum, d on't you think Murray would like to break the news to them himself?'

Iris looked crestfallen. 'Oh d ear, you're right. It's their news to tell, not mine.' She stared at him hopefully. 'When you see Murray, can you pretend you d on't know?'

'I think I can manage that.' Saul was good at pretend ing; he had pretend ed he was fine for months after Joelle d itched him.

'I'd better get tea on,' his mother said , and she bustled off back to the house.

Saul watched her go, smiling at the skip in her step. To his mother, family was everything, and the more family she had , the happier she was.

Murray, a father…? It was bound to happen at some point, and now that it had , Saul was even more convinced that he was right in wanting to strike out on his own.

Maybe it was time to talk to Kazz, and see what she had to say about it.

He might even tell her that he loved her.

–

Kazz stared at the message on her phone for the umpteenth time the following morning. It was a nice message, lovely in fact. But she could n't help feeling anything other than sad when she read it.

It was from Leanne, and it said *Woot! Woot! Murray is going to be a dad!*

Kazz hard ly knew Murray and his wife, but they seemed a nice couple and appeared to be very much in love. As d id Leanne and Rex, Stevie and Nick, Ed ie and She could go on, but it would only d epress her. Everyone else was in a happy stable relationship, except for her. Her relationship was on the rocks, and it was only a matter of time before Saul told her it was over – and she knew this because there was also another message on her phone, one she had n't been able to stop looking at.

It was from Saul.

> I'll bring us a takeaway this evening –
> there's something I want to talk to you
> about.

If she had received a message like that from Stevie or Rossiter, she would have immed iately messaged back, d emand ing to know what they wanted to talk about and haranguing them for being so mysterious and keeping her in the d ark.

But this was Saul. And she could guess what it was, so she had sent him a smiley face emoji and had left it at that.

Crumbs, the shop was quiet tod ay; it was alread y noon and apart from herself, no one had set foot insid e the bookshop. She would n't have mind ed , but the main street was fairly busy. There were plenty of people about, but none of them wanted what she was selling. It crossed her mind that she could start sourcing fresh stock since she had some time on her hand s, but her heart wasn't in it.

She was tired and upset, and the scarcity of customers had given her too much time to think. Her thoughts had n't been pleasant. Asid e from feeling so hurt that her very heart ached , she d id n't know how she could possibly carry on living in Tanglewood if Saul was with another woman. The thought of the two of them together mad e her feel sick to the bottom of her stomach.

She kept telling herself that maybe he wanted to talk about something else entirely, that he wasn't going to d ump her, but she d id n't believe it. After all, she had seen him with her own eyes. Even if he d id n't get back with Joelle, Kazz wasn't sure she would be able to continue living here without the man she loved . She would be better off returning to Lond on and forgetting that Saul Green existed .

Her eyes filled with tears and she blinked them away, refusing to cry. If a customer were to come in, she d id n't want them to find her bawling her eyes out, so in an attempt to d istract herself, she picked up a d uster and began flicking it over the shelves in a d esultory fashion.

But she had only managed a couple of shelves when her phone pinged with a message from Rossiter. Kazz read it with disbelief.

> Have you heard? All charges against Freddie have been dropped. He's reopening the restaurant. U should have had a letter and any wages due to you. What U think?

She read it again. This was too big for messaging, so she rang him. 'Can you talk? You're not at work, are you?' she asked.

'I'm on the sofa, reading this letter and thinking I need a vodka.'

'I haven't had a letter yet,' Kazz said. 'What does it say?'

'That he wants his staff back to help him make the restaurant even better than it was before. And he's offering more wages. I'm seriously thinking about it. What would you do? Do you think I should risk it?'

'How much more is he offering?'

'Twenty per cent more.'

'Bloody hell! That's not like Freddie. Go for it! Is he asking everyone to go work for him again, or is he cherry-picking?'

'Not sure. Why? Fed up with small-town life?'

'You could say that.'

'I'm not surprised. I thought you were mad when you told me you were moving to Trumpton.'

'Tanglewood,' Kazz corrected.

'Same thing. It's out in hicksville, and I bet you have to travel miles for a decent cup of coffee.'

'I can get one d ownstairs. Stevie might own a tea shop, but she d oes a mean latte.'

'Whatever.' Rossiter sighed . 'You could n't pay me enough to live there. So, back to the important stuff – are you seriously thinking about coming back to Lond on to work for Fred d ie again?'

For a couple of blessed minutes Saul had n't been in the forefront of Kazz's mind , but the memory of what she had seen yesterd ay, and what was going to happen tonight when he turned up at the flat, slammed into her. Fresh pain stabbed her in the heart and she almost wept.

'Yes, to coming back to Lond on,' she said . 'But as for working for Fred d ie again, I'm not sure…' She had enjoyed being her own boss and the thought of Fred d ie yelling at her d ay in, d ay out wasn't in the slightest bit appealing.

'You've got to! Without you, his Bord elaise sauce would taste like it came out of a packet, the place would go to the d ogs, and we would all be out of a job again!'

Kazz smiled , d espite the tears threatening to spill over. 'I'll wait until I get my letter, then I'll d ecid e,' she said , although she was pretty certain she *would* go back to her old job. Working for Fred d ie would mean that the pressure was off and she could look for another position from the safety of the one she had .

After the call end ed , Kazz d ropped into the gold wing-back chair and stared vacantly out of the wind ow. She was a jumble of emotion and ind ecision. She d id n't want to give up her bookshop and leave Tanglewood , but she d id n't see how she could remain, und er the circumstances. Everywhere she went would remind her of Saul and what she had lost.

And then there was the issue of seeing Saul himself: the village was too small not to bump into him every second d ay. It would be awful. Soul-d estroying. Unthinkable.

And now, mercy of mercies, she was being offered a way out. With the lease on the bookshop having only two weeks left to run, and with enough of her grand ad 's books sold to give her a bit of money to fall back on, she should be able to make the transition to Lond on smoothly enough.

She would contact a few of the second -hand book-shops in Hay-on-Wye and ask whether they would like to take any stock off her hand s, and it should be easy enough to d ispose of the furniture; there was certain to be a company that d id house clearances. They could have it for nothing, as long as they took it away.

Oh, God , this seemed so final. In a couple of weeks she could be back in Lond on, begging Rossiter to let her kip on his sofa until she could find a place of her own.

She hated having to think like this, but she felt better for having a plan in place should the worst happen this evening.

But she was clinging onto one little shred of hope: maybe Saul would have an explanation and his lunch with Joelle had been entirely innocent.

And it was that hope which stopped her from completely falling apart.

–

At least my friends want to speak to me, Kazz thought, an hour or so later when she saw Tia's name flash up on the screen of her phone. No one else wanted to know. Tell a lie, she'd had one customer, but he had n't wanted to buy a book. He had been looking for d oilies, having been sent out to buy some by his partner. With only a vague id ea that they were some kind of paper-thing, he had hoped Kazz stocked them. The d isappointment on his face when he'd d iscovered that she d id n't was probably echoed on her own.

So the call from Tia was very welcome, even though Kazz was so miserable that she was heartily sick of her own company.

'Hi, Tia, d id you have a good Christmas?' She tried to sound upbeat and normal, but it wasn't easy.

'Yes, thanks, I d id . You?'

'It was good .'

'Can I clarify something with you? Ed gar has heard that you're not going to renew your lease. Are you really giving up the bookshop?'

Kazz's mouth d ropped open. 'What makes him think that?' She had n't said a word to anyone, apart from Rossiter.

'He was at some d inner party and Ralph Booker, your land lord , was there. He mentioned that you had n't been in touch within the required timeframe.' Tia carried on blithely, 'I must ad mit that I was surprised to learn that someone else is taking it over when your term is up, but then you've always been ad amant that it was only a temporary thing, and it's good for the village that the shop won't be empty.'

Kazz was reeling. *Required timeframe?* What the hell? Was she supposed to know about this? 'Um, yeah,' she replied absently, hurrying out the back to her tiny office. She need ed to take a look at that lease.

Kazz opened the top d rawer of the d esk and took out a fold er, quickly flicking through the papers and d ocuments until she found the one she was looking for. Scanning it, she located the paragraph she need ed , and her heart sank. Oh hell, Tia was right; Kazz should have applied to the land lord for a new lease no later than four weeks prior to the end of the current one. If no notification was received , she would be d eemed to not wish to renew, and the property could be leased to any other interested party.

'Do you know who is taking it over?' she asked , aghast to think that her lovely shop would be selling something else in a few weeks.

'A cosmetics company, I believe. They're quite local, based in Hereford with branches all over the Marches and into Shropshire. Someone who used to live in Tangle-wood , Joelle Lawson, works for them. She's d one well for herself apparently; she started on the sales team and worked her way up. I'd heard a rumour she was seen in the village before Christmas, so that must be the reason why.'

Kazz stopped listening. The only thing she had heard was the name Joelle. And sud d enly everything fell into place.

Saul had betrayed her.

Tia was still talking. 'Are you going to look for a position in a kitchen? You'll d efinitely have to get yourself a car. Wherever you land a job, it won't probably be in Tanglewood .' When Kazz failed to answer, Tia asked , 'You *are* going to stay in Tanglewood , aren't you?'

'No.' Her voice was strangled , and she blinked away sud d en tears.

'Why not?' Tia d emand ed .

Kazz d id n't want to tell her about Saul. She could n't face the sympathy, even if it was given with the kind est of intentions. Or the pity. After all, she had been warned .

What better way to save face than to claim she had done what she had intended to do – namely, open a pop-up bookshop for Christmas in order to sell as many of her grand ad's books as possible. And now that she had achieved that, she would return to London and pick up her life where she'd left off. Everyone knew she was a chef: no one would think it strange that she was going to resume the job she had trained hard for and was good at.

Apart from Stevie and Leanne. Edie and Tia would probably also guess, but unless she confided in them, they wouldn't know for sure. Everyone else would assume she had been one of Saul's conquests and he'd moved on as he always did. It would be the truth.

Without the option of being able to extend her lease, the decision had effectively been taken out of Kazz's hands. Her days of owning a bookshop were numbered. Even if she were to stay in Tanglewood and not go running back to London, she would have to find a job.

At least working in Fredie's kitchen was a case of better the devil you know. She would have looked for a job in Tanglewood in a heartbeat if she could be assured of Saul's love, but…

'I'm returning to my old job in London,' she blurted. 'I'll be working in a Michelin star restaurant again.'

Chapter 27

There was no point in keeping the bookshop open any longer tod ay. Not only had Kazz not seen a single customer, but she was also in no fit state to serve one, even if one d id happen to appear. So she locked up and hurried back to the flat.

A letter waited for her, and as soon as Kazz saw the postmark, she guessed it was from Fred d ie, but she was too upset to open it there and then.

After she'd had a crying jag to top all crying jags, and feeling marginally calmer, she blew her nose, splashed water on her red , swollen face, and d ecid ed she would se how much more Fred d ie was going to pay her. It would be nice for her expertise and skill to be recognised , even if Fred d ie was increasing his former staff's salaries solely in ord er to try to tempt them back.

She eased her nail und er the flap and tore the envelope open, thinking that the extra money would come in hand y to help in her quest to find somewhere to live. She was d read ing it, though, because—

Kazz let out a horrified gasp. With a shaking hand , she read the letter again.

It wasn't from Fred d ie. Or rather, *was*, but it had come from him via a solicitor:

> *…Mr French thanks you for your service and wishes you all the best in your future endeavours.*

*Please find details of severance pay and additional
remuneration below. Yours sincerely…*

Kazz felt sick. She was being paid off! And the sum was
bloody paltry. The ungrateful little— After everything she
had done for him! She had put her heart and soul into
his damned restaurant. OK, maybe she had n't asked how
high every time he'd told her to jump, and maybe she had
argued with him more than had been wise, but someone
had to tell him that he should n't treat his staff like dirt.
The nasty little man was taking the opportunity to get rid
of her so he could hire a chef who was more likely to
dance to his tune.

Suddenly, it hit her that once again she did n't have a
job, and this time neither did she have a bookshop to fall
back on.

She was in the same position she had been in on that
fateful day nearly two months ago when her world had
imploded, and this time she had the added torment of a
broken heart.

When her phone rang, Kazz had to squash the urge to
throw it against the wall.

Oh, lord, it was her mum. After not telling her about
Tanglewood or the bookshop until she had been sure she
had good news to impart, Kazz now had to tell her that
the bookshop would be shutting its doors for good in two
weeks.

She should have stayed in London. She should have
listened to her common sense and not been swayed by
visions of her grandad and his shop.

'Mum, hi,' she said weakly.

'What's wrong?'

'Nothing—'

'Don't give me that, Karen. I can tell something's up by the tone of your voice. Are you ill?'

'I'm fine.'

'It's a fella, isn't it? It's always a fella. Don't look at me like that, Vince,' Diana added. 'He's rolling his eyes at me. Well, is it a man?'

'Yes, and no.'

'Spit it out – I haven't got all day.'

Taking a deep breath, Kazz told her everything. She held nothing back.

Then she wished she hadn't, when her mum said, 'Right, we're flying over. Vince, look up the flight times. I've got to pack,' and hung up.

Kazz was left staring at the phone with tears trickling down her face. Never had she needed her mum more.

–

Saul gritted his teeth, anger sweeping through him. Three sheep dead, seven injured. And one of them was Donald.

'The vet is on his way.' His father put a hand on his shoulder. 'Bloody dogs and their irresponsible bloody owners.'

It was horrific to see the devastation even a small dog could cause if it got amongst sheep. And it didn't take long for it to cause that mayhem either – a few minutes, perhaps. The dog's owner might not even be aware that their daft brush of a dog, who 'wouldn't hurt a fly', had savagely attacked ten sheep.

Saul would love to say that this was a one-off, but the scenario was all too common.

He got to his feet and wiped his hands on the backside of his overalls. He had better let Kazz know that he was

294

going to be late, and that if she was hungry she should go ahead and make herself something, because he d id n't know whether he would get to her before the takeaway closed . He had a feeling this was going to be a long night.

He took his phone out of his pocket, but before he could call her, it rang in his hand .

It was his sister, and he wond ered whether Mum had alread y told her. He wished Mum had n't said anything; there was nothing Leanne or anyone – except the vet – could d o. Anyway, she was probably in Scotland by now, so even if she had been able to d o something, she was too far away to d o it.

'Did you know that Kazz is moving back to Lond on?' Leanne d emand ed .

Saul d rew in a sharp breath. 'What? *No!* What are you talking about?'

'She's going back to her old job in the restaurant she used to work at.'

Saul staggered , shock slamming into him.

His father reached out a hand , grasping him by the elbow. 'What's wrong?'

'It's Kazz; she's going back to Lond on,' Saul muttered . Then he said into the phone, 'But what about the book-shop?'

'She's not renewing the lease.'

'How d o you know? Did she tell you?' And why the hell had n't she told *him*?

'Tia called me. She's just spoken to Kazz.' Leanne paused . 'There's more – it's being let to the company that Joelle Lawson works for. Were you aware of that?'

'No, why would I—?'

Leanne broke in, 'I thought she might have told you when you were having lunch.'

Saul felt sick, dread cupping his heart in clammy hands. 'How do you know I had lunch with her?'

'We saw you. Kazz and me. You and Joelle looked very cosy.'

He briefly closed his eyes, his stomach churning. 'It wasn't like that. Yes, she did mention that Rosy Glow was opening a branch in Tanglewood, but it never crossed my mind it would be where the bookshop is.' He dropped his head back and stared up at the sky, blinking back tears. 'I can't believe Kazz didn't tell me. I thought we had something special.'

To think that he had been considering telling her that he loved her.

Kazz had played him like a fiddle. Had he merely been an amusing interlude while she played at being a bookseller? Had he merely been someone to have a bit of fun with until it was time for her to return to her old life?

If he was honest, he wasn't entirely shocked to learn that she wanted to work in a kitchen again; she was far too talented a chef to sell dusty old books in a small village in the middle of nowhere. He must have been out of his mind to believe she would stay in Tanglewood, and even more stupid to think that he would be enough to keep her here.

Leanne was saying something, but he wasn't listening. 'I've got to go, the vet's here,' he lied, and ended the call with cold, stiff fingers.

The chill had gone right through him and had settled in every cell of his body.

Kazz would be leaving Tanglewood shortly and she would be taking his heart with her.

–

Kazz read the message from Vince. He and Mum were at Valencia Airport and their flight was due to take off in forty-five minutes. She did a quick calculation and realised they would be landing in just over three hours, assuming no delays. Vince had asked if she could sort out car hire or, failing that, if she could pick them up from the airport.

She was about to start checking Bristol Airport's website for car rentals, when hammering on the door made her jump and she let out a cry. Oh, God, it must be Saul. He was here. She wasn't ready for this; but then no one was ever ready to be dumped, were they?

But it wasn't Saul. The person who was standing on the top of the spiral staircase, grasping the hand rail and panting for breath, was Betty.

'Oh, um, hi, I… um… This isn't a good time, Betty,' Kazz stammered.

'I'd say it was the perfect time.' The old lady pushed past her into the flat. 'Stevie needs to do something about that metal monstrosity. It's bloody lethal. I nearly did myself a mischief coming up it. God help me when I go back down.'

'Er… Betty—'

Betty broke in before Kazz could finish her sentence. 'What's all this rubbish about you going back to London?'

The speed at which news travelled around Tanglewood never ceased to amaze Kazz. She didn't even bother asking Betty how she knew.

Betty carried on, 'I can't believe you're going to let your lovely little bookshop be turned into a shop selling cosmetics. If you ask me, people spend far too much time preening and primping as it is. They don't need any encouragement. What they *do* need is more books.

Read ing is far better for you than a bath bomb, or false eyelashes that make you look like a startled giraffe.'

All Kazz could d o was stare at the old lad y open-mouthed .

'Well?' Betty d emand ed . 'What have you got to say for yourself?'

'It's complicated .'

'Life is supposed to be complicated , young lad y. If it wasn't, it would be d ownright boring.'

'You d on't und erstand ,' Kazz said .

'Because I'm old , you mean?' Betty glowered at her.

'No! I'd never—'

'Good . Ageism isn't nice. I might have saggy boobs and varicose veins, but I've got all my marbles. Put the kettle on and make us a cup of tea. And while we d rink it, you can try to help a poor old woman und erstand all about young love.' The 'poor old woman' shucked off her coat and shoved it at Kazz, then plopped d own on the sofa. 'Chop, chop! I haven't got all d ay. You're not the only person who need s sorting out this evening.'

Feeling as though she had been thrust into a parallel universe, Kazz hung up Betty's coat, then went to make some tea.

When she returned to the living room, carrying two mugs, she found Betty with her feet on the coffee table and a d etermined expression on her face.

'You thought I was Saul, d id n't you?' the old lad y said , taking the mug with both hand s.

'Yes. I d on't want to be rud e, but I'm expecting him any minute, so—'

'He's not coming. Have you got any biscuits?'

Kazz blinked . 'I've got some gingerbread .'

'I'll give it a miss, thanks. By the end of the festive season, I'm sick to d eath of gingerbread . And mince pies. I'll have a bit of Christmas cake, though, if you've got some.' She looked hopeful.

'Sorry, I d on't. Betty, it's lovely to see you, but why are you here? And what d o you mean Saul isn't coming?'

'He's found out about you buggering off to Lond on and he's not happy.'

Kazz scowled . 'Huh! Well, I found out about him and his ex, so I'm not happy either.'

Not happy was an und erstatement. She was heart-broken. But she was also furious – mostly with herself, for not heed ing Leanne's warnings and also for giving her heart to a man who d id n't d eserve it.

'Which one?' Betty slurped her tea noisily.

'Which one what?'

'Which ex? If you're talking about the hund red s that came before you, they d on't matter. If you're talking about Joelle Lawson, she d oesn't matter either.'

'This is what you d on't und erstand ,' Kazz said with a d espond ent sigh. 'I saw Saul with her yesterd ay, having lunch.'

'So?'

'They looked very cosy.'

'*She* might have looked cosy – I would n't put anything past that one, she's a user – but I bet *he* d id n't.'

'He d id ! They were staring into each other's eyes and she had her hand on his arm.'

'Nah, that's not enough. Did you see them snogging?'

'No! They were in a restaurant.'

'I rest my case.'

'You're not in a courtroom, and you're not putting a case for the d efence.'

'Too right I'm not. I'm putting a case for love. Saul loves you.'

'How can you possibly know that?' Kazz demanded.

Betty tapped the side of her nose. 'I just do. You need to take my word for it. Anyway, let's get back to the bookshop. How did you let Joelle snatch the lease from under your nose?'

Kazz took a steadying breath. 'I was waiting until after Christmas to speak to the landlord. Or his solicitor I should say, because everything is dealt with through them.'

Betty tutted. 'Basically, you faffed around and left it too late. If you could negotiate another lease, would you?'

'I don't think so.'

Betty pressed her lips together and squinted. 'We're back to Saul and that Joelle woman, are we?' The old lady's sigh was loud. 'I wish you would believe me when I tell you he loves you.'

Kazz's gaze flickered to the ceiling, before coming to rest on Betty again. 'I think Saul has been feeding Joelle information about the bookshop and the lease.'

Betty's bark of laughter made her jump. 'Can you hear yourself? You're talking total rubbish. Why would she need to do that when she could contact the estate agent direct? If you search for commercial properties to let in Tanglewood, it's the first to come up. The other is that shop three doors down from the Hen and Duck, the one that used to be a pet shop.'

'Oh.'

'Yes, *oh*.'

'Maybe I did jump to the wrong conclusion,' Kazz admitted quietly.

'You *think*?'

'OK, no need to rub it in. It was an easy mistake to make.'

'It was a silly mistake.'

Kazz blinked away tears. 'It doesn't make any difference, though – he still had lunch with her and lied about it, the lease is due up, I don't have a job, and Stevie is going to need her flat back soon. And even if she doesn't, I can't afford the rent. Oh, and my mother and her partner are flying in from Valencia tonight and I need to sort out transport from the airport for them.'

Betty tipped the last of her tea into her mouth and put the mug down. With a bit of heaving, she hoisted herself off the sofa, then she turned to Kazz and stared her straight in the face.

'Is that all? Pfft. Come on, young lady, we've got work to do.'

Chapter 28

'Saul!' Betty shouted down the phone. 'I need a favour. A friend of mine will be landing at Bristol Airport and she needs a lift to Tanglewood. Can you do it?'

Saul gave Donald a pat on his woolly head and scrambled to his feet. The poor sheep had needed six stitches in his face and a cast on his leg. The vet had said he had most likely broken it in his haste to escape, but it was a clean break and the wound to his cheek would heal. After a shot of antibiotics, Donald was now in one of the lambing pens, munching on hay and sheep nuts, and looking considerably less sorry for himself than he had an hour ago.

Six of the seven ewes who had been attacked had also been treated for their injuries, but unfortunately the seventh had n't survived.

'Saul, are you there?' Betty sounded cross.

'I'm here. What day and time does your friend need to be collected?'

'Today. Her flight lands at twenty past ten.'

'*Tonight?* It's a bit short notice.'

'Can you do it?'

Saul did n't want to drive all the way to Bristol and back, but he knew he was unlikely to get much sleep tonight (if any) so it would give him something to do instead of lying awake, wallowing in misery. What he really felt like doing was find ing a nice d eep hole and hid ing in it for the next d ecad e or two, but as that wasn't an option, he may as well help Betty out. 'I can, but only because it's you.'

'You're a good lad . I knew I could rely on you. You're not half as bad as they say you are.'

Saul ignored the comment. 'What flight is she on, and what's her name? I'll write it on a piece of card .'

'No need , you can pick me up on the way to the airport. I'm coming with you.'

After he'd settled the rest of the injured sheep d own and d id the remaind er of his nightly chores, he had a shower and changed into clean clothes.

His mum said , 'You need to eat *something*. Let me make you a sand wich to take with you.'

Saul had n't wanted any of the stew she had kept back for him. Leanne's phone call had d riven his appetite away. 'No thanks, I'll take a flask of coffee with me, though. Not in that one!' he cried , as his mother picked up the engraved flask that Kazz had given him for Christmas.

'It's for using, not looking at,' Iris retorted . 'I bet Kazz d oesn't want it to sit on a shelf and not be used .'

'Not that one,' he repeated .

His mother shot him a curious look, but he d id n't care. He had enough remind ers of Kazz, without having one in the Land y with him. At least Betty sitting in the passenger seat might keep him from thinking about Kazz.

That's what he told himself, but he d id n't believe it. Nothing on earth could prevent him from thinking about the woman he loved and had lost.

When Saul pulled up alongsid e Betty's cottage, the d ownstairs lights were on. He gave a quick beep on the horn to let her know he was outsid e, then he got out and went to stand by the railings and stared across the d ark field to the river beyond . He could n't tell how high the water was, but it d id n't sound as though it was flowing particularly fast, d espite the run-off from the melting snow up in the mountains.

He heard Betty step out of her house and close the front d oor, but before he could hurry around to the passenger sid e, she had alread y managed to clamber in, so he hastened to the d river's sid e, opened the d oor and —

His heart gave a lurch, then skipped a beat.

Kazz was sitting in the passenger seat.

'What are you d oing here?' he asked , surprised at how calm he sound ed . Little of his inner turmoil showed .

'I'm coming to Bristol with you.'

'No, you're not.' Wearily, he leant against the d oor. 'I've got nothing to say to you, Kazz.'

'But I have something to say to *you*,' she said . She looked scared and was nibbling at her lip.

He d esperately wanted to take her in his arms and kiss that worried expression away, but he could n't allow her to inflict any more pain. 'Please get out of the car,' he said . 'It's been a long d ay and I want to go home.'

'I thought you were supposed to be going to the airport?' She sound ed panicked .

'So d id I.'

'You must go!'

'Why?'

'You've got to pick up my— Betty's friend .'

He flinched . 'I hate to break it to you, but Betty has set us up.' The interfering old so-and -so. He would have a few word s to say to her the next time he saw her.

'She has, but we still have to go to the airport. You really d o have to pick someone up.'

'Fine, but you're not coming with me. Say what you want to say, then get out.'

She hesitated . Her eyes were huge and glittered with unshed tears. He thought she was going to chicken out, and he assumed that if she d id , it could n't be that important.

But when she finally spoke, he und erstood that what she wanted to say was possibly the most important thing he had ever heard .

'I love you.'

–

Kazz was frozen in her seat, her d eclaration of love floating in the air between them. Saul seemed unable to respond and appeared just as frozen.

Had Betty got it wrong, Kazz wond ered . Was Saul horrified ? Was he frantically trying to think of how to respond ?

He closed his eyes; his mouth was a thin line, his jaw tense. A twitch had d eveloped in the corner of one eye and his should ers were rigid .

Then he opened his eyes and stared at her.

Unable to look away, she stared back.

Eventually, he spoke. 'Leanne seems to think you are going back to Lond on.'

Kazz gave a resigned shrug. 'Tia must have told her. It's a long story.'

'I've got all night.'

Betty rapping on the wind ow with her knuckles mad e her jump, and Kazz wound it d own.

Ignoring her, Betty said to Saul, 'I know you're a bloke and you have limited capabilities, but surely you can d rive and talk at the same time?' She tapped her watch. 'You'd better get a move on if you don't want to keep Kazz's mother waiting.'

Kazz winced as Saul shot her a frown. 'I thought I was meeting a friend of Betty's?'

'I said it was a long story.'

He continued to glower at her. 'Do you really love me, or are you saying that just to get me to drive to Bristol?'

'I would never do something like that!' Kazz was aghast he would think it. She was hurt, too.

Saul got in and started the engine. 'I had to be sure.'

'Don't bother!' she cried, tears gathering in her eyes. She reached for the door handle.

Saul said, 'I love you too.'

Kazz turned to stare at him. 'What did you say?' Her voice was a whisper of disbelief and hope.

'I love you.'

Betty gave a whoop, and Kazz jumped. Her heart hammering, she asked, 'Is that true?'

'Yes.' His voice was soft.

She gulped, the tears spilling over. Slumping into the seat, she felt giddy and weak with relief.

Saul loved her.

He said, 'I want to take you to bed and kiss your tears away, but I think we'd better get going. You don't want to keep your mum waiting.'

Kazz fished a tissue out of her pocket and blew into it. 'Better not. She's worried enough as it is.'

He sent her a curious look. 'I think we've got some catching up to do,' he said, putting the Landy into gear. 'I'll drive, you talk. Is that all right with you, Betty?'

Betty gave him a thumbs up. 'When you get back, give poor Donald a Jaffa Cake from me. I hope he's better soon.'

Saul blinked . 'How d o you know about Donald ?'

Betty tapped the sid e of her nose.

'I swear to God that woman is psychic,' Kazz muttered as the car pulled off.

'She certainly gives that impression,' Saul said .

'What's wrong with Donald ?' she asked .

'It looks like I'm going to have to talk as well as d rive.' Saul chuckled . 'You go first.'

So Kazz d id .

–

Kazz bounced from foot to foot as she craned her neck to see around the passengers trud ging wearily out of the security gate. She was so excited , she could n't keep still.

'Stop jiggling,' Saul grumbled as she trod on his foot for a second time.

Kazz stopped bouncing, and he put his arm around her and kissed her hair. She sighed with contentment.

She loved Saul and Saul loved her. They had each other, that was all that mattered . Everything else fad ed into insignificance: the bookshop, his search for a farm to rent, everything.

Those were things to think about tomorrow. Right now, Kazz could n't wait to see her mum.

'There she is!' she cried , spying her mother's worried face. Vince plod d ed behind , pulling a suitcase.

Kazz d arted forward and barrelled into her mother, wrapping her arms around her in an enormous hug.

Her mum patted her on the back, gently at first, but the pats became thumps as Diana wheezed , 'Karen, let me go – I can't breathe.'

Over her mum's shoulder she saw Saul approach Vince, holding out a hand to take the case.

Kazz released her hold and linked arms with her mum instead . 'It's so good to see you. I've missed you so much.'

'I've missed you too, my lovely girl.' Diana turned her attention to Saul, then back to Kazz. 'Have you two made up?'

'We have.' Kazz beamed at her.

Diana rolled her eyes. 'Well, at least that's one less problem we have to worry about. Now, all we've got to do is work out how you're going to keep your bookshop.'

Chapter 29

Kazz was more than a little surprised to see a customer waiting outsid e the bookshop when she opened up the next morning.

'I won't keep you a moment,' she said , hurrying insid e to switch the lights on and d isable the alarm.

She hastily took off her coat, and d umped it and her bag in the storeroom, then d ashed onto the shop floor.

'Did you have a nice Christmas?' she asked , recognising the eld erly gent as the man who had been told off by his wife for buying more books. She hoped he wasn't here to offer her any for sale. She might want to keep the bookshop going, but whether she would be able to was a d ifferent matter entirely – it would d epend on whether the former pet shop was still available and whether she would be able to afford the rent. And to ad d to her worries, she'd not had a single customer yesterd ay, which d id n't bod e well for the viability of her little business. Id eally, she need ed longer than the two weeks she had left on the lease before she committed herself to another.

Both Stevie and Leanne had told her that the period between Christmas and New Year wasn't brilliant for business, and the only reason that Ed ie's wed d ing shop was open was because she was frantically finishing the alterations on the d resses of those brid es who had d ecid ed

309

to get married on New Year's Eve, or New Year's Day in the case of one particular couple.

So yes, Kazz would like to give it longer, but she could n't.

It was a d ilemma she had been fretting over since she had opened her eyes this morning.

She had n't said anything to Saul, who looked as exhausted as she felt, bless him, and she'd sent him off to the farm with a coffee and a kiss. She had left her mum and Vince tucking into tea and toast, and she had n't said anything to them either.

The eld erly gentleman was wand ering around the shelves, stroking the books lovingly, and her heart was glad d ened to see someone who loved old books as much as she d id . Mind you, most people who entered her shop had a love of books, but this old chap seemed to love them more than most, she thought, as she saw him pick one up and sniff it before carefully returning it to the shelf.

'In answer to your question…' he began to say, strolling over to the counter where Kazz was making sure the card machine was working, in the hope he might buy some-thing. 'I d id have a nice Christmas, thank you. However, I've since heard some d isturbing news.'

'I am sorry,' she said . 'I hope it wasn't too upsetting?' Poor chap, he d id look rather cheesed off.

He placed both hand s flat on the counter and leant toward s her, his expression serious. 'I heard the bookshop is to close.'

To her cred it, Kazz d id n't flinch. The speed at which gossip travelled around the village was no longer a surprise. She'd have been more shocked if *he*adn't known.

She said , 'I know I asked you to give me a call after Christmas, but when I said that, I honestly d id n't expect it to close.'

'Why *are* you closing, if you d on't mind me asking?'

'I only had a short-term lease, so…' Kazz trailed off. She hated d isappointing people, but there was no point in giving him false hope that she would be able to take some books off his hand s. 'Have you tried any of the bookshops in Hay-on-Wye?' she asked . 'If you haven't, it may be worth giving them a go.'

'Did you try to renew the lease?' His eyes searched her face.

She blinked . He was being rather forward , wasn't he? 'Um, no.'

'Did you want to?'

'Yes?'

'Is that a question or a statement?'

'A statement. I d id ~~db~~ – want to renew it, or extend it, or whatever the correct terminology is.'

'Why d id n't you?'

Why all the questions, Kazz wanted to retort, but she d id n't want to offend him. He was only being curious. Nosey was a better d escription, but consid ering the number of people who were aware that she had intend ed to keep the bookshop open but had left it too late, he would probably know soon enough. She was surprised he d id n't know alread y.

'The gossip d rums not working this morning?' she quipped .

His expression d id n't change and , realising her flip-pancy wasn't to his liking, she explained , 'I left it too late. I'd planned on contacting the owner after Christmas, when I had a better id ea of… Never mind .' She d id n't want to d iscuss the bookshop's financial situation with a chap who'd just walked in off the street, no matter how nice he seemed , or tell him that she had d ropped the ball and had n't realised that she should have contacted the land lord before then. 'Someone got in before me,' she end ed .

'So I und erstand . Lipsticks and whatnot.'

'That's right.'

'I would prefer it to remain a bookshop, myself,' he said .

'As would I!' Kazz's reply was heartfelt. Even if it had n't been her business, she would take books over skincare any d ay. She said , 'Look, this probably won't come to anything, but there's an empty shop up the street that the bookshop might be able to relocate to. I stress *might* because I haven't looked into it yet. So, if you want to hang on for a couple of weeks, I might be able to buy some of your books from you then.'

At that, his eyes lit up and a smile spread across his lined face.

Not wanting to give him false hope, Kazz hastened to ad d , 'I'm not promising anything. Even if I d o relocate, I can't guarantee I will buy any books from you. I'll have to see them first.'

'You will.' The old chap sound ed confid ent.

Kazz thought it best not to argue. It would all come out in the wash, as her grand ad used to say. 'Why d on't you give me a call in a couple of weeks?' she suggested . 'I'll have a better id ea of what's happening by then.'

The old gent straightened up. He had yet to take his eyes off her and the intensity of his gaze was making her feel uncomfortable.

'I don't think we've been introduced,' he said, holding out his right hand. 'My name is Ralph Booker.'

Kazz took it, wondering why it sounded familiar. Then it came to her. That was the name on the lease agreement she had signed.

Ralph Booker owned this property!

–

Saul couldn't make head nor tail of what Kazz was trying to tell him. She was shrieking down the phone, gabbling so fast that he couldn't catch more than a word here and there.

'Kazz? Kazz! Calm down. I'm on my way.' Abandoning the tractor he was working on, he ran towards the yard.

'Where's the fire?' his dad yelled, as Saul wrenched the Land Rover's door open and flung himself into the driver's seat.

'Kazz needs me,' he called back.

'Should I come with you?'

'It's OK. I think it's good news.' He hoped it was, but it had been difficult to tell.

Saul made it to the high street in record time, parked up and raced inside the shop, skidding to a halt when he saw Kazz and an elderly gentleman calmly sitting in the wingback chairs and drinking tea. The old chap's face was familiar, but Saul couldn't think of his name.

'What the—' he began, running a hand through his hair.

Kazz got to her feet and walked towards him, and he assumed she was about to give him a hug, but she stopped a few paces short.

'Were you in the middle of something?' she asked, staring pointedly at his oil-covered hands.

'Yes, I was. What's wrong?'

'Nothing.'

'Nothing?' he repeated in confusion.

'Everything is *right*,' she said .

Saul puffed out his cheeks, then shrugged . 'I d on't follow.'

Kazz tilted her head in the old chap's d irection. 'This is Ralph Booker,' she said .

That was it! Mr Booker. 'I know. He lives in Langstone Lane.'

'That's right.' Mr Booker beamed at him.

Saul was becoming increasingly confused by the second , and it must have shown on his face.

'Do you know who owns this build ing?' Kazz asked . She was beaming too.

Saul said , 'I d on't, but I think you're about to tell me.'

'Mr Booker.'

'He d oes?'

'It looks like there's something the Tanglewood gossip waggon d oesn't know,' Kazz said .

Mr Booker spoke. 'I haven't broad cast it, if that's what you mean. And call me Ralph. It's silly to call me Mr Booker when we will be working together.'

Saul stared at him, baffled , then turned his attention back to Kazz. 'You're going to have to explain.'

'Mr – *Ralph* – hasn't signed the lease over to Rosy Glow yet. He says if I want to renew it, I can. He loves books, you see,' she ad d ed , as though that explained everything.

Saul stepped toward s the Chesterfield chair, and Kazz let out a shriek. 'Don't sit there! You're covered in oil.'

So he was. He leant against the counter instead , and wished he had a stiff d rink. Had he fallen d own a rabbit hole and had n't noticed ?

'Go on,' he urged cautiously, wond ering what other surprises she might have in store for him.

'Ralph came into the shop this morning. He had alread y been in once before, scoping it out.' She smiled ind ulgently at the old fellow. 'And he liked what he saw, so he wanted to ask me why I wasn't renewing the lease. When I explained , he told me that d ue to it being Christmas and the office being shut, his solicitor had n't d rawn up the new contract for Rosy Glow yet, so nothing has been signed .'

'Hang on, would n't the letting agent d o that?' Saul asked .

'Normally, yes, but I've always preferred my solicitor to d o it,' Ralph explained .

'That's lucky,' Saul said .

'Not lucky. Prud ent,' Ralph argued . 'I'm going to ask him to inform the other party that they won't be taking out the lease after all. He's going to d raw up a new one, with Kazz's name on it.'

'The bookshop is staying open!' Kazz cried . 'Isn't that marvellous?'

'It certainly is. If I wasn't so grimy, I'd give you a kiss.' Saul was so pleased for her. Kazz's d elight was plain to see. Then he remembered something. 'Did you say you and Ralph are going to be working together?' Surely not. He must have misheard and the old man had been referring to Kazz taking out the lease.

'That's right!' Kazz hugged herself in glee. 'Ralph knows as much about books as I d o – more, probably. And I was saying I need ed someone to run the shop while

I source fresh stock, but this way we can take it in turns to be in the shop or out buying. Although neither of us will have to d o any buying for a while because he's got over two thousand books he wants to sell, and that's just the start of it.'

'You're going into business together?' Saul clarified .

'Yes! Isn't that wond erful!'

Saul had to ad mit it was the perfect solution to the bookshop's problems, and he could n't be more thrilled for her. The joy he felt on seeing her so happy was tempered only by the realisation that his hopes of taking on a farm tenancy one d ay had gone up in smoke. How could he even consid er moving away from Tanglewood now?

But he d id n't care. Her happiness was all that mattered , and if he had to spend the rest of his life working on the family farm, so be it. At least he could put his savings toward s a home in the village – one that he and Kazz could live in together.

He wanted to start looking for suitable properties now, but he had a tractor to repair, and after that he intend ed taking Kazz, her mum and partner out for a slap-up meal to celebrate her incred ibly good news.

–

'Have you got five minutes?' Geoff asked , catching Saul as he was about to leave to fetch Kazz, Diana and Vince. His mum had invited them to have New Year's Day lunch at the farm.

'It'll have to be quick.'

'Come into the kitchen. There's something your mother and I need to d iscuss with you.'

Saul frowned . It sound ed serious, and his stomach d ropped to his boots. He hoped to God neither of them was ill, nor anyone else in the family. He thought of Murray and Ashley, who had just announced their pregnancy, and he prayed it wasn't bad news. They had n't returned from visiting her parents in Carmarthen yet, and Saul's heart was in his mouth as he followed his d ad into the kitchen.

His mother was sitting at the scarred old table. She looked solemn. Oh, God …

'Sit d own, Saul, there's something we need to tell you.'

Saul sat. Even if he had n't wanted to, his legs were shaking so much that he d id n't think they could hold him up. He plopped heavily into the chair and took a shaky breath.

'It's about Murray,' his mum began, and her eyes were suspiciously d amp. 'He's not coming back.'

'What! *No!* I d on't— He can't— Oh God .' Saul swallowed hard , trying to hold himself together for his parents' sake, although they appeared alarmingly calm. He guessed it was the shock. 'How d id it happen?' he choked out.

Iris frowned . 'How d id what happen?'

'Was it an accid ent or a… What d o they call it… a med ical episod e?'

His father, who was stand ing at his should er, said , 'Saul, what are you talking about?'

'Murray.' Had his parents gone mad ? 'You said he's—' Saul took a breath and forced the word s out, 'not coming back.'

'That's right. He and Ashley have d ecid ed to stay in Carmarthen and take over her parents' farm. Her d ad is getting on a bit now, and he had a fall on Boxing Day.'

Iris took up the baton. 'So her father asked whether Ashley and Murray would consid er running it.' She broke off to d ab at her eyes.

'Your mother is und erstand ably upset. She'll only have two chicks left within nagging d istance.'

Iris sniffed . 'I d on't nag, and they are your chicks too.'

Geoff sat d own and looked Saul in the eye. 'I know it's not been easy for you, but I hope you'll stay here and help me run this place. Please reconsid er taking out a tenancy.'

Saul was flabbergasted . He had told no one of his plans, apart from Kazz. *No one.* 'How d o you know that?' he d emand ed .

His mother gave him a watery smile. 'Betty – who else?'

–

'There's something I want to talk to you about,' Saul said , and Kazz's spirits sank. The last time he'd said that, she had been convinced he was about to d ump her.

'Spit it out,' she command ed , rolling onto her back and staring at the bed room ceiling. 'If you keep me in suspense, I swear you won't be getting any sex for a week.'

Saul gasped . 'That's harsh.'

'It's true. Now, what d o you want to talk to me about?'

'Donald .'

'Eh?'

'I think he's lonely.'

Kazz sat up. 'You're joking, right? He's got a whole herd of lad ies to keep him company.' He was thankfully recovering nicely from his horrifying ord eal and was now lord ing it over a field full of females.

'It's a flock, not a herd , and he's missinge, not the lad ies.'

'I'm not forcing you to spend every night in my flat,' she said , sticking her tongue out at him.

Since the night they had declared their love for each other, Saul hadn't spent a single night in his own bed in the farmhouse. Mind you, it hadn't been all rampant shenanigans under the covers, because her mum and Vince had only flown back to Spain today, so Kazz and Saul's bedroom antics had been rather subdued and somewhat curtailed.

'I want to spend every night with you. Heck, I want to spend every *second* with you,' Saul insisted.

'What are you trying to say?'

He sat up too, and scooted around in the bed so he was facing her. 'You know that Murray and Ashley are still in Carmarthen?' he began.

'Yeah, so?'

'He's staying there. He's not coming back to Tanglewood.'

'Do you mean never?'

'I dare say he'll be back for a visit.' Saul rolled his eyes, and Kazz thumped him on the arm.

'You know what I mean.'

'No, he's not coming back. Dad wants me to take over the running of the farm.'

'Are you happy about that?' she asked. He *looked* happy but she sensed there was something more.

'I am. The thing is… Murray's cottage will be empty, so I'm moving back in.'

'Does that mean I can have a sleepover at yours now and again?' she teased.

'You can have a sleepover every night, if you want. I'm asking you to move in with me. Come live in my cottage on the farm, with me and Donald.'

'I'm not living there with Donald,' she stated flatly.

'It's OK, he'll be in the field behind , not insid e the house.'

'Oh, in that case…' Kazz leant toward s him, lifting her chin.

His lips pressed against hers as he took her in his arms, kissing her d eeply and with such love and passion that he stole her breath. And as he laid her gently d own on the soft mattress, she knew life could n't get any better than this.

Epilogue

Kazz stirred sleepily, waking not to the sound of sleigh bells or Christmas carols, but to the irate bleating of a sheep who wanted his breakfast. Saul was alread y awake and he kissed her on the nose before slipping out of bed .

'I'll go feed Donald ,' he said . 'You have a lie-in.'

'Don't go,' she murmured , reaching for him, but Saul was too quick for her.

She was far too excited to go back to sleep, though. It was Christmas Day and she had presents to give – and receive.

As she shoved her feet into her pink slippers, she shouted d own the stairs, 'Don't forget to give him the peelings.'

Last night, she had prepared all the vegetables for Christmas lunch, and she had saved the peelings for Donald as a treat. Iris had merely shaken her head d espairingly when Kazz had bagged them up to bring back to the cottage with her. Kazz and Saul were joining Iris and Geoff for lunch, but this year it was Kazz who was d oing the cooking – after all, she may have a new career as a bookshop owner, but she liked to keep her hand in, and Saul certainly appreciated her d oing all the cooking, especially since he was hopeless in the kitchen. He was pretty good at d oing the laund ry, though, so she left that chore to him, along with the vacuuming and d usting.

They shared Donald's care, Kazz having grown quite fond of the cheeky animal. She had often caught herself talking to him as she pottered in her little vegetable patch, although she was careful to make sure he stayed out of it. She'd learnt from experience that he could decimate a row of peas in minutes, and she'd had to manhandle him out of it by grabbing hold of his fleecy backside and hauling him out. Since then, Kazz had insisted he wear a collar, similar to Tam's.

As she made the coffee, she found herself wondering where this year had gone. She couldn't believe that the bookshop was already a year old. Time had flown by so fast, and she wouldn't change a single thing. Coming to Tanglewood had been the best decision she had ever made.

The aroma of rich coffee filled the air, to mingle with the smell of cinnamon and vanilla from the baking she had done yesterday, and she gave a contented sigh, then yelped as a pair of arms encircled her waist.

'You shouldn't creep up on people,' she admonished, squirming around to give Saul a kiss. 'Merry Christmas, darling. I love you.'

'I love you more,' he said, his mouth on hers. He pulled away gently and stared out of the window. 'Look.'

It was snowing. Fat flakes were falling from a leaden sky and drifting lazily down to earth.

'Do you think it will stick?' Kazz hoped it would – snow on Christmas morning would be as perfect as icing on a fruit cake. And wonderfully magical.

'Probably not,' Saul said, pecking her on the nose and reaching for a mug. 'I need coffee and breakfast before I start my chores.'

'Haven't you forgotten something?' she teased.

'I don't think so.'

'What about opening our presents?'

He blinked at her. 'What makes you think I've got you a present?'

'I've seen it und er the tree.' Laughing, she d ragged him into the living room and head ed for the Christmas tree.

Presents were piled und erneath, and there was one in particular that she had her eye on. It was small and square, and had been hid d en und erneath the others. It was the only one without a tag.

Saul bent d own and rummaged through the pile. 'Here you go.' He pulled out a large flattish parcel and hand ed it to her.

Intrigued , Kazz tore it open, and squealed in d elight. It was a painting of her bookshop, and she simply loved it. 'Can I put it above the fireplace?' she asked .

'You can put it where you like. This is *your* home as much as mine.'

Kazz still had trouble believing it, even though she had been living in the converted barn for nearly a year. She was always careful to run any changes past Saul before she mad e them, such as red ecorating the main bed room, for instance – her taste and Ashley's were world s apart – and Saul always told her the same thing.

Saul loved his present from her (tickets to the Wales–England rugby match in Card iff), and once they had opened the rest of their gifts, Kazz began to gather up the d iscard ed wrapping paper.

'You've forgotten one,' Saul said , and she straightened up to find him hold ing the small box. The one that looked as though it could contain an item of jewellery – such as a ring.

Her heart thud d ing, she took it from him and sat d own on the rug to open it.

Saul was grinning wid ely, his excitement palpable, and Kazz felt her own build ing. Oh, my God , this was it.

She tore off the wrapping paper.

It d id n't look like the kind of box an expensive ring would come in…

Nervously, she opened it, and saw that she was right. It *wasn't* the kind of box a d iamond ring would be in, because the content *wasn't* a ring at all. It was a d og tag, with the word 'DONALD' on it, and a phone number.

Her d isappointment was so acute that she wanted to cry.

'I thought you could put it on Donald 's collar, since he's always escaping,' Saul was saying, and Kazz bit her lip to stop her chin from wobbling.

'Thank you,' she mumbled .

'Why d on't you put it on him now?' he suggested .

Kazz reluctantly removed the tag from the box and tried to summon a smile.

He stood up and held out his hand . She took it and allowed him to haul her to her feet and lead her outsid e to the pad d ock.

Donald was contented ly munching on the vegetable peelings, but was happy to saunter over in case the humans had something more tempting.

Kazz opened the gate and slipped insid e, Saul behind her.

'I'll hold him while you put the tag on his collar,' he said .

She held out her hand and Donald butted it gently. 'Merry Christmas, Donald . Look what Saul has bought you. People will know who to call the next time you get out.' Kazz thought the tag was a waste of time, because

Donald was instantly recognisable and everyone knew who he belonged to anyway.

She was just feeling for the buckle through the sheep's thick fleece when her fingers encountered something unexpected , and she bent d own for a closer look.

'That's od d , there's a piece of fabric attached to his collar.' Kazz und id the buckle and held up the collar. 'See?' The fabric was actually a navy velvet pouch, and she frowned in confusion. 'What's that d oing there?'

'No id ea.'

'There's something insid e.' She und id the cord and tipped the contents into the palm of her hand .

It was a d iamond ring.

Kazz blinked , then her heart began to race. Excitement surged through her and she gasped as Saul d ropped to one knee.

His eyes full of ad oration, he said , 'I love you with all my heart and I want to spend the rest of my life with you. Will you marry me?'

Of course she said yes. What else could she d o when he had mad e her the happiest woman in the world ?

As her soul brimmed with joy, she thought how lucky she was to have found him – how lucky they were to have found each other. And all because of Grand ad 's legacy.

As Saul slipped the beautiful ring on her finger, Kazz said a silent thank you to the man whose love of books had enabled her to find the love of her life.

Since that awful d ay in Lond on when she had lost her job and her home, her d ays had become much better, and she could n't wait to find out just how good the d ays, months and years ahead could really get.

Acknowledgements

There are always so many people involved in helping to turn one of my vague id eas into a book, and the one person who d eserves to be mentioned is my lovely ed itor, Emily, for helping me return to Tanglewood . I've long felt that I wasn't d one with this series, so it was an absolute joy to visit it again. The rest of the team also d eserve my thanks, as they work to polish my rough and sprawling d raft into a story fit to be published .

Donald Winchester (yes, you!) is to blame for the sheep, but the name is a fitting one, I believe.

My husband also need s to be thanked for supplying me with end less cups of tea, ensuring I step away from my computer now and again, and for loving me d espite the number of times I mutter to myself. He has more patience with me than I have with myself. My mum, who is my staunchest supporter (I d o pity the staff in her local library, for all the times she asks them to reserve one of my books – anyone would think I d on't give her a copy. I d o, honestly!), my d aughter who is my prid e and joy, my bestie Catherine Mills, and Poppy the d og, all help keep me sane and ground ed , Poppy especially – there is no love like the love of a d evoted pooch. And I can't not mention the Cariad Chapter of the Romantic Novelists Association – they have mad e me realise the importance and joy of having the support of author friend s.

But the most important people are my read ers. I write my stories for *you*.

Love,
Lilac xxx

Penguin Random House LLC
1745 Broadway
US-NY, 10019
US
https://www.penguinrandomhouse.com
1-800-733-3000

The authorized representative in the EU for product safety and compliance is

Penguin Random House Ireland
Morrison Chambers, 32 Nassau Street
D02 YH68
IE
https://eu-contact.penguin.ie

ISBN: 9798217269846
Release ID: 154078558